THE MEETING POINT

OLIVIA LARA

HEAD
ZEUS

An Aria Book

ALSO BY OLIVIA LARA

Someday in Paris

First published in the United Kingdom in 2021 by Head of Zeus Ltd
This paperback edition published in 2021 by Head of Zeus Ltd

975312468

A CIP catalogue record for this book is available from the British Library.

ISBN (E): 9781838933197
ISBN (PB): 9781800246263

Cover design © Beth Yirdaw

Aria
c/o Head of Zeus
First Floor East
5–8 Hardwick Street
London EC1R 4RG
www.ariafiction.com

To my dad,
Who loves books, the ocean,
And books by the ocean

ONE

The story goes like this.

Thirty-year-old Bartholomew von Coffenberg comes out of Madison Square Park Tower's underground garage in his red Corvette. The only child of an investment magnate, Bartholomew graduated from Harvard and now has a corner office at Goldman Sachs. He's in a rush to get to brunch at Elio's with his fiancée, Charlotte Astor. Charlotte is tall, slender, classy, and a successful attorney with a top law firm in NYC and the perfect match for him. Their parents made sure of this, just like they made sure the relationship was planned all the way to the wedding at the luxurious One and Only Reethi Resort and the honeymoon in the Maldives this summer.

What Bartholomew doesn't know is that his fiancée will not show up at Elio's. Instead, she will be on a plane to Italy to meet for the first time a man she fell in love with online.

A few streets away, thirty-four-year-old Natalie Bechamel enters a Starbucks on Park Avenue South. She's there every morning, and her order never changes—a grande, iced, sugar-free, vanilla latte with soymilk. Natalie is a widow and has two boys; one is eight, the other thirteen. She's been working as the personal assistant for the owner of IMG Models for years. The coffee's not for her; it's for her boss. She could never afford the $6 daily order, the $35 vegetarian lunch, or the eco-laundry where she drops his clothes on her way home. At 7 PM, Monday through Friday, Natalie picks up her boys from the upstairs neighbor and starts on dinner while helping the young one with homework and fighting with the teenager who misses his father and resents her. She never imagined life would look like this. She never imagined the kind, loving man she married would drink himself to death, leaving her all alone.

Natalie doesn't know yet that one evening very soon, as she crosses the street, a car will almost run her over. A red Corvette. That night will end with a bruised knee and a man driving her home while his eyes linger on her a bit too long. By Christmas, Natalie will fly with her two boys to the Maldives, where a happy and in love Bartholomew will say 'I do' to her and them forever.

* * *

My name is Maya Maas, and I write love stories. All the time and ever since I can remember.

Bartholomew and Natalie are just people I saw on the street. I don't know their real names or anything about their lives. What I do know is that they both seem lonely, and nothing makes me happier than imagining people are happy. And in love. And living happily ever after.

My 'silly little scribbles,' as my boyfriend David calls them, put a smile on my face and carried me forward through tough family times, school anxieties, making and losing friends, boyfriend dramas, life on my own, and job frustrations. Surrounded by books as a child, I didn't have many friends, but I had a big imagination, and that was enough for me. It still is. Writing also gives me an excuse to watch people —my favorite pastime. A random person on the street, a barista, or a bus driver all spark ideas. I love imagining who they are, their names, where they come from, and what they do. I usually put them in a tough spot and save them in the end and give them the smiles and laughter and love they yearn for.

I used to dream of becoming a published author. Years ago, I wrote a novel, then another, and sent them both to literary agencies. All I got in return was silence, polite nos, or painful critique I wasn't ready for. 'Too sappy, too unrealistic, too 1960s. Why do all your female characters search for love? Not all women need someone to complete them.'

I always thought you can have both. And you can be both. Being in love doesn't make you weak or dependent. Staring at the night sky together, holding hands, looking into each other's eyes gives you wings. It fills your heart and body with energy to accomplish everything else. I think so. I hope so. Yes, my characters all lived happily ever after, but I don't see anything wrong with that. There's enough sadness in the world as it is.

At first, I was determined to stand behind my stories and push forward. Still, even the most confident of us need reassurance, and mine never came. Instead, more critiques piled up. 'The market is too competitive, and these books don't have what it takes. There's nothing there. Cardboard characters, unrealistic plot. It suggests immaturity; lack of experience.'

That last rejection discouraged me. I started doubting whether I'd ever become a full-time writer, which was all I'd dreamed of since I was a little girl. At the same time, I knew I had to make a living, so journalism was the next best thing. I've put six years into my journalistic career, and all I have to show for it is a role as a junior reporter for a Brooklyn-based magazine.

I never attempted to pen another novel, but I continued with my stories. I don't care if they'll never be seen by anyone else but me. I'm not writing for an audience. I'm doing this for myself and because when I'm inspired, I can't help but write. Most of the time, inspiration hits when I meet people I wish had different lives: better, happier. Inconveniently, that seems to happen at the wrong time and in the wrong place. Last week, I shadowed a senior reporter—which means prepping interview questions and taking notes—when I saw a janitor in front of Yankee Stadium. I named him Ian. He ran after a loose dog and returned it to its owner, a sharply dressed businesswoman. Elizabeth, I thought, suited her perfectly. Minutes later, instead of taking notes during the interview, I was writing my best love story yet—Ian and Elizabeth's.

That's who I am. Happy in my made-up worlds where anything is possible. Where someone like me, like her, like him, can have everything. Saccharine and all.

TWO

I finally get to the front of the line in the Starbucks where I just saw 'Natalie Bechamel'.

"Good morning, Maya. What will it be today?" asks the barista with a smile.

"Hi, Kay." Kay has her own HEA that I wrote last year. Still waiting for it to happen.

"The usual," I say. "One Venti Frappuccino with extra whipped cream and chocolate sauce; one grande, quad, nonfat, one-pump, no-whip mocha; one Tall Chai Tea Latte, three pumps, skim milk, no foam, extra hot; one Venti Iced Ristretto, four-pump, sugar-free, cinnamon, Dolce Soy Skinny Latte; and one Venti Iced Skinny Hazelnut Macchiato, extra shot."

Always five, so I can't carry them in a drink tray. Because why make life easy?

Once at the office I place the cups on my desk and start making the rounds. Janice—my boss—gets the Frappuccino, then the rest go to our team. I'm still considered the junior around here, despite being with the magazine for almost four years.

We're about to have our morning meeting, and I already know what I'm getting. Either shadowing again or a neighborhood brawl, a briefing from a small local official, or a school sports team event. Now and then, if I insist, aka beg, I get to cover a book launch, but somehow, my articles never make the cut. Today of all days, I'm not upset about it though. I hope I get my assignment done quickly so I can be out of here on time. I have big plans tonight.

The moment I sit, Janice calls—yells—my name from across the corridor.

I take my notepad and rush to her, all ears.

"Remember I told you how we lost the story of Nakamura, the *New York Times* bestselling author who lives in Vermont and who's recently been nominated for a Pulitzer?"

I nod.

"Well, we just got another shot at it. Last-minute thing, and since nobody has ever interviewed him, this is an incredible opportunity for us."

I assume this means she's going to Vermont. "I'll book you on a flight for later today—"

"That's the thing. You've been asking me for your big story for years now."

Anything would seem big at this point. But this—this would be huge.

"What? You're giving me the assignment?"

The moment I've been waiting for for so long, and it comes at the worst of times. David and I haven't had a weekend away in ages. And the ones we've had didn't take us further than Connecticut or Rhode Island and only because he had friends there. We need this time alone to see where we stand and try and get that initial spark back.

"I thought you'd be happy about it," says Janice, raising an eyebrow.

"I am. Very happy. It's just that this weekend is my birthday, and I have plans."

Both her eyebrows are raised now and form a bothersome straight line. That's bad news.

"I'll go, of course. This is a big opportunity for me. Thank you."

"For our magazine. This exclusive interview could catapult us out of anonymity."

I'm still in shock. She's finally open to giving me a shot. I know I can't screw it up. Not if I want to be taken seriously as a journalist and do something with my writing.

"I'm giving you Mason," she says before walking away.

Mason is the magazine's photographer, occasional driver, and jack of all trades. Not my favorite character, especially after witnessing an unfortunate scene between him, his girlfriend, and her soon-to-be ex-husband, right here at the magazine. It ended with Mason hiding in the newsroom's bathroom until the other guy left. Of course I wrote a story about him. Gave him lots of lessons to learn—about being kind, brave, generous. And, eventually, I redeemed him. He ended up living happily with his new wife, getting ready to have a baby. In my story, at least. In real life, just a few months later, a woman came by the magazine, saying she was pregnant, and he refused to acknowledge the baby or help out in any way. The resemblance between that woman and how I pictured his wife was uncanny, but that was the only thing I got right.

Mason finds me in the kitchen.

"Are you ready? We have to get going; it's a long drive," he says, sounding annoyed.

"We're driving? That's six hours one way, at least."

He scoffs. "Tell me about it. You didn't think she'd pay for plane tickets, did you?"

"This is going to be tight. We have to get there, do the interview and return right away."

Mason starts laughing. "Why is that?"

"I'm going to San Francisco tonight."

"Not if you want to keep your job. The interview isn't scheduled until tomorrow afternoon. By the time we wrap up it'll be evening. We'll be back Sunday."

My stomach drops. "Sunday? Oh, no."

I've been planning this getaway for weeks, ever since I found out David was going to California for an interview, around my birthday. That's when I got the idea of surprising him and showing up in San Francisco for a weekend together. Just the two of us. I even bought a fancy dress and shoes. Thought I'd make an effort.

He makes a dismissive gesture with his arm. "Are you coming or not?"

"I need to go home and get my backpack. It's already packed."

"Make it fast. Give me your address, and I'll come to pick you up."

My surprise is never going to happen! Our perfect weekend and my perfect birthday. The first one in a long time. Gone.

THREE

The trip to Vermont is tedious and long. Still, we both survive, despite stopping somewhere in Massachusetts to grab fast food, which proves to be a bad idea, as I end up with a nasty stomachache. Also, I wish he'd let me drive. I forgot what an aggressive driver he is, and I end up spending most of the six hours there clutching my seat. The only positive thing of the whole drive is seeing a woman truck driver at the fast food stop and coming up with a cute little story about her.

* * *

In the morning, I'm sitting in the inn's lobby, putting the finishing touches on the truck driver's story in my notebook. I usually write longhand and then transcribe to my laptop.

Mason is out somewhere, undoubtedly charming a poor, unsuspecting woman. When my phone rings and it's a local number, my immediate thought is that he got into trouble. Hope I don't have to bail him out of jail or something. "Ms. Maas?" It's Nakamura's publicist. "Mr. Nakamura can't do the interview this evening, but if you can get to his house at ten-thirty, I'll try to get you in. I'll call to confirm."

This is perfect. I text Mason with the good news and twenty minutes later, we're parked in front of the iron gate that protects the author's massive property in Stowe.

"We're early, so I'm going to make a call," I say, getting out of the car.

"Alisa, I need your help," I say the moment she picks up.

Alisa is my best friend. We met because we lived in adjacent rooms on the college campus, and we got close because we were both English majors who shared a passion for collecting old books. We got along well but didn't become what we are today until after graduation when I ran into her in New York City one day.

I was in my early days with David and she was living with her now ex, Sebastian, who I knew from school. When I saw her that day, she was crying, so I asked her to join me for coffee and didn't give up until she told me what was wrong, despite her reticence. I found out Sebastian was emotionally abusive, he was gaslighting her, and she was slowly losing her grip on reality. I basically forced her to leave him, took her in and made sure she didn't go back to him. Although she tried a few times. Back then, Alisa was working as a junior editor at a publishing house in the city. When she told me about an opening for a paid internship in London, a few months later, I encouraged—read: bugged her—to take it. A fresh start she needed and deserved.

Ever since then we've been bound together by more than just our love of words and books. The distance didn't ruin our relationship, it made it stronger. The only problem we have is the time difference, but we make it work.

Alisa is now a senior commissioning editor and is in love

with a wonderful man who adores her. I'd say everything worked out for her—just as I hoped it would when I wrote the story of Alisa's amazing adventures in London. Even better than my story.

"How's California? Bright and sunny?" she asks. "Send me a photo."

"I'm not in California. Sorry, I meant to call you last night, but it was chaotic. I'm in Vermont on a last-minute assignment from Janice."

"What about your plans? Why do you let her push you around, Maya?"

"This is a big one, Alisa. I get to talk to Nakamura."

"It was about time you got a good one," she says and I'm thankful she knows who I'm talking about, and I don't have to explain.

"Yes. I'm in front of his house. That's why I need you, and I don't have much time."

"Oh, sorry. Yes. What can I do?"

"I need you to go online and find me a ticket for tonight from NY to SF. I don't have time to do research now and I'm afraid it'll be too late when I finish here. Please."

"So, you're still going?"

"I am, yes."

Alisa is not a big fan of David, and I know she's thinking I'm trying too hard.

"OK, then. I'll do it and send you the details."

"Thank you. You're the best!"

"Take care and good luck with Nakamura. I heard he's difficult."

"I hope not," I say, and she laughs.

I hang up when Mason bangs on the car window, showing me the watch. It's ten-thirty.

I press the buzzer. Nothing. I try again. No answer.

"I don't think he's here," I say as Mason gets his gear out of the car.

"Let's just wait then," he grumbles.

And we do. For an hour. Then another two. It's one-thirty already.

We go back to the car because our feet hurt from all the standing around and I call the publicist several times, but when she doesn't answer, I leave voicemails.

"What are we going to do?" I ask, panicking when I see it's already 2 PM.

Mason shrugs. A bomb could be dropping next to us and he would still be unfazed.

"I don't know, but you should think of something and fast. If we go back without an interview, we'll both lose our jobs."

"No, we won't," I say. "That's ridiculous. It's not our fault."

"I'm not even surprised by this. The guy is impossible. I heard he hung up on Janice."

Alisa was right. "You think she knew what we were in for?" I asked.

"For sure. Why do you think Janice gave you this assignment? Out of the goodness of her heart? That's why she didn't come. She doesn't like dealing with difficult people."

"If Janice knows how he is, she won't hold it against us."

"Dream on!" he says, continuing to play on his phone.

Another thirty minutes.

At one point, a black limousine pulls past us as the iron gates open. I jump out of the car and run toward it, with Mason behind me, but it continues up the driveway and the gates close.

A man gets out and I immediately recognize him from the photo I have.

"Mr. Nakamura. Mr. Nakamura," I say, the second time louder.

He doesn't even turn around to look at me.

"We're from *Brooklyn Times*. We had an interview scheduled for today."

He finally turns. "No comment."

"No comment?" I repeat quietly. What does that even mean? "We drove all the way from New York. Please, we won't take long," I say, my voice barely audible.

"No comment," he says again as he walks inside the house.

I wish I could be more combative. I turn to Mason. "Say something."

"What do you want me to say? I'm just the camera guy; you're the reporter."

Nakamura disappears inside just as my phone rings. It's his publicist and I tell her what just happened. "I'm sorry for the inconvenience. Let me talk to him," she says kindly. She sounds like a nice woman. I wonder what her life is like, having to deal with this man regularly. Being a brilliant author doesn't give him the right to treat people this way.

She calls back an hour later, by which point I'm hungry, cold, and I'm getting desperate.

"I'm sorry," she says. "I just found out he took an interview with another publication."

My jaw drops.

"What other publication? When?"

"This morning, apparently. *New York Lifestyle*."

Mason gives me an 'I told you so' look. "I'd say revamp that résumé."

"I'm sure Janice will understand," I say, trying to be hopeful.

* * *

She doesn't. When we call, Janice's reaction is one of the most violent, profanity-filled monologues I've ever had the displeasure of hearing. She calls us incapable, lazy, and as far away from journalists as she's ever seen. She tells us we're fired, and we owe her for the gas, accommodation and meals for this 'useless' trip.

A bit dazed by this new development, I get in the car, and we drive back to New York. When Mason starts telling me all about his freelancing plans and how this is a blessing in disguise, I turn on the radio. Not now, Mason.

We're minutes from my house when I notice the text Alisa sent. She booked me on the last flight of the night, and I realize that I shouldn't let losing my job ruin this for me. The surprise. My birthday. California.

FOUR

When I arrive in San Francisco, the weather is fantastic. Brilliant sunshine, short-sleeve temperature. Simply perfect.

I call and then text David, but there's no response. He doesn't know I'm here or how terrible the last twenty-four hours have been, I remind myself. I hope he's going to be excited when he sees me. He'll tell me everything will be fine, and I'll find another job quickly, and I'll smile, although I know it's a lie. It's hard to find another job when your previous boss hates you and is most likely not writing you a recommendation. But I don't want to think about this now. Also, I don't want to think that David might not be as supportive as I'm hoping. Our relationship has been struggling lately. No negative thoughts; just good vibes. I'll think about this beautiful day spent here. And how it will help us and how amazing and romantic it will be.

I congratulate myself on the idea as I sit on a bench in front of the airport and wait for David to see my messages and call me back. I didn't tell him in my text that I'm here.

Just that I have a surprise and he should get back to me ASAP.

There are so many people around, all rushing to get somewhere, maybe meet someone. If I stayed here, I'd have enough material for fifty stories. I pull my notebook and take a few notes.

I don't even realize when time passes, and when I recheck my phone, I notice it's been almost twenty minutes. And there's still no sign from him.

Knock knock, I text him.

Nothing. Five more minutes. Ten. Fifteen. It's now been over forty minutes. I text again.

Finally, my phone beeps. A message from David.

Who are you looking for?

I'm looking for a man, I text. The reply comes seconds later.

I'm a man, but I doubt you're looking for me

He's funny. I respond in the same tone.

How about this then? I'm looking for a love connection.

Sure, OK. Can you describe the owner of the phone please and give me a name?

Blond. Tall. Hunky. Surfer-like. David, the best boyfriend on the East Coast.

A few seconds later.

Now I know who it is. Are you guys still at Embarcadero?

He does have a talent for pushing things too far sometimes. Limits, David, limits.

Stop, I text back. But I don't get a chance to send it, because a new text arrives.

Does he want his phone or not?

My fingers clench on the phone. I don't know how to react. It's like I'm numb.

Who are you and why do you have David's phone? I don't understand.

I'm genuinely starting to panic, and I have a bad feeling about all this. I thought it was David making a joke, but now, I'm not sure it's him.

He left it in my car. You must be the blonde in the red dress? I'm the Lift driver who dropped you two off earlier. You guys were quite busy in the back seat; no wonder he forgot it.

The blonde? What blonde? This is either a sick joke or a terrible misunderstanding.

Not a blonde and I haven't worn a dress in ages. David was with a blonde in your car?

I take a deep breath, trying to calm down. What's going on? This can't be happening.

Oops. Sorry, he texts back.

Ooops, sorry? I feel like crying and screaming at the same time. Is this for real?

If you're not the woman I met, then who are you?

Just David's girlfriend of 5 years!! No big deal.

Now I'm starting to feel angry and humiliated. I take deep breaths, and my hands shake.

Maybe they were just friends, he texts.

I thought you said they were all over each other. That doesn't sound like friends.

He doesn't text back.

How naïve of me. Flying thousands of miles to surprise him on his 'business trip'. What a fool I've been. What a fool. Business trips, that's what they're called now?

The man texts me back. *Don't want to be insensitive, but what do you want me to do with the phone? Bring it to you?*

Sure. Whatever.

Where are you?

At the airport like an idiot. Just came from NYC to surprise him.

I'm really sorry, he texts. *I feel guilty now.*

A minute later. *How will I recognize you?*

Green-blue backpack, Guns N' Roses T-shirt and jeans. Brunette—NOT BLONDE, OK? Shoulder-length hair. Sunglasses. Sat right outside arrivals.

FIVE

If today was a story, it wouldn't be one I'd write. Even if I hated the main character.

An hour ago, I was waiting for David to call me back so I could reveal the big surprise. I was so excited. Fifteen minutes ago, I was trying not to cry in public—or to scream; it varied from moment to moment. I was so heartbroken, mad, and humiliated. And now, here I am. About to board an airport shuttle to Carmel by the Sea, a small oceanside town. Somewhere out there.

How did I get here? How did I get from recovering David's cell phone to not wanting anything to do with him? And why did I say yes to the Lift driver's suggestion that I should hop on a bus for three hours to go to a town I've never heard of?

It probably started with the realization that I was pathetic. Why would I want David's phone? To do what with? He was out there somewhere, busy cheating on me, and I was busy taking care of his belongings? I texted the driver back that he could keep it and do whatever he wanted with it. Somehow in our back and forth texts, it slipped that it's my birthday and how disappointing everything is and how I imagined the day would go.

I know a place just like you said you imagined California. Ocean, beach. If that's what you dreamed for your birthday, you should totally go. Spend the day there, he texted.

I could tell he felt sorry for me, and to be honest, I felt sorry for myself. What a crappy ending to a genuinely crappy twenty-four hours. Everything crumbled around me: my career, my love life, my accommodation—since the apartment is in David's name.

The driver's suggestion was kind, but it was also unusual, and I hesitated at first. But everything that could go wrong had already gone wrong. What else was there? The bus would break down? I'd be attacked by highway pirates? This wasn't more than the lesser of two evils scenario—sitting for twenty-four hours on a chair in front of an empty terminal and the unknown. And it's not like I accepted to spend the day with a complete stranger. He'll just be my guide from a distance. Crazy, as far as ideas go, but seemingly safe.

By the time you get to Carmel, I'll have an itinerary ready for you.

Why are you being so nice to me? I texted back.

Because nobody deserves to be unhappy on their birthday.

He seems like a good man. Taking the time to do this for me and keeping me company, even if it's a virtual company. All because I told him it's my birthday. There are still nice people left in this world. Am I a nice person? Would I have done this for someone else? I don't know. I've been so caught up in my life, I don't remember the last time I did something selfless. That's sad.

In line for the bus, I look around at couples and families.

I'm the only one who's alone. I hope this day won't turn into one of those cautionary stories you tell your kids.

I can't help but think... if I'd stayed home and waited for David, none of this would've happened. What am I saying? That I would've preferred I was cheated on as long as I didn't know it? What kind of person am I? Why would I want that? That's not love. Come to think of it, I don't even know if I've ever truly experienced love. I've cared about people, usually the wrong people. I've gotten used to them and our life together, but love... love is a big word.

At the first stop, a young woman wearing what looks like a bridesmaid dress gets on. She's barefoot. She takes the seat behind me and I unwittingly hear bits and pieces of the conversation with the man next to her. She's very chatty and in a few minutes, she tells him all about the ex who showed up and how she had to leave. Is she a runaway bridesmaid? I take out my notebook and jot down an idea for what I feel will be a great story, when I hear some more of their conversation. Now she's asking him about his life, and then they jump to their childhood. That was fast. I've never been that friendly toward people I've just met. Now they're playing a 'twenty questions' type of game and I chuckle. I have a feeling these two will not need one of my stories to find what they both seem to be looking for.

I call Alisa. I have to tell her what happened, and I bet she won't believe what I'm doing right now. I wonder if she'll say that I'm going entirely off the rails, or on the contrary, 'Good for you, girl!' I think the latter. Unfortunately, she doesn't answer, and I check the time; it's 3:30 PM in London. She must be in meetings.

It's been twenty minutes, but it feels like forever. The

row behind me is having a blast, now reaching 'the most embarrassing moments' category in their game.

When my phone beeps, I'm convinced it's Alisa, but it's the Lift driver.

Hope you brought a book. The drive is pretty dull. Sorry!

It's OK. I'm being entertained by two people who just met and are playing 20 questions.

What is it about telling all your secrets to a complete stranger? I always wondered if that's a myth or if it's true, he texts.

What?

They say it's easier to talk to someone you don't know in real life.

I wouldn't know. I've never tried that.

Me neither, he texts. *And anyway, I'm more of the two lies and one truth kind of guy.*

I thought it was two truths and one lie, I say.

Then I played it wrong all my life. Ha-ha.

Not my favorite game, I text.

I remember we used to play it in college, back in the early days of David and me. He refused to join and said it was stupid. So I started thinking it was stupid too and never got over it.

Oops. It sounds like we're running out of games. What about give me a number?

What?

I'm confused. Is he asking for my number? He already has it.

It's a game between strangers and it's pretty simple. You write down 50 questions. I write down 50 questions, and then you give me a number and I ask you the question attached to it. And vice versa. Nothing identifying like name or what you look like because the point is to get to know each other, not to stalk each other after.

I start laughing before getting nervous, and then eventually, I calm down. Just because he thought how this might sound and he's trying to make me feel comfortable gets him points.

Sounds like fun. Never heard of it, I say.

I just made it up.

I start laughing. I like him. I mean... I like that he makes me laugh. I have no new stories to write, no books to read, over two hours to kill, and the view is not much for now. Fields. Just fields as far as the eye can see. *Sure. Let's do it. Are we doing categories or just free for all?*

Categories? Why not? Let's go kitschy. Have you ever/would you ever, Do you, This or That, What's Your, How would you.

Give me 15 minutes, I text.

OK. And you go first, he texts back.

SIX

Why am I overthinking these questions? It's a game, Maya.
Who cares what you ask? Apparently, I do, and it takes me a
while to come up with fifty questions. Not because I can't
think of any, but because trying to imagine what kind of
person he is and what I should ask to get to know him—
without ever seeing him—is the reverse of how my imagination works. I usually see someone and then create a story
around that. Now I'll have to come up with a story from the
answers and then build the image to go with it. I know so far
that he's a Lift driver, he lives somewhere in Northern California, and he seems nice. That's all.

This exercise reminds me of Alisa and her online dating
adventures. Not that I'm thinking of him as an online date.
Not at all. There's no romantic interest here. I'm curious;
that's all there is to it. It's a new experience, and I'm allowing
myself to be... intrigued. Yes, that's the word. I'm intrigued.

Number 7, I text.

Have you ever eaten food that fell on the floor? he writes
back.

I chuckle. That's his question? OK...

Does the 5-second rule apply?

Outside of the 5-second rule.

Then no.

I did. Number 3.

Have you ever lied to your parents about where you're going?

Is it a trick question? Of course! But that was a long time ago.

That's a clue. A long time ago. He sounds older than I am. Although, if I think about it, high school was a long time ago for me too. *I didn't,* I say.

Then you're a much better person than I am.

I roll my eyes.

Or I was just a boring teenager. Number 13.

Have you ever done something you regretted? he texts.

That's a tough question. And kind of ironic.

Many times. Today for instance.

I hope you're not talking about this trip, he texts.

No.

I get a small tinge in my stomach and find myself smiling at the phone.

Good. Number 10, he says.

Time for some this or that. *Tea or Coffee?* I text.

Easy one. Coffee.

Same here. Do you have a favorite?

Strong coffee? And lots of it? he texts and then sends laughing emojis.

Totally with him on that one.

My turn. Number 21, I text.

Have you ever cheated? he asks.

No. Never, I say.

And it's true. I have never ever cheated on any of my boyfriends.

That was an insensitive question. I'm sorry. And I'm mad about what he did to you. It's unacceptable. Totally unacceptable, he texts back and despite the distance—who knows how big—I wish I could give him a hug.

A second text arrives seconds later. *I never cheated on anyone either. And never will.*

I read the text, and it gives me pause. I want to write something back, then I stop. It's like the awkward silence between two people who are face to face. Only we're not.

And a third text. *Number 15.*

Hope this doesn't count as cheating; it's a tiny tweak to the game. The real number 15 is: 'Would you ever swim with the sharks?' Instead, I ask, *Would you ever get married?*

The moment I press send, I regret it. He'll think I'm hitting on him. I shouldn't have done that; I don't even know where it came from. I guess I just... I just want to figure out if he's married. Why does it matter? It's not like... well, the harm's been done. I can't recall my text.

I hope I will. One day. When and if I find the right person, he answers a couple of minutes later. Those two minutes felt like two hours.

I don't know what to write back. I'd like to answer 'ditto' but he never asks, so I don't. Instead, I give him a new number: 31.

What's your biggest fear? he asks.

How much time do you have? I answer almost instantly.

As much as you do, he replies.

Not achieving my dreams, being forgotten, not being a good person, making mistakes, not being good enough, not being enough, ending up alone. The unknown, I text.

We're fear-twins, which is funny. I seriously doubt you'll end up alone and no one can measure your worth but yourself. Don't compare to others. As for the unknown, nothing worth achieving has been achieved by staying in your comfort zone. You're taking a step now. Heading into the unknown. Alone, he texts.

Not really alone. Did I thank you yet? I wouldn't have left the airport if it wasn't for you.

No need to thank me. I'm sure you would've done the same. Number 32.

Would I? The second time I'm asking myself this question in a few short hours, and it's something that hasn't crossed my mind before today. Maybe because I knew I wouldn't like the answer: I wouldn't have done the same. But I'd like to think that will change.

How would you describe yourself in 3 words, all starting with the same letter?

Moody. Mindful. Maximus.

Good ones. Like Maximus from The Gladiator?

He sends a grinning emoji. *Sorry, I meant Maximum. I hate autocorrect.*

Actually, I like that. Maximus. It suits you. I pride myself on being good at coming up with names for people. So, since I don't know your real name, can I call you Max?

Do you want to know my name? he texts, and I swallow nervously.

Do I? I do... Why not? What's the harm in that? I can't call him 'Mr. Driver'. And putting a name to what I already know about him will help me create a better picture of him.

You know what? Max it is. We said no personal stuff, so I want to stay true to our rules. Wouldn't want to ruin our game, he texts before I get the chance to reply.

Too bad. I really wanted to know. But I guess Max will do. For now.

Next stop is Carmel, I text.

Maybe we'll continue this later then. If you want to.

I smile from ear to ear. I hoped he'd say that. Where did the last two hours even go?

SEVEN

The moment I get off the bus, I know this place is unlike any other I've ever been to.

It reminds me of those made-up towns in movies that are fully constructed in a studio. The houses look like they've been drawn by an artist with too much imagination and a weakness for fairy tales. They're tiny and quirky and each of them has a plaque on the front with a name: The Sailboat, Souvenirs, Seventh Heaven, Sans Souci, Casablanca, Sea Horse. This is amazing.

My phone beeps. The Lift driver. Max, I remind myself, it's Max now.

The first thing is dropping your luggage somewhere. I assume you have luggage.

Just a backpack. I can carry it; I don't mind.

OK. Second thing is you're going to need a proper breakfast, he says.

I ate on the plane, I answer.

That's not food. I'm giving you two options: Bellini or Café Azure. Your pick.

How would I choose? I ask. *I don't know which one is better.*

Intuition. Don't women have that sixth sense?

Ha-ha. I doubt it applies to restaurants. I'll go with Café Azure. I've always wanted to go to Paris and this one sounds French.

Good choice. I'll send you the link on Google maps.

Dolores and Seventh. It's not far from where I am, and I take my time, walking and basking in the sun like a lizard. On the left side pretty houses, on the right side the ocean and a white-sanded beach like I've always dreamed of.

The temptation is too strong. I take my shoes off and walk in the sand.

If you take the Scenic Road Walkway, you could stop by the beach if you want. It's nice and it shouldn't be too busy now.

I gulp. Yes, that's exactly where I am.

Guess what I'm doing? I ask.

Running back to the station to catch the bus to San Francisco?

Why would I ever do that? It's beautiful here. No! I text.

I'm tempted to take a selfie, but instead, I just send a photo of the beach.

Nice! Breakfast will still be there when you're ready.

I sit in the warm sand. It's just me here, a couple walking their dog on my left and a man running to my right. It's so serene.

Number 44, I text.

Oh, good, I was afraid you didn't want to play anymore.

What's your favorite book? he asks.

I have so many. My absolute favorites are the ones I read

as a child. I'll say my top three are: The Secret Garden, Princess Bride, *and* A Wrinkle in Time.

Those are great books. Mine are oldies too, but more of the late teenage ones, like The Great Gatsby, To Kill A Mockingbird *and* Brave New World. *Number 29.*

Have you ever seen a ghost? I text.

I don't know if I believe in ghosts, but I hope there is something after this. Not that I'm excited at the prospect of getting stuck here and haunting people, LOL. Have you?

I don't know. Maybe. When I look in the mirror in the morning before I put on makeup.

He sends laughing emojis. *Self-deprecation is endearing.*

I feel my face getting hot. If I had a mirror, I'd probably see my cheeks are red.

After a while, I put my shoes back on and walk in the direction of the breakfast place.

Café Azure is a cozy café—I'm sure peaceful when it's not so packed like today. It also has a few tables on the sidewalk, and I stay outside. I've always wanted to eat like the Parisians.

A young woman greets me with a smile. "Welcome to Café Azure. What can I get you?"

"Good morning," I say and realize I'm mirroring her smile. "Not sure what's good here. Someone recommended it. Do you still serve breakfast?"

"We sure do. How hungry are you?"

"Starving," I say. "I only had plane food."

"Say no more. Do you prefer eggs or oats and fruit?"

"They all sound good," I say, my stomach now grumbling.

"Leave it to me then," she says and walks back in.

Minutes later, she returns with a large glass of a red

drink. "*Compote de saison*," she says. "Cherry. It's my favorite."

A good drink, a spot in the sun, a flurry of people up and down the street. Each with their own story. Since I sat down, I've jotted down ideas for three stories already. And the ideas keep coming. I usually get one, not twenty of them. I'm so busy writing—almost like I'm in a frenzy—that I don't even see her standing in front of me with a large platter.

"Breakfast is served," she says, with the same warm smile.

Two eggs, baguette, butter, different kinds of cheese and hams and fresh fruit. Oh, my. And it's all so delicious, I eat without stopping.

I don't remember the last time I sat alone at a table without feeling uncomfortable. But here, it seems that nobody cares. There are plenty of singles and people look relaxed and not judgmental. It makes me feel better about my situation. I keep going back to it, even if I don't want to. I take a big gulp of the compote and whisper, 'Happy birthday, Maya'.

And I'm not alone, am I? I'm texting Max, and at the same time, he texts me.

Mine is: *Thank you, you were right. This café is something else.*

His: *What do you think? Did you make a good choice?*

Then we both send smiling emojis and I smile in real life too.

When you're ready, your second stop awaits you, he texts.
Ready.
San Carlos Borromeo de Carmelo Mission. It's a fifteen-minute walk.

I'm putting my phone in my pocket when it rings and I'm so startled, I let out a shriek. Why is he calling? I'm not ready to hear his voice. What would I even say to him? My hands are clammy and I'm so nervous, I don't even check to see if it's him or not.

"Sorry I missed your call."

I breathe, relieved when I hear Alisa's voice.

"I was in an editorial meeting and then had to see a client. How's Mr. Fancy Pants? Hope he's kissing the ground you walk on for all you went through to surprise him," she says.

"He's kissing something alright, but it has nothing to do with me," I say.

"W—what are you talking about? What's going on?" she asks.

"He's cheating on me. I'm still processing, to be honest. He's here with someone else."

"Oh my God! Did you catch him with another woman? Maya, I'm so sorry. I'll kill him!"

"Not if I do it first," I say. More than anything, I'm angry, and I realize that now. I feel betrayed and made a fool of. I feel like I wasted so much of my life for no reason. "I didn't catch him, but someone saw him."

"My heart breaks for you," she says. "What did you do? Are you staying in San Francisco until tomorrow or going back earlier? This is horrible. I'm so sorry you're all alone there."

"I'm not all alone."

"Oh?"

"I met someone," I say and then snicker. "I didn't actually meet someone. It's a long story, though, so I'll tell you more when we Skype."

"I wanted to say, but I didn't want to seem mean."

"What?"

"You don't sound totally destroyed over David. You're perky."

"Perky? Me?"

"Why can't you tell me now?" she asks. "I want to know all about it."

"Because I just arrived at the church and there's a 'no cell phones' sign on the door.

"The church? Are you marrying someone you just met?"

I start laughing. "Sure, because that's exactly the kind of thing I'd do. No marrying in the cards, relax. Just visiting. It's like a museum."

She lets out a loud sigh. "And you're alright? You're safe? You don't need anything?"

"I am perfectly safe, and I will call you when I get back to New York tomorrow."

"I love you," she says.

EIGHT

The mission is beautiful. I take a guided tour and it's incredible how so much history is bottled up in this building. It dates from back in the 1700s.

An hour later, I emerge from the dark church and back into the sun and immediately turn my phone on again, feeling a bit of excitement. Has he texted me while I was in there? Should I text him? And that little feeling in my stomach makes me smile. I haven't been this anxious since I was a teenager and was waiting by the landline for my crush to call.

I do have a text from him. *How do you feel about biking?*

A big smile on my face.

In general?

No. *In particular. Ha-ha.*

I haven't ridden a bike since I was a child. Not sure if I still know how.

Do you know the expression, 'it's like riding a bike?'

Yes. But I don't think it applies to me.

You'll be fine. Plus, it's electric, so won't be as hard. 201 Mission Street.

As you wish, I text. Will he get the Princess Bride reference? He will, I think, and my certainty gives me pause.

I hope you'll be a fool. That's the best thing you can be, he texts back.

I hold my breath. This is what gives me pause the most. Not only that he obviously got the reference, but that he answered with his Great Gatsby one, which I immediately got.

Don't be too impressed, he texts back, as if reading my mind. *I have a photographic memory. I never forget anything I read.* I am even more impressed now, I think, and smile to myself.

* * *

I'm at the corner of Ocean Avenue and Mission Street, in front of a shop that faces Red Eagle Lane and across from Tiffany's. This town is as eclectic as they come. There are maybe eight or nine people on bikes and moving between us, a man dressed in a bright red T-shirt waves his arms above his head. "Everyone ready?"

An elderly couple cheers as they hold hands even on bikes. It's lovely to see. Will it be bizarre if I take out my notebook from my backpack and write something on it? I have to do it.

"Hands on the handlebar," I hear right behind me as the redshirt man spots my notebook.

I smile innocently and stuff it in the backpack. "Writers write," I mumble, amused.

Before entering Pebble Beach, we take Scenic Road to cycle along what the guide tells us is the most beautiful stretch of coastal roadway in the US: 17 Mile Drive. It's breathtaking. We pass the golf course, the Lone Cypress Tree where we stop, and I take a few photos with my phone. I text one to Max, who sends back smileys and asks me if I'm having a good time.

A blast!

Did you know this is the most photographed tree in the world?

I didn't. Had no idea. Just like I had no idea that a day that started so disastrously would take me here. Despite the pain and the uncertainty of my future and the regret for the last four years—both at work and with David—I find myself smiling from ear to ear as Max and I text back and forth. I do not feel alone at all, as hard as that is to explain, even to myself.

The group is now at the Ghost Tree and Cypress Point Lookout, where we stop again. There are seals and otters on the large rocks in the ocean and the view and this moment take my breath away. This is by far the most amazing adventure I've ever been on.

We head on to Fanshell Cove, Seal Point, Point Joe and eventually to Spanish Bay. The group stops at the beach where there are lots of stacking stones and I take tons of photos. I'm sorry I didn't bring my camera with me and even sadder it's in David's apartment, because I can't even call it my own anymore. Whatever happens after today, I need to get my things out of there. Where to though, that's the question. I guess back to my mom's house? Moving back to Hartford isn't something I ever thought I'd do, but then again, I should stop planning for anything, as it's fairly obvious by now it's completely pointless and it only leads to disappointment.

Knowing Max is a text away, giving me directions and

helping me navigate this day is comforting. I feel safe and not lonely at all, although I'm practically alone here. And one of the best parts about this day and the greatest surprise for sure is how much I'm enjoying getting to know him. I find myself wondering when the tour will end—although I'm having a great time—so I can sit somewhere and talk to him again. And I don't remember the last time I felt like this.

I say goodbye to my cycling buddies and text Max.

What an amazing town this is!

I'm glad you like it. It's one of the prettiest in the Bay Area. Some say the prettiest. Do you want to relax a little? Catch your breath?

Yes, please, I say.

When I look at my watch, I can't believe this whole cycling tour was three hours.

It's mid-afternoon now and the sun is not so strong anymore. I've finished the two water bottles I bought for the ride—thankfully the guide reminded us to get some—and I'm thirsty and tired. But a good kind of tired. I'm still smiling and in awe of everything.

I think I know the answer to this question, but here it goes: the beach with snacks and a drink OR a terrace?

The beach, I answer without hesitation.

I only got to spend those few minutes on the beach earlier in the morning, and I'm dying to go back. I grew up dreaming about it. After I moved to New York for college, I never saw the ocean except for the occasional Long Island trip. And I had never seen the Pacific until now.

Max tells me where I can get something to drink and the fastest way to Carmel Beach.

Impressive how he gets all of his directions so right, but,

as a Lift driver, you kind of have to know your way around, don't you?

I text him from the shop the moment I see a rack full of sunglasses.

What do you think? I ask and send him three photos with three different pairs. I'm holding them in my hand, not wearing them, since we're staying away from anything personal.

Get the pink ones. Seeing life through rose-colored glasses is allowed on one's birthday.

Back on the beach, I lie in the sand, staring at the clouds and listening to the waves. I could see myself living here. My life would be so different, wouldn't it? New York is always in such a rush. Time seems to stand still here. It gives you room to catch your breath.

Whose turn is it? I ask.

Yours if you want.

Alright. Let's go with number 22.

What's your pet peeve? he asks.

This is like the list of fears. Too many to count. But I'll try: loud chewing, being late, people who say honestly before telling a blatant lie, and those who say literally before a non-literal thing, people stopping suddenly in the middle of the street.

That last one is such a NYC pet peeve, he says. *And it's a good thing we don't know each other in real life because I'm that guy who chews loudly, is always late and says literally and honestly all the time. Honestly.*

Ha-ha-ha. I don't believe you, I text.

Why not? he asks.

You just don't seem like that type of person.

What type is that?

The obnoxious one.

I just fooled you because I'm a master texter.

Although I'm pretty sure it's a joke, it does make me think. And it's never a good thing when I think. Because I don't just think. I overthink and then I analyze and overanalyze. Normally, I'd talk to Alisa about this, but it's midnight in London, and her phone goes to voicemail. So I'm left to do this by myself. What if he just has a great way with words? This man I don't know. We've now been talking for seven hours and I've found out more about him than I did about David in the first seven months of our relationship. Yet, I don't really know him. I picture him in a certain way, but he could be way different. His voice might be squeaky or deep. His mannerisms might be maddening. Age is just a number, so whether he's in his twenties or his thirties that wouldn't make a difference—and I doubt he's older than that. There's just something about our conversation so far that makes me believe we might be relatively close in age. Could we be friends if we met face to face? Would I want us to be friends? I don't know why I keep going back to this. As we're texting now, I'm even trying to write down some thoughts about him. What kind of character would he be? What kind of story would I give him?

And the funniest, funniest thing happens. I'm jealous of the woman character I would pair him with. This is ridiculous, but it's what I feel.

I look at my phone and I'm tempted to call. I'll just wait until he says hello so I can hear his voice. Then I'll know if his voice matches his personality. What am I? Five? Calling and hanging up? No. I'm not going to call him to hear his voice or for any other reason. It wouldn't be appropriate, and it would most likely ruin everything. Anyway, he would've called me if he wanted to. Why didn't he want to?

Now I'm in my head like I always am. Does he have a family? He's not married, I know that—or I think I know. But maybe he was married before, maybe he has children, old parents who need care, or needs to take rides instead of texting with me. Or just do something else today. Am I imposing on his time? Maybe I should cut him loose. He might feel like he owes me something, and he clearly doesn't. He's done enough for me as it is. Much more than anyone— especially a complete stranger—ever did before.

I was thinking, you know you don't have to keep me virtual company all day. If you have other things to do, you can just tell me the names of the places in advance, I say.

Are you trying to get rid of me? he texts.

I rush to answer. I don't want him to think that's what I want. *No, no. Not at all. I'm quite enjoying your company.*

Am I flirting with him? Is that flirting? I'm so obviously not good at it, if I don't even know what it sounds like.

Good. Because I'm enjoying yours as well and I'm not planning on going anywhere.

I look at the phone and smile. The kind of smile I shouldn't have after today.

NINE

Are you ready for one more tour? he texts.

Yes, I am. Where do we go now?

The moment I hit send, I realize what I just said. Where do *we* go. It'd make me laugh if it didn't feel so true. Whoever he is and wherever he is, it's as if we're doing all these things together. Going from place to place, sharing these incredible experiences. And I'm loving it.

It's been hours since I last thought about David and all thanks to Max. How funny life is.

Fairy Tale Houses, he texts.

Wait, are those the few houses I saw when I got off the bus?

Those are just the touristy ones. Just wait and see, he says.

I like that he seems to know when to push back on me, and he doesn't do it aggressively but kind of in an attractive, taking-charge way.

Patience is not a virtue I possess, I send back with a grinning face.

Some things are worth waiting for, he texts together with a smiley wearing sunglasses.

I gulp. I think I read something else into that text. I don't know why.

Head on to Carmel Plaza, across from Devendorf Park on Ocean Ave, between Junipero and Mission. Look for the Trumpeter bronze statue and fountain in front of Kate Spade.

I follow his directions and arrive in front of the Trumpeter ten minutes later.

Now cross Ocean Avenue at Junipero and walk through Devendorf Park. Exit on Sixth.

Where to now?

You're a fast walker, he texts and sends me a running emoji.

I'm excited to get there, I text.

Cross Junipero to Surf and Sand Liquors. Right after is Torres Street. Turn left and walk up the hill. Across from the parking area of the Best Western you'll see it.

Oh, wow! What is this?

It's an amazing little house and it does truly look like it's from a fairy tale. And I know exactly from which one the moment I see it. Hansel and Gretel. When I get closer to the entrance, I smile to myself. The plaque says 'Hansel'. It looks like a real-life gingerbread house, with a cute light-green rounded door and matching window frames. *So beautiful*. It's not perfect and seems a little skewed, which makes it even more charming.

It's beautiful, isn't it? he texts.

A couple of minutes later, he texts again.

Let's walk back down the hill and turn left on Sixth Avenue. On the corner of Torres and Sixth is the historic Grant Wallace House, a Tudor Storybook style.

I love how he refers to all this as if we're in it together. Just like I accidentally did.

It looks like an elf house.

I laugh and stare at it in awe and then, of course, I take photos and send him one.

It does.

Next door is The Woods, which I take a photo of.

I walk back on Torres to Sixth Avenue and turn right and I see a house with a large sign in front that says, 'Hugh Comstock Residence'. Then 'Comstock Studio'.

Who is Hugh Comstock? I ask. Is it the architect who made all these houses?

He is the one who made all the original cottages back in the 20s, but he was no architect. He was just a guy who came to Carmel, fell madly in love, got married, and when his new wife said she wanted a fairy house in the woods, he got to work. She was an artist I think; she was making dolls and wanted to showcase them. And then everyone loved the little house so much, they all wanted one.

That's the cutest story ever. Almost, if not cuter than my own stories. See? So these things do happen. Not just in my imagination.

Did you notice how they're not level? he texts. *They're quirky.*

It's like searching for 'skewed' in Google and seeing the page tilt to the side.

Ha! Exactly. That same feeling, he says.

I like them even more because of that and knowing he wasn't trained to do this, and he made the first one out of love. It's amazing!

I walk from cottage to cottage until I reach a dreamy one

with a narrow arched three-light casement window with a heart shape cut out.

It's like he built all of them for her dolls. They seem so tiny.

Yes. Some are incredibly small. That one is less than 400 square feet, he texts.

I hold my breath. That one? How would he even know what I'm looking at right now?

I have a strange feeling and turn and look around. There's nobody on the street, except for a man and a woman talking at the corner of the intersecting road.

Which one?

A minute passes. No answer.

TEN

The one I just told you about. The Woods, he responds a couple of minutes later.

I passed it already. I'm at the heart-shaped one, I respond and instead of feeling relieved, I feel disappointed. For a second, I thought that maybe... I don't know what I thought. I think it was more than a thought, it was hope. A hopeless romantic's hope. Sometimes I have a hard time separating my imagination from the reality of this life. Where things like this don't happen.

Our House, he says.

Our House, yes. It's surely the most beautiful one I've seen today. Absolutely dreamy.

I still feel the disappointment. How silly of me to think such things. What did I imagine? That he's somewhere around? That's ridiculous. Just because someone is kind doesn't mean there's more to it. And how would I even react if he was here? Would I be scared or nervous or excited? Why would I be scared? Alisa would tell me to get out of here; that he could be anyone, a psycho, a stalker. But he's not anyone, is he? He's Max. And I know Max. Not sure where all these questions are coming from, but now's not a good time for this. I'm having so much fun. Someone is nice enough to guide me through all this, someone who didn't want me to be miserable and spend the day alone in the airport. This might be a fairy-tale town, but my life is not a fairy tale. It's not one of my stories. Silly thoughts from a silly woman.

I'm kind of hungry, I say after I see a few more houses.

Was hoping you'd say that. I have just the place for dinner.

Hope it's not fancy because I'm not dressed the part. Or if it is, I could go change. You know what? I would like to change. Been in these clothes for too many hours.

He tells me where I can change—the bathroom of an inn close by—and I'm pleasantly surprised they treat me like I'm a paying customer and nobody's giving me the stink eye. The woman at the front desk even compliments me on my outfit and wishes me a wonderful evening. I've changed into a black romper I had with me for my night out with David—ugh—put on a pair of flats and pulled my hair up in a bun. Glad for that lady's nice words. Don't entirely believe them, but this is a step up from my ripped jeans and Converse.

Where to? I text Max.

Mission Ranch Hotel and Restaurant. It's on Dolores.

Right-o, I reply and make my way to the restaurant.

About to take a left turn, I spot a truly magnificent two-story house.

I send him a photo. *You missed one. I thought Our House was my favorite, but I was wrong. This one! This one is it.*

Describe it to me, he asks.

I'm usually good at describing things, but this perfect little cottage is just beyond words. How could you possibly not live a fairy-tale life here?

It still has the look and feel of a cottage, but it's a bit taller, with a tiny balcony on the second floor—just big enough for two chairs—and white and blue flowers in pots, an arch above the front gate and tall walls protecting it from curious eyes, like mine.

I jump to see the yard. Behind it... there's the ocean. The views you must have from here.

I can imagine myself watering the flowers every morning before having coffee on what I hope must be an ocean-facing terrace in the back. Feet up, no worries in the world, I add.

That's Dolce Far Niente, he texts back. *You have good taste.*

When I arrive at the restaurant, the place is full. And it's marvelous.

The hostess asks me for my name, then I see her looking in a big notebook.

"I don't have a reservation," I say, awkwardly smiling and wondering if this is the first stop on today's incredible itinerary that won't work out. All the tables are taken by sharply dressed men and women; couples, families. I definitely feel my romper—satin or not—is underwhelming for the occasion.

I look out the window and the view is breathtaking. A man explains to a woman, while they're also waiting for a table, "That's Point Lobos, and the Carmel River Beach."

So that's what I've been gawking at. I can also see the Pacific Ocean from where I am, and I suspect the views are equally amazing from everywhere in this fancy restaurant. The property itself seems to stretch for acres and acres, as far as you can see.

I hear a piano playing and wonder if there are speakers in the waiting area, but no. To my left there's a Piano Bar and a man in a tuxedo is playing 'Close to You' by the Carpenters.

The hostess comes my way with a tray with two glasses of wine—red and white. I take a step back to make room for her to pass, but she stops in front of me.

"Would you like something to drink, miss?"

I nod nervously and grab the red wine.

"On the house," the woman says with a sleek smile as if sensing my worry about how much all this is going to cost me. "Your table will be ready in a few minutes," she adds, which is quite surprising given how busy it is.

The hostess keeps her word. Shortly after, she returns and leads me to a window table.

"Our restaurant offers the most spectacular views on the Monterey Peninsula. Those are the Santa Lucia Mountains in the distance and that is Point Lobos," she explains with a smile.

I nod and smile back. "Beautiful," I say in a low voice.

A waiter comes by before I even get the chance to properly look at the menu. When I ask what he recommends, he kindly gives me five options but mentions the filet mignon twice.

"Filet mignon in red wine and roasted shallot glaze, seasonal vegetable, potato gratin," he adds. "The chef's specialty."

"Filet mignon it is," I agree.

"Have you been here before, miss?" he asks, holding a fishbowl filled with folded notes.

"No, it's my first time. What is that?" I ask, pointing at the bowl.

"It's something special we do for our customers," he says and hands it to me. "You need to pick one. It's your fortune, miss."

I've only experienced this with Chinese restaurants, but I'm not complaining; I like fortunes.

"They're said to be true, these ones," he says, before leaving.

> *Love, because it is the only true adventure.*

I can't help but smile. Not that I believe in fortune cookies, Asian or American, but this time, I want to think this is some sort of sign. Just this once.

Did you get your fortune? he texts me a bit later.

I did.

Was it a good one?

An unexpectedly good one, I text. *Just like today.*

You know so many details about Carmel. Do you spend a lot of time here? I ask.

I know it's a personal question; it's just, he's like a bona fide guide.

Everyone who lives in the Bay Area knows Carmel. I'll let you enjoy dinner and not bug you with messages, he says.

Who am I going to play the game with then? Maybe I should ask someone here. See if they'd want to, I tease.

Am I flirting with him? My cheeks are hot again, so I must be.

No, don't do that, he responds in seconds.

Give me a number. It's your turn.

Number 44.

I type and send. *Do you have a secret you've never shared with anyone?*

It's a couple of minutes before he replies. *If I share it, it wouldn't be a secret, now would it?*

It's true. But I'm not anyone.

Here I go. I did it again. I'm not a flirt or a tease. There's just something about this unconventional, unexpected arrangement of ours that's both exhilarating and freeing. And it makes me say and do things I wouldn't do in my everyday life.

No, you're not. But this is one secret I'm not yet ready to share.

Is it something bad? I ask.

Are you asking if I'm wanted by the Police or on the FBI's Top 50?

Are you?

No. I might make their top 100 though.

I hold my breath. I'm ninety-nine percent sure he's kidding.

Just kidding. No, it's nothing bad.

I let go of the breath. We continue talking all through dinner and I make sure to thank him for an absolutely perfect choice.

The dinner is indeed exquisite. The food finger-licking, the wine—though I'm not an expert—a perfect pairing. And with that view and the sun setting over the Pacific Ocean, I find that I'm feeling content and I might even say happy. I'm alone, but not uncomfortable as I'd normally be. And not lonely, although I should be. Because I'm only physically alone. Going from being 'alone in two' with David to tonight, it's like being bumped from coach to first class.

Let's raise a glass, he texts as the dinner is coming to an end. *It's your birthday after all.*

I've known for quite a few hours I would've loved if he was here with me, but this is the first moment I actually start typing that message to him.

I wish we could toast in person.

I delete it. I write it again. I can't. It's just not who I am. And if he wanted to, he would've suggested it. He obviously doesn't want to. I delete it again and push my phone away.

Do you think you have the energy for one more thing or would you like me to suggest a place where you can sleep for the night? There's that inn where you went—

I'm not tired. I hope that didn't sound too desperate or eager.

I don't want the night to be over. I don't want to think about what's next. Returning to New York. I'm not ready.

Great, I was hoping for that. On weekends there are bonfires on the beach. The closest one to you is at 10th Avenue and Scenic Road. I think you'll enjoy it.

I've never been to a bonfire. I'd love to; great idea.

Pretty much everything I did today was an absolute first. Not pretty much. Everything.

ELEVEN

There are quite a few people around the beach fire and at first, I feel uneasy. It's the middle of the night, nobody knows exactly where I am—except for Max—and anything could happen. But they're all so friendly and welcoming, I start to relax a bit.

I sit next to a guy with a guitar, who tells me his name is Remy. A bit of a player; you can tell ten seconds into the conversation. He also thinks he's the next Elvis, so there's that. I try to cut our chat short when he asks me 'how a beautiful girl like me is alone on a Sunday night?'

Remy stares into my eyes for a long minute before grabbing his guitar and blowing me a kiss. "The next one is for the lovely Maya whose eyes are like the ocean," he says out loud, and everyone turns to look at him.

He starts playing, 'Can't Help Falling in Love', and while I smile and act flattered, inside, I'm rolling my eyes.

Across from me, on the other side of the fire, a woman and two men are talking and laughing. They seem to be having a great time. When Remy starts playing, they all stop talking, although I'm not sure if they're listening to him or not. He's not bad; a bit karaoke-sounding, but not awful. I try not to look in Remy's direction and encourage him, so I stare at the fire instead. One of the men who's sitting across from me must be doing the same, because our eyes meet for a second. The wind blows the high flames and makes shadows dance, his face only lit up for a moment. He gets up and walks away and I look away. That was an intense stare. I wonder if he was thinking this is all amusing, with Remy making a spectacle and me being the target.

How wrong is it that I wish Max would look into my eyes like that? I wish he was here and that feeling is getting stronger and stronger as the night advances. I've tried to put the thought out of my mind, but this incredible day is coming to an end and the excitement and adventure are almost over and I feel wistful.

I so want to talk to him, to see him. And I love our game, but I wish we could just talk without numbers and questions. Just talk the night away. But I wouldn't know where to start and what to say, so I go back to the only thing I can.

Give me a number, I text.

33, he texts back.

Oh, this should take you a while to tell me all about. The question is: What's your favorite day? Of all days. Could be early childhood or anything. I'm sure you have tons.

You're wrong, he texts almost instantaneously.

You don't have tons?

It won't take me a while to tell you all about it.

How come?

Because it's today. Today is my favorite day, he texts.

I gulp. I'm jumping out of my skin with excitement and nervousness and all the possible and impossible feelings I didn't even know I could have. Did he say what I think he said? I reread the last messages three times to make sure I didn't misunderstand. All I want to type back is: 'Mine too. Of all days. It's my favorite day, and you are the most inter-esting, selfless, funniest man I've ever talked to.' I'm holding my phone and in the middle of the song, in front of that beautiful fire, I just start typing and press send so fast, I don't allow myself to change my mind this time. It's now or never.

Please don't take this the wrong way... Is it strange if I say I wish you were here? I don't know you, but you are the reason for this beautiful day and although I'm not alone and I'm not even lonely—surprisingly for me—I would've loved to share all these amazing things... with the person who made it all possible.

This is kind of crazy, isn't it? And risky. No, it's not risky. Why would it be? I'd feel it if something was wrong. No, this is me wanting to thank a kind man in person. That's all. Right. Who am I kidding? I'm dying to meet him in real life because I already feel like I know him. I've already been 'meeting' him and getting to know him all day. If we were next to each other, we'd just continue where we left off with our conversation. Unless it would be awkward. I don't know. I hope not. Did I just do this? I check my messages. Yes. Sent.

I take a deep breath and a shiver goes down my spine. I'm so incredibly nervous.

It's been minutes and no reply. It usually takes him seconds. I ruined everything, didn't I? Maybe I should text him and say I was kidding. Or ask directly if he wants to meet. Maybe my message just confused him. Can I be that direct though? I can't. I want to but I can't. It's not in my nature. Today, well, yesterday since it's past midnight, was utterly out of my character. Being alone in a new place, doing all these things, not me.

So, I do what I'm best at. Chicken out. Retreat.

I'm sorry. I didn't mean to make you feel awkward. It's just that nobody has ever done anything this nice for me and I'm a bit woozy from all the wine and beer. Been drinking a lot at the bonfire. I just meant that I'm grateful, that's all. It would be totally strange if you were here. We don't even know each other. Please ignore what I said.

He doesn't respond to that either. What did I do? That's why I never act like this; that's why it's better to stay in your lane and mind your own. Not dream too high, not imagine crazy things. Magical, over-the-top, once-in-a-lifetime things are not for me.

The fire is getting smaller. Some people leave; others lie in the sand and fall asleep. Remy finally gave up on trying to convince me to go to an after-hours bar and left. Thankfully.

I'm sad. And now I do feel lonely. And stupid. I should leave, get some sleep before my flight. That's when my phone finally beeps.

Not strange or awkward. I wish I was next to you at the bonfire too.

I can't help but grin. But what took him so long? He must think about all the things I'm thinking too. He must think this is crazy. We don't even know each other.

What should I reply? What more can I say? I think my message was clear enough. If he's not suggesting anything, it's because he doesn't want to for whatever reason.

The fire is almost gone now. I'm getting up.

And my phone beeps again.

Give me a number, he says.

Now? He wants a number now? I don't want to play

anymore. Maybe it's all a game to him, and perhaps it should've been for me too, but that bus—ha!—had left the station hours ago.

I sigh, and despite myself, I text: 49.

The question is: Would you ever consider meeting me in person? he texts.

I don't think I've ever felt what I'm feeling reading these words. A mix of disbelief with excitement, joy, nerves, happiness. Is it happiness? Must be. Then I'm starting to doubt everything as usual.

Was that really the question at number 49?

No.

I chuckle, my hands still shaking, holding the phone.

And when I say 'ever', I mean today. Just so that's clear. If you're not too tired and can make it a little longer, the sunrise on Carmel Beach is a once-in-a-lifetime sight. It's at six. I would love to... if the answer is yes, meet you there. There are some large rocks—you can't miss them—and right next to them, an old bench.

I read and can't help letting out a gasp. My hands are shaking even harder now, and I have a massive pit in my stomach. This is all so new to me—this feeling. And I can't stand still, but I have to calm down and think.

I walk toward the ocean. In the darkness, the waves swoosh and a shadow moves in front of me. I immediately turn around and go the opposite way, to the beach's edge and the lights. Once there, I sit on the low concrete wall and start typing. It might be the craziest thing I've ever done, but I'd hate myself if I didn't take a chance on this. On me. On him. On this day.

Sorry it took me a while to answer. I've just been thinking. I don't usually do this; I want you to know that. But there's something about today that's different. I guess this is my complicated way of saying yes. I'd love to spend the last hour of my birthday watching the sunrise... with you. I'll be there at six.

Technically not my birthday anymore, but... still part of the amazing twenty-four-hour birthday adventure, so I'll take it. I guess any excuse to see him, meet him, is acceptable.

I press send.

And then immediately add: *Do you want to know what my question #50 was?*

TWELVE

I open my eyes and realize I am lying on the beach. The last thing I remember is sending the text, then sitting in the sand, waiting for him to reply, but he never did. That must've been hours ago. Did I fall asleep here? Great, my first night of being homeless. My backpack is still next to me, so at least I didn't get robbed. When I try to get up, something falls in the sand. It's a dark-colored hoodie and definitely not mine. It's too big and too... gray for me to ever wear anything like this. Someone must've put it over me while I was sleeping. A shiver passes through my body at the thought that people saw me like this and took pity on me.

I check my watch; it's five-thirty. The sun isn't up yet, and it's chilly. Hope I didn't catch a cold, I think and thank whoever gave me their hoodie. Carmel truly is a nice place with nice people. At first, I'm thinking of leaving the hoodie on the bench so whoever left it can get it back. But on impulse, I put it in the pocket of my backpack. A souvenir from Carmel.

My phone is in my handbag; I slept with my head on it,

and I now have a massive headache. I take it out, and it's almost out of battery.

No text, but I do have missed calls from him—ten of them.

Why did he call instead of texting? We said 6 AM. I'm not late yet, am I? The last call is from a few minutes ago. What if he can't make it and wanted to tell me?

I imagined we'd see and hear each other face to face, but this is not one of my stories where every scene is written to perfection. I have to call him back and see what's going on.

I take a deep breath and press call. It rings once and before it rings a second time, I hear his voice, do a double take, look at my phone, and then put it back at my ear.

"Maya, Maya, can you hear me?"

"David—" I say and can't continue.

David got his phone back. How? When? What happened? What does this mean?

"Are you OK? Where are you? Why didn't you tell me you were coming?"

"I tried, but you didn't answer your phone."

"I lost it. Just got it back."

Did he get it back straight from Max? Did Max leave it somewhere for him?

"How did you get your phone back?"

"Does it matter? I forgot it in a Lift yesterday."

He's acting like nothing's wrong. Like he did nothing.

"Where are you?" he asks, his tone edgy. "Are you still at the airport—?"

Where else would a stupid woman like me be? At the airport, waiting for him.

"No, I'm not."

"Then where are you?" he repeats.

"Carmel. You wouldn't know it."

"What are you doing in Carmel?" he asks.

I don't respond. I don't have to justify myself to him.

"I'm in Monterey," he says, then I hear him talking to someone before talking to me again. "I'll be in Carmel in less than ten minutes. Meet me at Hotel Marin."

"David—"

He hung up.

Meet him? I don't want to meet him. What is he going to say? That it wasn't him with that woman? The only person I'm going to meet is Max, at six, at the bench. Is this what I want? I don't know anymore. With David on his way here, things feel different. It's like a wake-up call. 'Hello, this is your reality. What are you doing?' Am I brave enough to go through with this? It's all so different in the daylight. As if I was living in this carefully constructed yet fragile bubble for the last day and now that the sun is almost up, the bubble has popped. I look a mess, I haven't showered in a day, I have sand in my hair. I have sand everywhere. If I meet Max like this, he'll take one look at me and run the other way.

Should I get on the bus and return to New York alone? But what will I do there? I have no place to live; I have no job. No, it'll be Hartford and staying with my mom for a while.

It's five-forty-five. What should I do? What am I doing?

Minutes pass, and the more I think about it, the more I panic.

I try to picture his face, waiting for me on the bench. I try to imagine his reaction when he sees me. I look down at my clothes and almost gag.

What if I'm going to regret this? What if this man is the one I was meant to meet? What if what I felt yesterday is the beginning of a love story unlike any other? The kind I write about. What if it could happen to me? I smile, thinking how I'm going to tell Alisa how he and I met.

With a swift move, I grab my backpack and run across the street to the Starbucks. Thank God for Starbucks. Nothing else seems open. I run into the bathroom, wash my face, clean up as best as I can, brush my teeth and change. Seven minutes all in all.

I run back out, ignoring the curious looks the barista is giving me.

I have to do this. It's five-fifty-five. I should go; just risk it.

What's the worst that can happen? When something feels so right, it can't be wrong.

I put on my backpack and start walking back to the rocks he told me about; to the bench.

The streets are empty; it's still so early.

My hands are shaking, I'm so nervous, but I can do this. I can.

THIRTEEN

I see the bench in the distance and then hear the car stopping next to me.

It's too late.

David's coming toward me. The moment he's at an arm's length, he lunges at me and grabs me in a tight hug. And then his lips are on mine. I don't even have time to react.

"What do you think you're doing?" I ask and push him away.

"Kissing you—what does it look like? Happy birthday, Maya. Sorry I missed it."

"I'm sorry for a lot of things too."

"You're acting weird, first on the phone and now."

"You shouldn't have come," I say.

"Why? I apologized already for not answering your calls and ruining your birthday."

"I actually had the best birthday of my life. Without you."

"You're particularly nasty this morning."

"And you're acting particularly innocent," I snap back.

"Am I missing something?"

"From what I heard, you're missing a blonde hanging on to you."

He frowns.

"Out of words? Can't think of a quick lie?" I say.

"I can't think of anything because I don't know what you're talking about."

"It's fine. I honestly didn't expect you to admit it."

"Admit what? What's this blonde thing?"

"Someone saw you with a woman yesterday."

He shrugs. "So what?"

"So what? Now that's new."

"I'm always with someone. If there was some blonde woman, although I don't particularly remember, it was someone from work."

"Someone from work you couldn't keep your hands off? And you were all over each other? Interesting colleagues you have."

"Did you see that, Maya? Did you see me with another woman?"

I feel so frustrated. "No."

"Then it could've very well been a lie. Who told you this? I thought you didn't know anyone in California."

"Is that what you were counting on?"

"I wasn't counting on anything because I didn't know you were coming. This is absurd."

"So you're saying you weren't in a Lift yesterday with a woman, hugging and God knows what else."

"In a Lift," he says and stops. His nostrils flare, his face turns a shade of burgundy. "I knew there was something off about that guy. First of all, I think he was deranged. I almost called the police on him when he wouldn't return my phone. Did he tell you all this nonsense?"

"Yes, and it's not nonsense. Why would he lie? He doesn't even know me."

"Because he was a wacko. I'd be more concerned with the fact that he followed you here. You're lucky he didn't hurt you or kidnap you or something."

"He didn't follow me anywhere."

"Then how did you talk to him? I should've called the cops on him."

"We talked on the phone," I say.

Not even. I never even got to hear Max's voice...

I lean to the side and look behind David. The bench is empty; there's nobody there. Where is he? Did he change his mind?

David grabs my shoulders, and I try to break away, but he's too strong.

"There *was* no woman whatsoever. In a Lift or anywhere else. It's all a lie. I was at work or in work meetings all day yesterday. I met someone at Embarcadero, then went back to the office and out for a work dinner. That's all."

He takes a step back. "I'm offended by your accusations. I thought you knew me better."

He sounds upset and disappointed. Was I wrong and he's telling the truth? Did Max lie to me? Or maybe it was an honest mistake; maybe he got men mixed up and what he saw was another blond guy with a blonde woman. It's possible. Improbable, but possible.

"Let's just call my office. They'll confirm where I was yesterday. It will be awkward, but I'll do it to end this. But if I'm honest, this is hurtful. How are we together if you don't trust me, and instead, you believe a stranger, a complete lunatic?"

David is nothing if not convincing; after all, he convinces

people for a living. He's a litigation lawyer and a good one at that. I'm starting to have doubts. If he's willing to call his work, then he must be telling the truth. Right?

"I'll call now and wake up my boss if I have to because you clearly don't believe me. But after this, we should reconsider our relationship. I don't know if I can be with someone who doesn't trust me."

I look again at the bench and check the time. There's no one on it or near it. Six-fifteen. I turn to my left, my right. It's just us two here and some early risers jogging or walking their dogs. A man walking in the other direction, away from the rocks. A woman running past us. He's not coming and my heart sinks.

Maybe you dodged a bullet, Maya, I say to myself. Perhaps it's for the better...

This could've never worked. These things never last; they're like summer romances. No, they're fairy tales. Maybe that's what this was: a fairy tale—virtual as it was—condensed into one perfect day. One of my perfect stories. And now we've reached 'the end'.

What now? What are my options? Only two: to believe or not to believe David.

David is about to dial a number when I stop him.

I take a deep breath. "No, it's OK," I say. "I believe you."

I want to. I'm trying to.

"I'm sorry," I say. "I shouldn't have doubted you."

"Have I ever given you reasons to doubt me? Never," he says, sounding sure of himself again. "Did I ask what you did all day yesterday or where you spent the night?"

It's my turn to look away.

He tilts his head. "Should I?"

"Should you what?"

"Ask you what you've been doing the last twenty-four hours in California?"

I wrap my perfect day and put it in a box somewhere deep in my heart. Mine alone.

"I explored this town. I didn't know what else to do," I say, not looking him in the eye.

He checks his watch. "We have to get going. My flight is in two hours. Are you on the same one? If not, we should change it, so we're going back together." He kisses me again and holds me in his arms. "I missed you," he says.

"Let's go back home," I say.

A YEAR LATER

FOURTEEN

I'm not happy. I'm not even close to happy. Not event content.

If someone asked me to sum up the last year in a word, I'd choose regret. Or anger. Still can't decide on only one. Regret that I believed David. Anger that I believed him. Regret that Max didn't show up. Anger that he didn't show up. Regret that I let myself be fooled into believing in a fantasy that made me see life through rose-colored glasses. Anger at the pink glasses. Regret that I came back. Anger that I came back.

I've thought about him and that day ad nauseam. I analyzed every second, every text message. I remembered every feeling and sensation, every one of my smiles. Something like this can drive even a strong person crazy. And I'm not that strong.

When David and I returned to New York, I felt stuck. Like a hamster who never gets anywhere despite running on the spinning wheel incessantly. The only thing it manages to accomplish is getting tired. Same with me. Only that for hamsters it's minutes or hours; for me it's been a year. Round and round.

I couldn't get a job for a month after my return, which made me feel like such a failure. Like I assumed she would, Janice refused to give me a recommendation, and nobody would hire me. My only option was to grovel and ask her if she'd rehire me. It was one of the most humiliating experiences of my life. She never let me forget this 'immense favor' she did for me.

Quickly after that, life went back to what it had been before Carmel, but more and more, as time passed, I noticed something was different, almost invisible at first. And it wasn't on the outside looking in, but on the inside looking out. Maybe nobody perceived the change, but I felt it. The apartment was the same, my job was the same, and David was the same. The only thing that changed in the equation of my life was me, apparently.

I didn't know what was wrong for a while; I just knew that I felt sad and lonely.

At first, I blamed the job. The hours were worse than before, the pay stayed abysmal, the assignments were only leftovers from the other reporters. Yes, the job was making me miserable.

I blamed NYC. It felt dirty, noisy and overcrowded all of a sudden. The winter was too long, the summer too hot. But a city doesn't make you happy or unhappy. A city is just a city.

I blamed my relationship with David. It wasn't perfect before Carmel, but there was nothing wrong with it either. Now, there *was* something wrong: the shadow of a doubt. Although I tried, I never fully trusted him again after Carmel. The first few weeks back, I avoided bringing it up, but you can only pretend you're OK for so long. When I finally asked, the fights started, the accusations, the blaming game. He accused me of being crazy and looking for reasons to belittle him, of not caring; he accused me of many things. I called him a hypocrite. I accused him of cheating, lying to me, never having time for us. I dug up Carmel again and again. After a while, the fighting stopped. I don't think either of us had any energy left. All that seems to be left between us is an awkward silence over dinner, kisses I avoid, and sleeping on the couch.

My mom keeps probing, as any mother does when she feels something is off.

"I'm just tired," I usually reply.

I am tired. Of everything. But I'm also a coward. The question that's been nagging at me lately is: am I more coward or more tired?

Leaving David would be hard both emotionally and logistically and I keep asking myself if the logistics are the reason I'm still in the relationship. Isn't that why I chose not to break up with him last year? Because I had no home, no job, and he was the safe choice? Well, nothing changed. I have a job, sure, but I could never afford to live in the city with the money I make. And what would I even tell him? I'm leaving you because you cheated on me last year? Because I don't love you anymore? Why did I stay for so long? And when did I stop loving him? The bigger question is: did I ever love him?

The more I think about it, the more I realize that day in Carmel ruined me because it offered me a glimpse into something I've always wanted. Those intense feelings, the butterflies, the nervousness, the smiles, the incredible conversations, the excitement, the possibilities, and that unique sensation that you're lighter than the air and happier than you've ever been. Those are the exact things I gave my characters... story after story. And I had them. For one day.

Only after Carmel did I realize just how much I wanted all those things. I still want them. I still think about him. Wonder. Try to imagine his face, his voice. I try to come up with excuses for why he didn't come. Why he never contacted me although he had my phone number. I had an excuse. I don't have his phone number; I don't even know what his real name is. What would I do? Return to California and talk to all the Lift drivers in the Bay Area?

Besides, he stood me up. That thought still hurts so badly. I wished so many times he would just text me and tell me why. Or tell me it meant nothing. Or that he lied about being single and he's married. Or that he came, saw me, and decided I wasn't what he was looking for. Something. Anything. So I can move on.

I was there. He wasn't. And despite all this time that has passed, I still can't wrap my head around it. I know what I felt and I thought he felt the same way. How could I have been so wrong? I just want answers. I want to look into his eyes, listen to what he has to say, no matter how painful or difficult, then turn around and leave, knowing I did everything I could.

That's all I want. A chance for closure. But that moment will probably never come.

I look at the calendar on the wall and flip the page for May. I can't believe it's already June and I didn't even realize it. My birthday is less than three weeks away, and I can't help but let out a loud sigh. I wish I was a different person. I wish I was the person I briefly became on my birthday, a year ago. That brave, reckless, adventurous, not-afraid-to-be-alone, flirty, fun person.

David walks into the kitchen and I start doing the dishes to avoid a conversation.

"Can you stop that for a minute?" he asks, his tone different than usual.

I turn and the look in his eyes matches his tone.

"Yes?" I say and wipe my hands.

He wants to break up. I knew this day would come, but it's still not easy.

"I've been thinking about this for a while now—" He stops. "Us. What we're doing."

Here it comes.

"I think we should get married," he says after a moment.

I stare. "Married?"

"We've been together for five years, and I want kids while I'm still young. My career is going great; we can sell this place and buy a house in the suburbs."

I'm still staring.

"Married," I repeat. I realize I sound dumb. It's just that this is so unexpected. "But our relationship hasn't been going well," I say. "Why would we get married?"

"I think it's been a bit tricky because we've been together for so long but haven't committed. And the more I thought about it, the more I realized it's never going to be perfect. You're not perfect; I'm not perfect. And you know what? Perfection is boring."

My head is spinning. Married to David? We barely kiss anymore, and although we share a bed a few nights a week, it hasn't been the same in months. There was no sign this was going to happen. I can't marry him. Can I? People do get married for all sorts of reasons. Caring about each other. I do care about him. Financial stability, which I would have with him. Good-looking kids. I would have that too. A nice house. Yes, I'm sure. I guess if you put all these things on a list, they'd make sense. But what about love? What about trust? What about imagining growing old with that person and smiling, not cringing?

"I didn't get you a ring. I thought we could go together to Tiffany's and you can pick it. I'm not sure which one you'd want."

What about knowing each other's likes and dislikes?

"David, look, I—"

"Don't give me an answer now. Think about it. I'll be back tonight, and—"

"Where are you going?"

"To the Yankees game with Jason, remember?"

I don't remember. Maybe he told me, but like with most things lately, I've filtered it out.

"Are we happy together? I mean—"

He frowns. "I'm happy."

I'm genuinely shocked. "With me?"

"Yes, with you. Are you not happy? If you're not happy, why are we still together?"

That's a good question. A valid question.

"I love you," he says and I want to say it back. It's that easy. Just say, 'I love you too.' But the words don't come out.

"Tomorrow, let's go ring shopping."

He leans down to kiss me and I let him.

I feel nothing. This is bad. Worse than I thought.

* * *

An hour later, he's ready to leave.

I've always thought we are all born equal. Equal parts coward, equal parts brave. In time, our personality, our experiences push the scale one way or another. Am I braver or more coward? Tonight has shown me that although I might have changed in the last year, a lot has stayed the same. I am still more coward. So, I don't tell him what I want to. What I've wanted to tell him for a year.

There's nothing left between us.

SIXTEEN

I know what I must do. I think I've known it for a while...

As soon as he leaves, I call my mother. I usually call her on Saturdays and we already spoke yesterday, so she'll immediately know that something is off.

"Don't tell me? You're not coming next weekend?" she asks.

"Actually, I was thinking I'd come over today."

"Is everything alright?"

"Yes. Just fine."

"Is David coming?"

"No. He's away." I stop. "He asked me to marry him." I don't know why I tell her that.

"Finally! So happy for you, Maya. I can't wait to see the ring and tell everyone."

"I haven't given him an answer yet. I don't—"

"You don't what?"

"I don't know what to do."

"I see. I thought this was a sure thing. Your relationship. When two people are together for five years—"

I interrupt her. "I know, Mom. I know."

She must suspect I've been struggling lately. That I have doubts. Maybe she doesn't know the cause, but a mother always senses these things.

"Everything's going to be fine," she says. "I'm sure you'll make the right decision."

"I hope so."

"Are you coming just for the day?"

"I have some figuring out to do and might stay a bit longer if that's alright with you."

"Of course it is. However long you need. But what about your job?"

My job has been making my skin crawl more and more lately. It's always bothered me, but it's gotten worse since I came back. The newsroom is toxic. That whole environment is toxic. If someone doesn't cry on any given day, it means they were either on vacation or took Xanax in the morning. It's just not a place where you'd want to go and definitely not a place where you should spend twelve hours a day if not more. Five years. I've been there for almost as long as I've been with David. I only now make the correlation between the two.

"I have a ton of vacation days accumulated. I'll ask for time off. Maybe a week or so."

I feel relieved that I thought of this. I do need a break from that place. Although a week won't work miracles, it's better than nothing.

"Great idea. I'm so excited you're coming. We'll do girls' stuff. Mani-pedis, go to the movies. It's been so long since we've had a full week, just the two of us."

"Yes, Mom," I say robotically. I need some alone time to

think and I don't know if I'll be the best company, but I don't want to make her sad.

"Just come home, darling," says my mother. "We'll talk everything through."

"Thank you, Mom."

"Don't thank me. You're always welcome here. This is your home, no matter what."

I'd argue against it. There were many times when I felt that if anything happened, I would not be able to go home, that I would not be welcomed with open arms. And it wasn't just a hunch. It was the reality of my late teens and early twenties. My relationship with my mother was rocky through high school, almost nonexistent in college. Only a couple of years after I graduated it started, slowly, to patch together. It's been better lately.

The one with my father never recovered from the fallout ten years ago. One of the reasons I gave David another chance after what happened in Carmel was my father. I was sixteen when he cheated on my mother and denied it, just like David. Only my mother didn't forgive him—or try to—she kicked him out. He seemed depressed for a while, but that didn't last long. A few months later, I found out he was remarrying and his new wife was expecting a child. I accused my mother of throwing him into the arms of another woman. I accused him of never loving us. I haven't talked to my father in nine years and haven't seen him in just as long. And he didn't make an effort either. As if his new family was more important than us.

I had blamed my mother for breaking up our family for so long that when I was faced with that same choice, I made my decision as if to prove I'd always been right. What I ended up doing was proving it was my mother who was right all along.

You can't keep someone tied to you just because you have a home together, and you've spent years together. You can't pretend to believe someone if deep down in your heart you don't trust them. Trust, once lost, it's almost always lost forever. And most of all, you can't force yourself to love someone.

* * *

I look around the apartment and make a mental list. All my stuff should fit in two suitcases. My books in boxes, and whatever else is left, I'll just put it in the trunk of my car.

At the bottom of a drawer, I find my old notebooks. Seeing them makes me sad. I could hardly write any of my stories this past year. The one thing I did write is hidden in a thick yellow envelope among them. My manuscript; the fastest 80,000 words I ever wrote. The story of that day in Carmel, of us. I promised myself I wouldn't write another novel, but I couldn't *not* write this one. I couldn't sleep, and couldn't do anything else until I finished it. Well, except for the ending. I couldn't bring myself to mirror real life and break my character's heart like that. It was too cruel. But every other option also seemed unrealistic and far-fetched. So, it's almost finished.

I never showed it to anyone, especially not to Alisa. I know she'd have the absolute best intentions and she'd be nice about it, but I don't think I could take yet another disappointment. This story is too important for me and I won't let anyone tell me it's not good enough. I place the manuscript with my 'important' documents folder and put it in a box. Then I change my mind and move it to one of the suitcases. I'm not letting it out of my sight.

* * *

Three hours later, I'm all packed, and my letter to David is sitting on the kitchen table.

David,

I'm sorry. I wish I could start this letter with something other than regret, but—

I'm sorry I haven't been more honest about my feelings over the last year. I'm sorry I couldn't tell you all this to your face. You know I'm always much better in writing. I tend to get flustered face to face and I back down, let myself be influenced and persuaded. And I guess that's why I'm doing it now. Because you cannot look into my eyes and convince me to give this another chance. I haven't been happy. It's hard to explain why, but it's not only your fault. I did accuse you of cheating and was never able to get past that, but that's not the only reason.

You see, that day in California, I met someone. Someone who changed my life and I've been feeling rather lost since then. I feel trapped in our life. In New York. In my job. I need to get away and start fresh. You deserve someone who is just like you: they know who they are and what they want, and they are set on getting it no matter what. You deserve someone who loves you above everything else. I'm afraid and I'm sorry to say, that person is not me.

I'm struggling with what I want and who I want to be. I know I'm kind of old for this and I should have it all clear by now, but I don't. I'm struggling with what kind of relationship I want and what I think I should feel for the other person to be sure they are the one for me.

I'm not certain you cheated on me. Either way, I should've been strong that day and ended it, but I wasn't, and I'm sorry I dragged this on for as long as I did, when deep down I knew there was no road ahead for the two of us, together.

I know you will be OK and you will find your happiness. I'm sorry it wasn't with me.

Goodbye,

Maya

Maybe my departure will surprise him. Perhaps my letter will make him sad at first. But after he gives it some thought, I'm sure he'll feel relieved. We're not right for each other and although I don't hold grudges, I do have regrets. One in particular.

The backpack I had with me in Carmel last year is by the door. Seeing it there, remembering that day, I realize how much the last three hundred days have weighed me down.

Maybe at twenty-two, I was too young to know. At twenty-three I thought I was in love, at twenty-four I was blinded by the possibilities, and at twenty-five, he made promises I wanted to believe. Maybe at twenty-six I still hoped. But at twenty-seven, I knew what I should've done, and I didn't do it. This is my regret. Not wasting five years but one. And undoubtedly, never having the opportunity to get that one year back, the year that could've forever changed my life.

SEVENTEEN

I'm taking a final look around the apartment. Half a decade comes with some nostalgia for sure. I thought I was happy here for a while. Things were good. Fresh out of college, starting my journalism career, I was in a relationship with a man all my girlfriends wanted to date.

We're not the same people we used to be back in 2013. I'm not the same person.

I'm about to go out the door when my cell rings. It's Alisa.

She sounds agitated, and her voice is pitchy—a sign that she's excited about something.

"You won't believe what I'm reading now."

"What?"

A locked-room mystery? A baffling disappearance? Definitely another submission she's enthusiastic about. Alisa now handles the Thriller/Mystery Fiction Division for her publisher. She's been on a roll lately, signing new authors left and right. I got to read some of those early copies—she always mails them to me—and every time I do, I understand why she wants to sign those authors right away, and I get jealous and insecure all over again.

"Listen, OK? This is Max Meridian's story, a thirty-something unlucky in love Californian who has big dreams of becoming a successful artist but works as a rideshare driver to make a living. On a day like any other, while Max is on his way to pick up a client, a phone rings inside his car. A woman is calling. When Max answers, he doesn't imagine that in the next twenty-four hours, this woman will mend his lonely heart and make him believe again in the magic of love and fate. Will this story end tragically or with a happily ever after when the morning comes and he doesn't meet her as planned? Inspired by the real-life love story of a young artist the author has known all of his life. This is a deeply touching and spellbindingly beautiful novel about the kind of love that once found, cannot ever be forgotten, about the magic of serendipity and the heartbreak of ill timing."

I gasp. "What is this?"

"The blurb for a book that's about to be published."

"A book? One of your books?"

Such a dumb reaction, but my brain is completely blocked.

"Does this sound like a thriller to you? Nothing to do with me or our imprint. I just heard about it from a scout I met who couldn't stop raving about it so I got her to send me the blurb. Apparently, the man who wrote the novel is a New York Times bestselling author, but I'm not up to date with romance authors. His name is Ethan Delphy."

"Ethan Delphy," I repeat. "Can you please read the whole thing again? And slowly."

She chuckles. "Sure."

When she finishes, I'm just as shocked as I was the first time she read it.

After I finished my manuscript, I wrote a blurb for it as a way of killing time. I don't know if I kept it, but it sounded just like this one. Except it wasn't the story of Max Meridian, the driver who meets a woman, it was the story of Dawn Davis who meets a driver in California.

I'm speechless.

"It's uncanny, isn't it? The resemblance to your Carmel story."

Over the last year, Alisa has had to suffer through countless retellings, late-night analyses over Skype and ridiculous never-ending scenarios about that day.

"Yes, it's uncanny."

"It could be a coincidence," she says.

"Max Meridian," I repeat his name and start laughing.

It's definitely a nervous laugh.

"Melodic name," says Alisa.

"That's not the point. Remember why I called him Max?"

"The Gladiator?"

"And what was his full name?"

"I don't know. Maximus something."

"Meridius," I say.

"Jeez. The guy has a sense of humor," she says.

"What did you say the author's name is?"

"Ethan Delphy. Have you heard of him? Read any of his books?" she asks.

"No. I don't think so. I just... I'm so confused. I don't understand how this Ethan Delphy guy found out about my day."

"I just read it to you. Inspired by the real-life love story of a young artist the author has known all of his life. I guess

Max, or whatever his name is, and the writer are friends. If I was a writer, I could've written the story too. I know all the details. Maybe even better than you."

"No, you wouldn't have," I say firmly.

"Why?"

"Because it's not your story to tell."

"You sound grumpy. I thought you'd be happy. You've been fixated on this man and that day. This is good news. We can reach out to Ethan Delphy, ask for the dude's contact details, talk to him and that's that. Finally getting what you want."

"Yes, sure, I guess. Can I call you a bit later?" I ask.

"Sure. I'll do some digging in the meantime."

I think I should be happy like Alisa says, but instead, I'm numb. I'm having difficulty breathing as if a heavy weight is sitting on my chest.

I've spent this past year coming up with reasons why Max didn't show up, why he didn't contact me. I was convinced something must've happened. It sounds like nothing happened; he just made the decision not to come. But why? I don't understand.

Just like I don't understand why he'd tell someone about our day. It's called a magical love story that changed him forever. So he did fall in love with me just like I fell in love with him. Then what happened? I need to know. I need to understand. I want him, whoever he is, to look into my eyes and tell me. He owes me at least that.

Alisa calls again. "I emailed his editor, but it's Sunday so she might not respond. She's in New York so it's still early though. I asked for Ethan Delphy's email address."

"Do you think you could get the book?"

"I'm going to try to get an early review copy, yes. What's

the plan? You want to read the book before you get in touch with him?"

"I don't know if I want to learn the truth from a book or if it's better to hear it from him."

"Keep in mind this is a work of fiction. I don't know Delphy's style, but he might've added or removed events or reinterpreted them. He wouldn't be a writer otherwise," she says. "OK, I'll talk to you later." She chuckles. "Hey, this feels like a secret mission."

"Except that it isn't. It's my life," I say bitterly.

"Sorry, I didn't mean—"

"No, it's OK. *I'm* sorry. I'm still trying to process all this. I'm grateful, Alisa, for everything. Don't know what I'd do without you."

"Don't mention it. I'd love to help and get you two in front of each other."

EIGHTEEN

I grab my backpack and go downstairs, get into my beat-up Elantra. I'm holding my phone in one hand and propping myself on the wheel with the other; I just don't know what to do. Should I drive to my mother's and continue the search from there or stay here? If this Ethan guy lives in New York, like most writers I know, then perhaps it's easier if I'm here too.

I google the author's name on my phone and get a ton of links. He wrote and published three novels; this would be his fourth. The other three were love stories too. On Wikipedia, I see the first photo, not that I'm particularly interested in how he looks. It's one of those 'at your desk, act professional and writerly' images. He has dark hair, cut short, a bushy dark beard, eyes of an undefined color, perhaps brown, behind the kind of glasses people wear for kicks—thick, dark frames, 'intellectual' written all over them. And to top it all, he's wearing a black polo neck. He has a slight, lopsided smile.

I stare at the photo; this is the man who's writing my story. He doesn't look like he knows anything about love and the more I think about it, the more I get worked up. I never agreed to anyone sharing my day in Carmel with the world. Maybe I want to keep it all to myself. It's a private thing. That's why I didn't send my manuscript out. Maybe. Never mind my reasons. The bottom line is that this is a beautiful yet painful matter of the heart. And it's mine. Mine and Max's. Definitely not Ethan Delphy's.

I read on.

Ethan Delphy is an American novelist and screenwriter. He has published three novels and one non-fiction book, all of which have been *New York Times* bestsellers, with over 5 million copies sold worldwide in more than 25 languages.

Born: August 8, 1985 (age 33 years), Carmel by the Sea

Spouse: Isabella Delphy (m. 2014)

Books: *Need No Words, Early Summer Dreams, A Million Minutes*

Early life

Ethan Delphy was born to Tim Delphy, an investigative journalist, and Anne Marie Delphy (née Thoene), a baker and restaurateur. Ethan has a twin sister, Celine Delphy who runs the family business—an Art Nouveau café in the Bay Area.

Delphy is of French, English, and Irish ancestry.

He was raised in Carmel by the Sea where he was active in sports during school. He subsequently attended UCLA, graduating with an English major and then got an MFA in Creative Writing from UC Irvine.

Personal life

In 2013, while vacationing in Europe, he met his future wife, Isabella Andres of Madrid, Spain. Delphy and Andres were married on September 1, 2014. They live in Carmel by the Sea.

Career

Delphy began writing in his first year of college. He is said to base his stories on real events and his characters on real people. He calls his impressive circle of friends and acquaintances 'an unending, ever-surprising source of inspiration'.

Published works

2012: *Need No Words*

2013: *Early Summer Dreams*

2014: *A Million Minutes*

(upcoming) 2019: *June After Midnight*

I hate the title. *June After Midnight*. It's so irrelevant and bland.

And my plan to stay here because he might be here is obviously a bust. Wikipedia says he lives in Carmel. It makes me wonder if 'Max' lives in Carmel too. That would explain why he knew the town inside and out.

Carmel is a small town, maybe three thousand people. If I went there... how hard could it be to find a famous author? He probably stands in the town square with blinking lights on his head. "It's me! The talented, successful, rich writer who steals other people's stories!"

What am I saying? No, going there to find him would be crazy.

The more I think about the book, the more I get worked up, and all my anger is targeted at the writer. Who gave him the right to tell my story? Is he even a good writer? Did he do a good job? If it's my story, our story, then I'm part of it. How could he possibly get right how I felt that day and what it meant to me? How that town and that man changed me forever?

I mumble to myself and notice a woman passing by who gives me a strange look.

"This is New York. I'm allowed to talk to myself in my car," I say to her through the window.

I look again at the writer's photo. So stuck up.

"His impressive circle of friends," I mumble. "Who says that?"

He should've asked for my permission. I'm a journalist; I know how this works. One source of information is not enough, and it doesn't make a story. You need to have at least two. He should've contacted me and asked me about it, and I would've gotten the chance to tell him, 'NO. No, you can't write about my life'.

So frustrating that he knows what I don't. He knows what happened. Why Max didn't show up. Why he broke my heart. What happened to him after. I punch the wheel. I don't care how many books he wrote and how many millions he sold. This is not his story to tell. It's mine. And I wrote it. I hate this guy!

NINETEEN

I find his social media profiles. All with the same photo, all of them just promoting his books. No email address listed anywhere, no nothing.

Then articles in newspapers and magazines. Most of them talk about his books, have reviews or news. *People Magazine, Huffington Post, Chicago Tribune*. None of the articles are recent. The latest one is from early 2016 from what I can tell. He's mentioned in passing. There's a photo that basically everyone republished of him and an attractive young woman. Arm in arm at an awards ceremony. The caption says, "Ethan and Isabella Delphy, March 2016." She's grinning; he's again sort-of-smiling. Or maybe that's how he smiles.

She's in a long, light blue dress, and he's wearing a two-piece dark suit, and compared to her he seems tall. She's much younger than him. Maybe early twenties.

I can't help but stare at how fancy she is. For what it's worth, they look like a match. At least in the way they dress. I look down at my jean overalls and I don't need to see myself in the car's mirror to know my hair is a mess—let's call it a ponytail. I would never look this good, even if I had to go to the Oscars. The whole 'I clean up nicely' doesn't apply to everyone.

He's facing the camera. With that beard and the fancy glasses, he looks like one of those guys in aftershave commercials. For some reason, I pictured all Carmel men to be the full 'T-shirt, flip-flops, sunglasses, and tousled hair' package. I hope that's how Max is.

Alisa texts. It's a screenshot of a webpage. A two-month book tour for *June After Midnight* that starts in less than three weeks; on my birthday, to be exact. The first stop is Carmel by the Sea, then SF, LA, Phoenix, Austin, Houston, New Orleans, Jacksonville, Savannah, Charlotte, Richmond, Baltimore, Philadelphia, NYC, Hartford, Boston, Portland, Chicago and Seattle.

She calls me.

"OK, so here's what I have so far. Max is most certainly a friend, which confirms what we knew. I found some mentions of how he uses his social circle for inspiration."

"I saw that too," I say.

"I also found a press release. They're making a movie for one of his books and he's set to leave for New Zealand right after the book tour I just sent over. He'll be gone for a while."

"He can go to Antarctica for five years for all I care. He can probe the penguins for stories, see how that goes."

"Are you OK?" she asks.

"Fine. Just having a bit of a meltdown."

"Why? What's wrong?"

"The whole idea of this book, parading my feelings out to the world, unnerves me. I don't want to find out the truth at the same time a million other people do. I deserve better."

"That's why I'm trying to get you his email and the book. Try to calm down, please."

"I'm calm," I say, while having a very public tantrum in the middle of the Upper East Side. And on a Sunday no less. I'm taking this very well...

"The only reason I told you about the book tour and the movie is that it might be harder to get answers from him once he's on the road. But, that's over two weeks away; plenty of time."

"Plenty," I repeat.

"Wait," she says. "Just got a reply from his agent's assistant. She says he can be contacted directly via his author's website. And if it's related to movie rights blah blah and translation rights et cetera, we should contact X and Y. Unrelated. OK, so go to his website."

"I was just there and didn't see an email. Let me check again. I'll put you on speaker."

"OK."

I go back to his website and click on every button and link until, finally, at the bottom of his 'about' page, which is a rehash of the Wikipedia info, I see a basic contact form.

Want to get in touch? I might not be able to answer each and every message, and even if I do reply, it might take me a while to get to it, but here it goes.

And then the form is a three-field thing: name, email address, message.

"I found a contact form, not an email address."

She groans. "It's better than nothing and I know how much you hate waiting. It'll buy us some time while I continue trying to get an actual email address for him. As an alternative, you can reach out to him via social. I'm sure he's on there."

"That's a good idea," I say and then stop. "What should I write in the form?"

She snickers. "Say who you are and tell him you met a man in Carmel last year and you don't know his name and you'd like to get in touch. Ask if he can send you Max's real name and his email address or something. Keep it short and simple."

"That makes sense," I say, feeling like I'm about to hyperventilate.

"OK, OK, I'll talk to you later."

"You call me the minute he replies, OK?"

"Don't hold your breath. I don't think Mr. Important checks that mailbox too frequently."

"You never know," says Alisa.

TWENTY

'Mr. Delphy'. 'Dear Mr. Delphy.' No. No dears. I keep writing and deleting, writing and deleting, until I finally manage to come up with a decent message and press 'submit' before changing my mind and starting over.

I should call Janice, but I keep putting it off.

Better yet, I should get on the road and drive to Hartford. It's getting late.

Enough excitement for one day, I say to myself as I get onto FDR Drive before taking the exit toward New Haven.

* * *

I just entered Connecticut, and I'm about an hour from Hartford when my phone lets me know I have a new email. There's a sign for a gas station and I pull in in a shady area next to a truck.

I click on my inbox, hoping but getting myself ready for a spam email.

From: contact@ethandelphy.com
To: Maya Maas
Subject: RE: contact details needed
Dear Maya,

Thank you for your message. We always appreciate when Ethan Delphy's readers reach out as I know he loves to hear from his fans. I'm sorry to tell you that your request for information is not something we can help with. The author's sources of inspiration and the people behind his characters cannot be disclosed.

I wish you a wonderful weekend, and thank you for being an Ethan Delphy fan!

Nikky Hurlock,
PR/PA

Fan? I'm not a fan. What in my message made her think I'm a fan? And this guy is not James Patterson or Danielle Steel to have a PR/PA answering his emails for him.

I reply.

Could I possibly speak directly with Mr. Delphy? He might have a different answer once I tell him all the details.

I buy a cup of coffee from the gas station and sit in the parking lot for a few minutes before getting back on the road. If she says no, I can try social media, I guess. Otherwise, what are my options? Stalk him?

Ten minutes later, just as I'm about to leave, my phone beeps. A new email.

The book tour for *June After Midnight* is approaching. If you're in any of these locations (schedule attached), you can definitely stop by and say hello. Ethan is a lovely and friendly author who always takes time to talk to his readers.

Nikky

A lovely and friendly author. Sure. If you say so.

The attachment is the tour flier. Thanks, that's not helpful, is it? Already had this, and I don't want to wait until the book is out to talk to him. I waited a year to find out what happened. That's enough waiting.

"I heard back," I say as soon as Alisa picks up.

"What did he say? Did you find out Max's name? Address?"

"No. Delphy didn't even answer my message himself. He had an assistant answer."

"OK, and what did they say?"

"It's confidential, and if I want to talk to him, I should go to a book signing."

"I was afraid that might happen. Sorry, Maya. So, are you going?"

"The first one is on June 17. I'll lose my mind until then."

"We'll hopefully get the book in the meantime, so you'll have that to keep you busy."

I pause. A thousand crazy ideas going through my head. "I wonder—"

"Yes?"

"Do you think it would be completely insane if I went there?"

"For his book launch?"

"No. Now. He lives in Carmel, doesn't he? How hard can it be to find him?"

Silence.

"You think it's crazy, don't you?"

"A bit. On the other hand, I know how much this means to you, so it's less crazy from that perspective. That day is all you've been talking about for a year. People get over these things much faster. The fact that he's still so important to you and now this book... maybe it's a sign."

"I was thinking the same thing. The day I decide to leave David, boom! It happens."

"Wait, what? You left David? When and why didn't you tell me?"

"Wow, yes, you don't know. With all this Ethan Delphy excitement, I just—"

"What happened?"

"He sort of proposed. In his own way."

"That's ironic, isn't it? I never imagined it would take a marriage proposal for you to dump him. Are you OK?" she asks.

"I am. I actually am."

"But where are you going to live?"

"I'll be fine. I'm at a gas station between New York and Connecticut, on my way to Hartford to stay with my mom for a few days. But now—"

"Now, you'll find the exit to New York, then the one for JFK, and that's that."

I let out a sigh.

"I know you're over-analyzing things right now because that's who you are. But don't. Just do it. It's better than not knowing, right? Even if the answers you'll get are not the ones you're hoping for, at least you'll get closure."

I chuckle nervously. "I know you're right. I guess I'm just anxious about meeting him and terrified of finding out he didn't show up because he realized that day meant nothing."

"Maya, he told the story to a guy who wrote a novel about it. I think that qualifies as meaning something. I have to get my hands on a copy. Or two; I want to read it too. I'll try another editor, just in case. I hope they'll send the PDF and not the actual book, but just in case, call me when you get to California and give me the hotel's address, OK?"

"OK," I say.

"Call me anyway or text me. I want to know how it goes."

"I will."

"Good luck. And stop worrying."

TWENTY-ONE

I call Janice, but in her usual style, she doesn't even let me speak.

"I was about to dial your number. Do you have plans tomorrow morning?" she asks. "Andy is busy; I'm away for the weekend, Debbie is sick. I need you to go to Long Island."

"I'm on my way to Hartford," I say, hoping she will find someone else to ask.

"That's fine. It's not so far. Can't you just drive over? It's a one-hour thing. In and out."

"I can't, sorry, I have plans."

"Maya, have we not talked about this before?"

I'm sure we have. Every time I needed to do something, I had to ask Janice for permission. Going to my mother's birthday, a friend's wedding, even sleeping in on a Sunday.

"I'll email you the details," she says.

"Wait, Janice—" I hesitate. "I can't go to Long Island this weekend and that's why I called. I need to take time off—a week or so. You see, David and I—"

"Who?"

"David. My boyfriend."

Not like I mentioned his name a few hundred times in the last five years.

"We broke up and I can't stay in New York because I don't have an apartment."

"Why are you telling me this? I'm not going to take you in," she says and laughs.

"I just wanted you to know I'll be staying with my mother in Hartford. I can't drive to New York from there daily, so I need time off. Besides, I haven't had a vacation in four years."

"You can move wherever you please. If you want to make the one-hundred-plus-miles drive back and forth from Connecticut to New York each day, that's fine with me."

"That's the point. I can't."

If she's this aggressive when I explain a personal issue, I wonder how she would've reacted if I told her I'm going to California to meet a man. This woman is something else.

"What do you think this is? A telecommute job?"

"No, I don't think that. I just need a week of vacation."

I feel my voice is starting to crack.

"You're so disrespectful. I gave you a second chance and everyone told me it was a mistake. There you go. Now you're proving their point; you didn't deserve my pity."

We all have a breaking point. It's that moment when you forget you're a coward. You forget there are consequences, you have no back-up plan, and your decision will cost you.

"I work harder than anyone else. I'm there first and leave last. I write the most material, and I'm paid the least," I say, my jaw clenched. I'm unsure if I do it not to scream or not to cry.

"Stop whining. Everyone works hard. Go to Long Island, and I'll see you tomorrow."

"No!"

"No?"

"No."

"Are you trying to get fired?"

"Who's going to do all the work if you fire me?"

"You are an ungrateful little brat. I *should* fire you."

"You can't, because I quit!"

"What?"

"You heard me. I quit. I should've done it a long time ago."

She hangs up.

TWENTY-TWO

It suddenly hits me. I left David. I quit my job. I'm about to find out who Max is. My life has changed drastically in twenty-four hours. Again. It's like a cycle. Once a year, something related to Carmel pops up, and it's like a whirlwind.

I'm alone, unemployed, with barely any money in the bank, no prospects, and about to go chasing a man who wants nothing to do with me by all accounts. Crazy much?

There is a moment when I consider driving back, ripping the letter for David and just pretending like it didn't happen. But that moment passes. I've done the right thing. For both of us. Just like I've done the right thing with Janice. Just like I'm doing the right thing by driving to the airport. I have to do this. I HAVE to. For myself. For the last year and all the sleepless nights. For what I felt that day and ever since.

I hesitate again when I stop at a UPS store and mail my book boxes to Hartford. It costs me a fortune. Not a good time to be spending right now.

I hesitate again as I'm standing in line at the counter at the airport and buying my one-way ticket with two stopovers

—the cheapest I could get on such short notice—to San Francisco.

I hesitate when I call my mother and tell her about my change of plans.

"Won't make it home this weekend after all. Sorry, Mom. I'm headed for the airport."

"Airport? Where are you going?"

"California," I say. "To meet—"

I'm about to say 'friends', but I hate lying. Hate it! I crack down and tell her the truth.

"Let me see if I got this. You're going to California to find a man you spent a day with, without talking to him or seeing him, and all that happened while you were with David."

"Sort of. It's complicated."

"Maya, he could be a total psycho. You realize that, right?"

"He's not a psycho. Mom, have a little faith in me."

"Honey, your decisions when it comes to men aren't—"

"It's different this time."

"Why?"

"Because I don't think I truly loved any of my previous boyfriends. Maybe I was in love with them in the beginning, but then I knew it wasn't going to work out."

"And you think you love this man you don't even know?"

"I don't know. But I owe it to myself to at least meet him face to face and talk to him."

"Honey, why don't you come over, spend the weekend, and let's talk about it. Is this because of David? This is such a rash decision, and it doesn't sound like you."

That's a good thing. Because she's right. The 'me' she knows only made crappy decisions all of her adult life. I'm happy to exchange that version of myself any day.

I hesitate many times, despite telling my mother I'm sure about what I'm doing.

But an hour later, I'm on the plane, we take off, and I see my reflection in the small, round window and the silly grin on my face, and I feel proud. I feel reckless and brave and excited. I'm taking a risk. And at least for a moment, as brief as it is, there's no hesitation and all that lies ahead is a world of possibilities.

I haven't felt this free since I boarded a bus and headed into the unknown. So free!

TWENTY-THREE
JUNE 3

It's Monday afternoon when I finally land in San Francisco. The moment I turn on my phone I see I have two missed calls from David and two voicemails. I delete them without listening. If I don't talk to him, he'll get over it faster. Besides, this is too fresh for me to be strong about it. I worry about how I will react if I answer.

I get my suitcases onto a luggage cart and make my way to the front of the Arrivals building. It's all so familiar. The last time I was here, things took an unexpected turn. And now, here I am again, things reversed. My life already took an unexpected turn.

There are so many rideshare cars in front of the airport and I can't help but think back. And wonder. What if? Although I know that would be too much of a coincidence. I'm tempted to request a Lift to take me to Carmel, but when I open the app and see how much that costs, I change my mind. There's a 0.01 percent chance he would be my driver, and I can't spend money I don't have on those odds. I've taken enough risks in twenty-four hours and spent a few hundred dollars of my limited funds—limited is a mild statement. I need to budget wisely for a place to stay while I'm here, eat and still have enough for the return ticket to New York.

* * *

I decide in favor of the bus. The same bus I took a year ago.

The three-hour drive to Carmel feels so incredibly long this time. I'm looking out the window, remembering last year and realizing how different it all is. I feel alone now. Not for a minute did I feel alone back then. Because he was there, somewhere, texting me every few minutes, seconds sometimes, making me smile, revealing himself to me slowly.

The timing of me being here so close to my birthday feels surreal. Maybe some things do happen on their own timeline and follow their own rules I don't particularly understand.

I get my notebook out, open it and then close it again. Outside of work assignments and my manuscript, I haven't been able to write anything this past year. Every time I saw someone and thought they could be a character in one of my stories, my next thought was, 'but it will never work out, so what's the point?'

For three-quarters of the way to my destination, I feel somewhat calm, but as it gets darker and Carmel is approaching, I'm starting to feel again those nerves I first felt when Alisa called me. That mix of disbelief and worry. He's my 'one that got away'. He truly is. And being back here, so close to him, about to meet him—hopefully—feels like breaking one of those unwritten rules that says you leave the ones that got away alone. They got away for a reason. It also goes against what I've always believed in, which is 'what is meant to happen will happen no matter what you do'. Well, if I don't stop in Carmel now and go looking for him, it won't happen. I can't believe I feel so torn, and I hesitate again. Where's that confidence I felt on the plane? Where's brave Maya? I'm a bundle of worries, nerves and what-ifs.

"Next stop, Carmel by the Sea," announces the driver.

After going back and forth on my decision a few times, I know what I want to do.

"Anyone for Carmel?"

He looks in the mirror at all of us. There's not that many people left—maybe six or so.

I raise my hand.

TWENTY-FOUR

I find my way to the inn as if I've been there a hundred times, not once. It feels so nice to be here and have this familiar feeling. I don't usually get attached to places—or people—that fast, but this small town has left a strong and obviously lasting impression on me. Maybe just the adventure, the almost magical—fairy-tale-like—feel of that day, perhaps just its beauty and serenity, the friendly people, the ocean, the hope of a life I didn't even know I wanted.

"Good evening," says the woman at the front desk as I put down my luggage. I hope they have a vacant room. After all, this is an oceanside town, and it must be popular in the summer if it's anything like Cape Cod or Newport on the East Coast.

I look up at the price list on the wall. I can afford it for three nights; four, if I don't eat anything. That should be fine; I doubt I'll need more time.

"Good evening. I was wondering if you have a room. Three nights for now, but it might be more; I won't know until tomorrow."

"I have good news and bad news," she says. "We do have a room, but only for two nights. We have two large groups of tourists arriving Tuesday. The madness started on Memorial Day and it won't stop until Labor Day."

Not exactly what I want to hear, but at least I have a place to sleep for now. I'll have to go around town tomorrow and find other options.

"That's fine," I say. "I'll take it."

I give her my ID and my credit card and after a few short minutes, she gives me a key. Room number 7.

"Are you on vacation?" she asks. "Will anyone be joining you?"

"No. It's just me," I say.

I'm not comfortable talking to strangers. I try not to come off as unpleasant or too good for chats, but it's just who I am. I guess that's why I hold on so tight when I do get close to someone. Because it's hard for me to warm up to people and let them in. It's strange, if I think about it, given my profession in the last five years. As a journalist, you have to talk to a lot of folks. But that's just a job, not real life.

It was one of the things that struck me last year, when I arrived in Carmel. How quickly I became comfortable smiling at and talking to strangers all throughout that day. Almost as if someone else inhabited my body or I had left all my insecurities and inhibitions at the airport, and a different Maya boarded the bus.

The most surprising of all, was how lightning fast I became familiar with Max, talking to him about anything and everything. How easily I let him in. Maybe it's because we only texted. I don't think I would've ever been that open and flirty or agreed to meet him in real life.

I've thought about it many times, wondering if I would've

gone through with it if David hadn't shown up. Maybe I would've chickened out anyway or hid somewhere to see what he looked like and then left. I don't know. My behavior that day was so out of character, it still haunts me. Anything could've happened, but I didn't see the dangers of it. I only saw the excitement, the adventure. I do remember I was happy. Although alone in a new place, I was so absorbed by my surroundings and my growing fascination with him, that I let down my guard and didn't put up the walls I usually surround myself with. I was so curious about how that text 'relationship' would translate into real life. It's maybe because I've never hit it off with someone so quickly, someone with a similar—albeit quirky—sense of humor, someone who seemed genuinely kind and just right for me. I've never felt so much in such a short amount of time for someone.

Look at me now, a year later. The mere thought of standing in front of him makes my heart gallop, my hands sweaty, and my stomach do somersaults. I still can't believe I'm so close to meeting him.

* * *

It's too late in the evening to start my search now, though, so I ask the same woman who gave me the room—who introduces herself as Susan—if I can have something to eat at the inn. "Even if it's just a sandwich or a soup that'll be fine," I say and she tells me there are a couple of options I could choose from if I move quickly. "The kitchen closes in thirty minutes," she says.

I sit alone in a small dining room with a pretty view of the inn's garden and ten minutes later, Susan brings me a Cobb salad, which I finish in a hurry.

Tomorrow's a big day and I need to take a shower and get some sleep.

I text my mother to let her know I arrived safely and that I'll call her on Saturday, as usual. It's around eleven at night when I call Alisa, right before going to bed.

"All good. Got here, have a room at an inn," I say.

"Great. I was about to call you. How was the flight? You sound tired."

"I am beat. Any news?"

"No, It's only 7 AM," she says. "The day is just starting."

True. I always forget about the time difference. "Let me know, OK?"

"Of course. You let me know too, promise?"

"Promise."

TWENTY-FIVE

JUNE 4

"Good morning," says Susan with a big smile and I can't help but smile too. It's Carmel, what can I say? Even if you don't want to smile, you smile. It's like a reflex.

She's a woman in her fifties, wearing a pair of shorts, a sleeveless shirt with gold sequins and flip-flops. I wonder if everyone in Carmel is as bohemian, and based on what I remember, I think they are. I wouldn't mind living here. What am I saying? I'm only here for a few days.

"Will you have breakfast today?" asks Susan.

"Maybe just a coffee. I have to be somewhere soon," I say.

"Do you need me to call you a cab or are you using that phone thing? My son is on it."

"Lift?" I ask, gulping.

"Yes! That's the one. Funny name."

The idea of taking a Lift is making my heart beat faster. It did even in New York, which didn't make any sense. I hope my agony will end soon, so I won't feel this anxious every time I see a rideshare driver or someone simply brings up the topic.

"No, it's fine, thank you. I'll walk," I say.

"Alright then. Let me bring you that coffee," she says, again smiling.

Susan not only brings me a cup of coffee—a good, strong one—but also a large plate of mini sandwiches with melted cheese and ham and fruit. I must look like I need all this food. The truth is I've been losing weight lately and I didn't have that much to lose in the first place.

David calls again, but I reject his call. I wish he'd stop. I'm in a good mood and feel so close to finding out who Max is. I can't have anything or anyone get in the way of that.

* * *

Half an hour later, I'm standing in front of the bookstore. It was my first thought when I tried to make my 'plan of attack' for finding Ethan Delphy. If he's so famous and lives here, the booksellers must know where I can find him.

I walk over to the romance shelf but can't find any of his books.

"Excuse me," I say to the bookseller. "Do you have, by any chance, Ethan Delphy's books?"

I don't want to come on too strong, so I'll just act interested in getting his autograph or something after buying the novels. I don't know yet. I haven't thought this part through.

The woman grins. "Ethan's, of course," she says and walks over to the bestseller section. "All three of them and we're counting down the days to his fourth."

She's visibly excited. "He's a big celebrity around here. And not just here, obviously. But we're extra overjoyed because he's one of our own."

Extra overjoyed, oh my. The woman is in her sixties, so

she must've known him since he was a child. No wonder she's so starry-eyed and proud like a mamma bear. Carmel is the size of a block in New York. I exaggerate, but it's small, none-theless. They all must know each other.

"He's such a nice, humble young man. He didn't let all the success go to his head."

I do my best to keep a straight face and stay within my 'fan' act.

I buy all three books.

"You can pre-order a copy of his new novel now-if you want," says the woman.

I obviously plan on reading it way before June 17, but this will show my interest.

"Yes, of course, I'll do that."

She takes my details and when we get to the mailing address, I pause. I don't have an address. "Can I just pick it up when it's available?"

Not that I'll still be here on June 17, I mean... I don't know, but I don't think so. What would I do in Carmel for two weeks? I don't have money to last me that long in California, that's for sure. I barely have enough for four to five nights at the inn and if I add food and so on, it's less. Maybe I should've planned this better.

"I'm sorry, I thought you were a tourist. It's just that I never saw you before. That changes things. Did you know Ethan's going to be doing a book launch event in our bookstore?"

"Is he, really?"

I knew it was in Carmel but didn't know it was this particular bookstore. Although, now that I think about it, there are only two in town, so I had a fifty-fifty chance.

"Yes. He always does the first event at home. You should

come. Get his autograph too and maybe a photo with Ethan. He's so nice. He takes photos with everyone."

"I wish I could read his new book sooner. So excited about it," I say, testing the waters.

"It's worth the wait, trust me. I read it," she says and winks. "His best yet. So lovely."

"You have? Could I maybe get your copy then? I'll pay for it."

The woman chuckles lightly. "Sorry, no. It's only for, you know, booksellers and select people. It was an early version. Absolutely lovely," she adds, dreamy eyes and all.

Select people. I should be one of the select people. It's my story! Mine.

"You should definitely come to the book signing event. June 17," she says. "Not long now. You have to register online though. We might have a spot left," she says although I didn't indicate I want to get on the list. What I want is to meet him now. And read the book now.

"It's a long, long list," she says as she's looking at something on the computer.

I try not to roll my eyes, imagining crowds of women—I don't know why I think they're mostly women—crowding this small bookstore, as he's reading some mumbo jumbo from his undoubtedly pretentious literary works. His photo is on the back of both books. The Steve Jobs one. I stop myself from chuckling.

She nods. "You're in luck; we have a few seats open. I'll add your name."

"Thank you," I say, all smiles.

"Very well then," says the woman, ready to move on to the next customer.

"You said Ethan Delphy lives in town?" I ask in my most innocent tone.

"They all moved down to Florida a few years ago. But he comes back to see his sister and of course, to launch his books," she says, grinning proudly.

I frown. Then what am I doing here? I can't stay until June 17. "His sister?"

"Yes, she owns the coffee shop at Seventh and Dolores."

I'm bummed about this. But at least I have something to work with.

Outside the bookstore, I catch my breath. I was never one for manipulating people to get what I want and was even accused by Janice of being incapable of getting more than the obvious answers from politicians. *Take that, Janice. I can be deceiving too.* Not sure that's something to be proud of, maybe only because I proved her wrong.

It's about a ten-minute walk to the coffee shop. Good. I have time to clear my head. Calm my nerves. Come up with a plan. The idea of having to manipulate yet another person makes me queasy. The idea of using this guy's sister, who would soon find out the truth, is profoundly uncomfortable. *You'd better be worth it, Ethan Delphy, and tell me what I need to know,* I think as I make my way to Dolores Avenue.

TWENTY-SIX

I call Alisa on my way to the café, but she doesn't pick up. She might be in a meeting.

I text her instead.

Got something from the bookstore. Bad news. Delphy's not here but his sister has a café in town. Fingers crossed. Call me. No, better text. Not sure who will be around.

I'm standing in the middle of the street, at the intersection of Seventh and Dolores. I'm right across from the coffee shop and my face drops. Café Azure. It's Café Azure.

Max gave me two options and I chose the place owned by his friend's sister. Really? What was the other one? His friend's brother? Mother? I would hate to think he played me and got me here so they could all check me out and see if I was 'worth it'. No, I can't believe Max would do that. On the other hand, how would I know what Max would do?

The place was super nice, I remember that. The tables in front of Café Azure are all taken up, and there are a couple more now than I remember. I walk in, although I don't have a clear plan just yet. She might not be here and even if she is and I find out who she is, how do I go from that to asking where I can find her brother? Inside, it's even busier than last year; the line goes almost all the way to the door.

Behind the counter, I see a woman, who just like this place, is familiar. Is she the one who served me last year? Or maybe I met her somewhere in town. I was so focused on my adventure and my texting, that although I met many people, my brain put everything but Max into a big 'Carmel' bubble. Names, faces, places.

It's almost ten minutes until I finally reach the front of the line.

"Hi," I say, still studying her, unsure if my memory serves me right.

"Hello," she says, looking at me with the same expression I probably have.

"I know you," she says. "Wait, don't tell me." She squints.

I laugh. "I was here exactly a year ago. Maybe that's why."

She smiles. "The Parisian girl," she says, an air of recognition on her face. "Yes. I didn't know your name, but I called you the Parisian girl. You just had that air about you, sitting out there at that table," she says and points to where I had my breakfast last year.

"Your memory is excellent."

"You reminded me of myself when I lived in Paris."

"You lived in Paris?" I ask with a mix of admiration and envy. "That must've been so wonderful. I've always wanted to visit."

"You should," she says. "I was an exchange student there for a semester. It feels like a lifetime ago," she says with a slight smile.

I doubt it could've been that long. She can't be older than twenty-five, twenty-six maybe.

"Wish it was longer than just a few months," she says, visibly nostalgic. "But look at me, talking and talking. What can I get for you today—" She pauses.

"Maya," I say. "Although I like Parisian girl too."

She laughs. "Maya. So nice to have a name to go with the pretty face," she says kindly. "Thank you for coming back," she adds.

"I'll just have a coffee. Double shot espresso with regular milk," I say, looking up at the menu written in chalk and then, gazing at the display fridge on my right, I'm tempted. "Can I also have a brie and avocado sandwich?"

"Sure," she says, then scours the café, "Look, a table just cleared. I'll clean it up for you in no time," she says. There are now ten, maybe twelve people in line behind me.

There doesn't seem to be anyone else working here, which seems crazy to me given how busy this place is. Is Ethan's sister a scrooge? Shocker. She's obviously over-working this poor woman. It's a bustling café. I doubt one person can handle all this madness and keep their sanity or physical health.

I hear some grumbling behind me, and I know the other customers are not happy that she just left and went to get a table ready. The pretty woman must've heard it too, because she turns toward the line, as she's wiping my table, and with a big smile says, "I'll be just a minute. Thank you for your patience."

The grumbling continues though.

* * *

It's not the same as being outside in the sun and looking at passersby, but I'm enjoying my lunch and the atmosphere, nevertheless, despite the crowds. Good music, a shelf of books, one with newspapers and magazines. I wonder if living in Carmel feels like you're always on vacation or if it's just the summer and the tourists that are making it seem that way.

With its people and its bohemian vibe, this town fascinates me now just as much as it did last year, and I realize how much I've missed it.

I'm staring absentmindedly out the window when I see a man parking across the street and getting out of his car. My heart skips a beat. Is that a Lift sticker on his window? I'm not surprised I'm having this reaction here in Carmel—where Max probably works and lives—but remembering I reacted the same way in New York makes me cringe. There was no point doing it there, obviously, but I just couldn't help it. I lean to the side to see better. It is a Lift sticker; I didn't imagine it. The man crosses the street and walks straight to the café's entrance.

I freeze.

He's about the right age—or so I think. He's in his mid-thirties maybe, good-looking. Not that it was a pre-requisite, but he is. He's now standing in line and I shamelessly stare. Not too tall, average build, which means the wind won't blow him away but you won't find him in the gym every day either. He's tanned and has light-colored hair. He kind of reminds me of David with that surfer look but that's where the similarities end.

He gets to the front of the line and orders and I'm still staring and my ears prickle, trying to hear his voice. Would I even know if it's him by his voice? I don't know and I can't hear anything anyway; the place is too loud.

When he looks around, trying to find a table, all I want to do is grab him and say, 'Hey, you can sit here with me. Are you him?'

Our eyes meet and he doesn't look away for a few seconds. Is it him? Did he recognize me? How could he? He doesn't know what I look like.

I get up and I'm about to do something even crazier than coming all the way to Carmel. I'm about to just go to him and ask, when he turns around and leaves. And before I know it, his car speeds away.

TWENTY-SEVEN

It takes me minutes to recover. I don't know why, but I just... I thought that it might be him. How incredible would it be if I randomly find him on my first day here?

But I don't know if it's him, and I can't do this to myself whenever I see a Lift driver. I'm sure there's more than one in Carmel.

There's no sign of Ethan's twin, Celine, so I have to come up with a plan. Another plan.

The line calms down after a while, and I make my way to the press shelf to see if they have any local papers. Maybe, I don't know, maybe there's something in there about him. An event, a reading, or whatever it is that authors do. A party I could go to, uninvited. I chuckle to myself. Where are these crazy thoughts coming from?

The server stops by to ask if I need anything else and if I'm enjoying the food, just as I'm closing the second magazine. Nothing about him in either of them.

And just as I'm telling her I'm all set and wonder if I

should ask about the owner and how to do it, I hear a man calling out, "Celine!"

My head snaps in the direction of the voice.

The server turns too. "Just give me a minute, Hugo," she says, and then turning to me with a big smile on her face, "Duty calls."

My face drops. She's Celine. She's Ethan's twin sister. My God, she looks fantastic for thirty-three. I look old compared to her.

I met her last year and I didn't know who she was. Funny if not ironic. I study her, trying to find similarities with the man in the photo. She's tall, slender and has light brown hair with sandy highlights, and light brown-amber eyes. She's very pretty. He probably has brown eyes too and that short hair in the photo is most surely brown. So, I guess they do look alike.

As the fascination fades, I'm left with the question—now what? Should I ask about her brother? And how? If I tell her the truth, it might not go well. If I say I'm a fan, it won't help because I doubt she'll offer any information about Ethan. She seems nice, and I don't want to lie to her, but I don't know what to do. I should've thought about all these things before I came. I get that I went from never doing anything in the spur of the moment to doing everything in the spur of the moment, but this is simply stupid.

I text Alisa and tell her Ethan's sister is the woman I met last year. *Fate,* Alisa texts back.

Sure. Yes. Delayed fate, but still counts.

So, did you find out anything from her?

I don't know how to ask.

I don't know Miss 'I'm on a mission'. Is the sister friendly? Just chat her up.

Me and chatting someone up.

You can do it. Didn't you say you're a different person in Carmel? Be that person!

I bought his earlier books. What if I put one on the table? Maybe she'll say something.

You might as well just call yourself his biggest fan and beg for an autograph.

Very helpful, I say.

Yes, priceless. Now go talk to her.

Talk to her about what? Hey, how's your brother? Still writing books? You know where I could find him? There's some stuff we need to talk about.

Nope, not going to happen.

TWENTY-EIGHT

I'm staring into the distance, trying to come up with an idea, and I see a piece of paper taped to the café's front window. So this is what that man was looking at. Oh, well, my story was better.

The paper is facing outside, and I'm making an effort to read it backward.

Help Wanted
Seasonal employment, June–August
Flexible Schedule and Shifts 8 AM–12 AM
Inquire inside.

OK. OK. I could try. This could be an option. No crazier than my other ideas. After all, I need the money and it would justify why I'm here, plus she'll surely mention her brother at some point.

Celine is cleaning the table next to mine.

"I saw you're looking to hire," I say, pointing at the window.

She nods. "Haven't had much luck with seasonal staff. Had a girl here for a couple of weeks, but it didn't work out."

"I'm actually looking for a job. A temporary job."

"Really?" she says, sounding as surprised as she looks.

"I'm in town for a little while and I need to make some money, while I take care of some personal stuff," I say, realizing how shady that sounds. It's not a complete lie, more like a lie by omission. I do need to take care of personal stuff and I do need a job. "I could help out until you find someone better," I say, trying to convince her because she seems to hesitate.

"That's not why I didn't jump up and down when you told me," she says, with a wide smile. "It's just that I usually only get students or drifters showing interest. Obviously, I'd love to get some help, but do you have any experience?"

I smile innocently. "I used to work at Starbucks in college. That's about it."

"More than all the other candidates I had this season," she says, laughing. "I'm in dire need of help, to be honest. My brother has been pestering me to get someone here for ages, but it's hard to find qualified personnel once the season starts. I'd do it by myself, but between Memorial and Labor Day it's a bit brutal. It's good for business but hard to manage alone."

I smile. "So, I'm in?"

"You most definitely are. If you want to."

I am tempted to hug her, but instead I just thank her maybe a few too many times.

"The pay is—" She pauses. "I'm sorry. I'm afraid it will offend you," she says.

"Why would it offend me?"

"It's $25 per hour plus any tips you make."

"It's better than I thought," I say and I'm honest. I do

quick math; it's just a bit shy of my fancy journalistic job in New York. And there were definitely no tips there.

"Good to hear," she says.

"I assume there is a test on the job," I say.

"Just a few hours. And paid," she says. "Half a shift. Anyhow, I'm sure you'll do great."

I appreciate the vote of confidence. I'm not as sure as she is, and I don't know about great, but I'll definitely do my best.

"When would you want me to start?"

"Now? As in, today? Or tomorrow? Whenever you want."

"I can start now," I say.

"Perfect. We can finish the trial period this evening. If it all goes well—which I'm sure will happen—do you know for how many hours a day you'd like to work? Four? More?"

"How about I work for however many hours you need me?" I say.

I don't have a reason—*yet*—not to be here all day. When that reason shows up—hopefully soon—we'll discuss this again. Besides, I want to make sure I'm in Celine's good graces.

Her eyes widen. "That's too good of an offer to pass up. Be careful, I might take you up on that and decide I need you here from 8 AM to midnight."

I laugh. "That's fine."

No difference versus my job in New York. I wasn't making coffee for sixteen hours, but I was up on my feet for just as long in a job I loathed. This can't be any worse.

She seems excited, and that makes me feel even more guilty. She seems like such a kind person—her only fault is that she's related to Ethan Delphy—who doesn't deserve being used like this. But I plan on giving this job my absolute best, and hopefully, she'll soon find someone who's here to stay for the summer.

Celine is explaining everything with patience and a permanent smile.

"Is there a uniform or something I need to wear?"

She smirks. "Look at me. Do you think you need a uniform?"

She's wearing a long purple and green tie-dye dress and sandals to match it. Celine and Carmel make me think of the flower power movement and Scott McKenzie's song, and I'm tempted to put a flower in my hair and dance on the street. What's gotten into me?

"I'll just need an ID and some info for the paperwork, but we can deal with that later. It's all online anyway. Should be painless."

"Sure," I say and give her my driver's license so she can make a copy.

"Alright, just so you know, people here come for dinner as early as four. We have a couple of hours now before it gets busy again. It's the perfect time to show you the ropes."

My phone rings. It's David again and I reject his call. A minute later he texts, asking me to stop ignoring him. I was strong enough to leave, but I don't want to have to hear promises and excuses, because undoubtedly that's what he's going for. Although I haven't officially left him before, we've had plenty of fights and all of them ended with: 'It will be different. Let's give it another try'. Every single time.

"Everything alright?" asks Celine.

I put my phone away and nod.

She takes me in the back and walks me through the kitchen, where everything is made from scratch with fresh ingredients. She shows me where things go in the walk-in pantry and fridge and assures me she won't ask me to cook anything—unless I want to. I'm sure I won't because I'm beyond clumsy around sharp or hot things. She shows me the baking area and finally the espresso and coffee machines. I pay close attention to all the details, although I don't think she'll ask me to make coffee. Probably just take orders, serve customers, and clean tables.

It's been seven years since I've done this and I'm a little nervous, but Celine is doing a great job of sharing all the details and reassuring me she will help me with anything I need.

"You'll do great and our customers are easygoing so you won't have any problems. There is the odd tourist who has a short temper or doesn't have patience if the line is long, but I can take them on. And if anything, just keep your cool, stay calm, and if you can... smile."

I show my teeth like a monkey.

"That should do it," she says and bursts into laughter.

It's now four o'clock. I think I'm ready. Let the games begin.

TWENTY-NINE

I have walked more miles in these fifteen hundred square feet for the last six hours than in the previous six months in all of New York.

There were no problem customers, only pleasant clients, which was perfect for getting my feet wet. I've already learned the names of five of them who Celine says are regulars.

My cheeks hurt from smiling, and I'm finding myself saying 'thank you' and 'have a nice day' in my mind every few seconds. But I enjoyed it, which is surprising. The first couple of hours were tough, I'll admit. Not that I'm unpleasant, it's just that being *this* pleasant doesn't come naturally. Making small talk, waiting for people to choose their food, repeating the orders to make sure I got them right, smiling. But I mimicked the way Celine talked to customers, and based on what she just told me five minutes ago—"People love you"—I think I did OK.

"You don't have to stay if you're tired," she says after the last customers leave.

"We have to clean up," I say stoically and start wiping down the tables.

"I imagine it's quite a lot for your first day," she says.

"First day? Does that mean there's going to be a second? Did I get the job?"

"Of course. You did great today."

"Thank you," I say, trying to sound more enthusiastic than exhausted.

"Thank *you*. You did great, and don't feel like you need to put on a brave face for me. I'm tired too, but I'm used to it. I've been doing this for twelve years."

"That's a long time."

"Yes, it is," she says, deep in thought.

She seems to love doing it, but it's almost as if she yearns for more.

"Is Café Azure yours?" I ask.

"My grandparents opened it in 1955, my parents took over, and now it's my turn."

"That's so nice that it stayed in the family."

"It is. It's also a big responsibility."

"I'm sure. But you do enjoy it, right? You're great at it, and your baking and cooking skills are amazing. Not to mention your coffee. Delicious!"

She chuckles. "Recipes passed from generation to generation. I learned them when I was a kid; I could do them with my eyes closed."

"I've never known my way around a kitchen," I say, a bit ashamed.

"I'd be happy to teach you."

"One day, maybe," I say and then realize our arrangement is only for a short while, just until I talk to her brother and find Max, so that day will probably never come.

* * *

We finish cleaning and lock up.

"Which way are you going?" she asks, in front of the café.

"Not sure. Left, I think. I'm at The Lantern Inn."

"Susan's place. OK. How long do you plan to stay here?"

I hesitate.

"I'm sorry, I didn't mean to pry. Just thinking that it might not be practical to stay at an inn if you're going to be here for a while." She winks. "It's lovely but not cheap."

I smile. "That's true, but I'm only staying there for another night. Tomorrow I have to find something else. Even if I could afford it, she's fully booked."

"Not surprised. And did you rent a place already?"

"Actually, I wanted to ask if it would be OK if I bring my suitcases to work tomorrow; I'll put them somewhere in the back. And then maybe on my lunch break—if I have one—or after work, I could go around town to look for a room to rent somewhere."

"No problem. You can leave them in the back office. And take all the time you need."

She looks like she wants to say something else but doesn't.

"Appreciate that. I'll see you at eight. Good night, Celine," I say, and I'm about to leave.

"Good night. Maya—" she says and stops. "Not sure if you'd be interested, but I have two spare bedrooms. I live alone in my family's house, so you can rent one if you want."

"That'd be amazing," I say.

She smiles. "They're obviously not as nice as Susan's, but they're not bad either."

Celine's kindness is the type that renders one speechless and is causing me confusion. My opinion of Ethan Delphy is definitely not a good one. I imagine it'll get worse once I meet him, just from what I know so far. I wonder how twins can be so different.

"I bet they're great. But, are you sure? I mean, you just met me."

"That's not technically correct. I've known you for a year," she says with a big smile. "Usually, landlords rent to people they've never met, so this is a step up," she says. "I already have your info for the application from earlier today, so it should be an easy process."

"I'm speechless. You're a lifesaver," I say.

"Just wait until you live with me for a few days. You might change your mind." She laughs. "I'm not the most organized person."

"That's fine. I'm used to—"

I want to say cleaning after David. He was the biggest slob in the history of slobs.

"Would you like to come by, take a look, and see if you even like the place?"

"Now?"

"Yes, now. Since you have to leave the inn in the morning, you don't have much time."

"Of course. I'd love to," I say and as we start walking, I repeat, "That's so nice of you."

"I have my selfish reasons too. It gets lonely in that house, all by myself. With Ethan gone, all I have is Marcel—"

I know her brother doesn't live here. The question is, when will he come back? Is this a good time to ask? And who is Marcel? I give her a questioning look.

"Ethan is my brother and Marcel is my cat. He's an old grump."

"Your brother or the cat?"

"Both," she says, laughing, and I laugh too.

"So your brother doesn't live in Carmel?" I ask as we make our way through narrow streets lit by pale yellow lamps.

"Technically, he does, but he travels a lot. The last time I saw him was Christmas. He now stays with our parents in Florida," says Celine as she turns right on a narrow road. "But he'll be back soon. You might meet him if you're still here."

Celine points at a cottage like the ones I admired last year. "This is it."

"It's beautiful," I say.

"And old. It needs some love. I'm doing a thing here a thing there, but—"

We walk into a flower garden, which is a bit wild but cared for. The cottage has a beach house vibe, with its white and blue in the living room and the 'sitting room', which leads to a massive terrace with an ocean view. The double oven and stainless steel appliances in the kitchen are clearly Celine's touch.

"Let me show you the bedrooms," she says, and I follow her.

The first one has a more traditional look than the rest of the house, with heavier-set furniture. There's a massive king-size bed in the center, a leather armchair and a small round table by the window. I like it, although it's a bit dark.

"And the second one," she says as we walk into a much lighter, albeit smaller room. A queen-size bed, a bay window overlooking the beach, light blue drapes, and off-white curtains.

Two of the walls are covered in shelves and crammed with books. The room is painted a light shade of blue. If I had my own beach house, this is precisely what you'd see in it.

Except for the books, they'd be organized by color or by genre, depending on my mood.

"I love this room," I say, and judging by Celine's smile, she's not surprised.

"It's settled then," she says. "I'll finish the paperwork tonight, both for the job and the room. Weekly rental, right?" she asks.

"Yes, please. Because I don't know—"

"How long you'll be in town. I know. I remember what you said." She rubs her hands together. "Tomorrow morning, you should be all set. What's that saying? Killing two birds with one stone?"

I laugh. "I got lucky today."

"The stars aligned," she says, smiling.

Although today didn't go as expected, I feel strangely at peace. This small town, this kind woman, the cozy café, this charming cottage, the sound of the waves crashing on the rocks below, make me feel inexplicably at home. As if I'm exactly where I'm supposed to be. I don't know what it means, and I don't know what tomorrow will bring or how or when I will meet Ethan Delphy and how that meeting will go, but for now, today, tonight, I smile. The world is still full of possibilities. No doors have been closed for me today. On the contrary, they opened.

THIRTY

I return to the inn before midnight and Susan, who's still awake, greets me at the door.

I nod and cover my mouth as I yawn. I'm exhausted.

"I'm sorry to bother you at this hour with this, but I just wanted to remind you that check-out is tomorrow before eleven," she says.

"Yes. No bother. I'll be ready before eight."

"Sad to see you go," she says, sounding sincere. "Did you find another place to stay?"

"I did, yes, close by."

"That's wonderful. I'm so glad."

I smile, thank her, say good night and head straight for my room.

Before falling asleep, I remember I didn't tell Alisa what happened so I call her and we talk for a few minutes. As in, I talk and she listens.

"I told you to talk to the woman, not get her to hire you."

"I didn't know how else to get close to her. I couldn't just come out and ask. Plus, I need the money and a reason to stay."

"You have a talent for complicating things. Was it worth it? Did you learn where he is?"

"Yes. In Florida."

"In Florida?" She sounds shocked. "What are you still doing there then?"

"Well, Max is here somewhere, and Celine said her brother is coming soon. Oh, and she had rooms to rent, so I'm moving in with her. I'm still in shock at how kind she is."

"Can I envy you for a second? Yesterday you left New York with nothing, and now you have a job, a place to live, and it sounds like a new friend."

"I don't know about friend, but she's nice. How these two are related, I have no idea."

"I know you are set against her brother, but you don't even know him, right?"

"I don't need to know him. He stole my story. Besides, I saw his photo, I read about him. What else is there to know?"

"Prejudiced much?"

"Stop!"

"By the way, I'm calling an assistant editor at his publishing house this afternoon. Didn't hear back from the other girls on the copy. What's your fancy-schmancy address by the ocean?"

I give her the address.

"Oh my God," she says seconds later. "Now I really hate you. I just google mapped it and did the satellite view. Are you kidding me? It's right on the ocean."

"Hop on a plane and come on over. Maybe this way I get to see you. It's only been, what, eighteen months?"

She sighs. "I wish I could. Too much work to do, can't take a holiday now."

"I know. OK. I have to go to sleep. Tomorrow is my first full day at my new job."

"So funny to hear that. You, a barista. Please don't repeat your Starbucks misadventures. We all know how those turned out. Poor Celine doesn't know what she's getting herself into."

I snicker. "Hey, I'm not that bad."

"Aha. Sure. Good night," she says.

"Have a great day, Alisa. And text me if you have news. Don't care what time it is."

THIRTY-ONE
JUNE 5

Susan is checking someone in when I bring my luggage downstairs.

My phone beeps and it's a text message from a local number.

Good morning. Your paperwork is done, and everything looks good. I've left a key for you under the front doormat if you want to drop off your luggage before work. I'll see you soon. Celine.

This is a great way to start the day.

"Good morning," says Susan. "What a lovely day. The sun is up, the coffee is made, and biscuits are in the oven," she declares, satisfied.

"That's what that is," I say with a smile. "I smelled something delicious the moment I opened my eyes."

"Do you have time for breakfast?" she asks.

By the time I took a shower and packed it was already seven.

"I have to be at work soon, but thank you."

"I didn't know you worked in town," she says. "Thought you were just visiting."

"I just started at Café Azure."

"Celine's place?" she says, sounding surprised. "That's lovely."

She asks me to wait a couple of minutes and returns with a paper cup with a lid on and a food container. Both are hot and judging by the smell... it's coffee and fresh biscuits. I don't think Susan is used to taking no for an answer. She puts them on the desk and winks. "You can share them with Celine," she says, pointing at the food box, "compliments of the chef. Ask her if my biscuits are better than hers; she's always welcome to borrow my recipe." She chuckles.

"I will," I say.

I check out and after Susan hugs me once inside the inn and a second time in the front yard, we wave goodbye.

"You sure you don't need a ride? I can call a cab for you."

"I'm sure. It's close.

"OK. Well, don't be a stranger. We'd love to have you back," she says and gives me a pamphlet. "We have all sorts of fun activities planned this summer."

* * *

I get to Celine's house and drop off my suitcases by the door.

It's a ten-minute walk to Café Azure, at least that's what the maps app on my phone says. I don't remember how we got here last night; I was just following Celine and not paying attention to street names. I'm probably taking a longer route, but I'm so enjoying this right now. I pass by places that are familiar from last year and find myself smiling. I see the beach and I'm so tempted to go to that spot—THE SPOT—

but I'm not yet ready to see it again. I turn right on Tenth Avenue, then left onto Monte Verde Street and before I know it, I'm on Seventh Avenue, in front of the coffee shop. At the corner, I see him. The Lift driver from the other day. He's wearing a pair of skinny jeans, a Hawaiian shirt and aviator sunglasses. He's going into a small restaurant across the street from Café Azure, and without even thinking, I follow him. I look at the name above: Bellini. Are you kidding me? The first breakfast choice he gave me last year. Does he work here? Does he own it? Is that why?

My heart is beating out of my chest. I pretend to be looking at the menu while I scour the inside of the restaurant, but I can't see him anywhere.

"Hi, can I help you? Would you like to be seated?" a young woman asks as I see him, from the corner of my eye, back out on the street, getting into his car.

I point to him. "Is that the owner?" I ask her.

She looks in the direction I'm pointing then back at me.

"Would you like to see the owner? Something wrong? I can ask her to come," she says.

I shake my head. "No, no, it's fine. You don't know who he is?" I ask again.

"Who?"

He's long gone. Ugh, never mind. I make my excuses and drag my feet to Café Azure. I will find him. If that's him, I will find him. He's here somewhere.

Café Azure is already busy, not as bad as yesterday at lunch, but it's pretty crowded.

"Good morning," I say to Celine the moment I reach the counter.

A couple is debating muffins or cereal for their kids and not paying attention to us.

"Go-o-o-o-d morning," she says in a sing-song voice. "Boy, am I glad to see you."

She nods at the long line and whispers, "Don't you dare ask how I got on without you."

"Wasn't planning to," I say. "What do you need me to do?"

"Hold the front of the house, please. I have things in the oven," she says.

"On it," I say, trying to remember everything I learned from her yesterday.

"By the way, this is for you," I say, and give her the food container. "From Susan."

"Freshly baked biscuits? Some things never change," she says with a strange smile and takes the box in the back.

THIRTY-TWO

I meet a few more of the regulars. Some come in for breakfast; some are here just for lunch. Celine knows each and every one of their names, their families, what they do. I'm at the 'let's make an effort and remember their first name' level, so I have a way to go.

I've gotten to know Anna; she's a painter. Her arms are covered in random colors, her clothes as well. This morning she came in with a blue streak on her forehead. Celine told her about it, but Anna didn't seem to mind. She's about my age and wears her long black hair in two braids and both yesterday and today she came in overalls. Celine told me she has a small gallery on Ocean Avenue. I might stop by one day. Watching her, I wish I could write again; she'd be the type of character I'd enjoy giving a happily ever after to.

For dinner, it's just as crowded as yesterday, and Celine tells me starting tomorrow, it'll get progressively busier by the day.

"Don't even get me started on the Fourth of July," she says. "You'll see. It's madness."

I don't want to contradict her or remind her it's improbable that I'll be working here in July. I'd rather not think about it and take one day at a time, which is a new concept for me.

We're almost done with dinner and as I'm cleaning up a table, David calls again. It's the fifth time today. I don't want to do this. I should change my number or block him.

I'm a bit cranky because I feel like he's pulling me back, just by insisting, and there's nothing to pull me back to. I don't understand why he doesn't just move on. Celine must notice something is off, because she asks if I'm OK.

"I'm fine, sorry, it has nothing to do with you or the job. It's complicated."

"If you want to talk about it," she says, "know that I'm good with complicated."

Maybe I will. One day. Just not today.

* * *

We walk back together. Thanks to her jokes and generally upbeat disposition, my mood changes almost immediately. I'm worried a bit though. It's been a full day, she hasn't brought up her brother at all and because it's been so busy at the café, we didn't have time to chat. I have to ask her. I have to know.

"Let me get your room ready," she says the moment we get to the house and disappears from the living room before I have the opportunity to respond.

I sit on the couch, not knowing what to do.

"All set. You can take your luggage into your room, change, make yourself at home." She smiles. "Have you been sitting there since I left? Make yourself at home, just don't leave the terrace doors open because Marcel has Houdini tendencies. Are you hungry?" she asks.

"Not really," I say.

"You have to eat something. A fainting employee is of no use to me," she says with a wink. "How about a cold-cut platter, wine and for entertainment, a movie?"

"You're going out of your way to be the perfect host," I say.

"At least for tonight," she says with a big smile. "Want to make a good first impression."

I laugh. "That sounds great."

"I'll get the food ready. If you want to change, shower, unpack, we have time. When you're done, can you pick the movie? I have all the streaming apps you could possibly want."

I laugh quietly.

"What can I say? I lead an exciting life. The remote is there," she says and points toward the table in front of the couch.

I take my suitcases to my room. Celine has changed the sheets, and there's a pleasant coconut smell in the air—I see the plug-in air freshener by the door. There's a set of brand new towels on the side of the tub in my en-suite bathroom and everything is so clean and inviting.

I must repay Celine's kindness somehow. You don't often meet people like her.

I take a quick shower, change and leave the unpacking until later. I choose three movies: *Love Affair* from 1939, *The Last Time I saw Paris* from 1954 and *A Star is Born* from 1937. She goes for *Love Affair*, which is my first choice too. We're at the part where Irene Dunne is on the couch and I remember that was one of my crazy scenarios. What if something happened to Max and that's why he didn't come, and he didn't call? Alisa told me it was doubtful, and she was right. Nothing happened. He just chose not to show up.

Alisa texts me. *No news from me. Yet. How was your first day?*

Good. Long. My feet hurt.

What are you doing?

Just finished dinner and now watching a movie.

Alone?

With Celine.

Aha. No news?

Not yet. Didn't want to be too obvious and ask her anything just yet.

But you know you have to, right? Alrighty. Night night.

Both Celine and I cry at the end of the movie. We all have baggage, and as we grow older, it gets heavier. I wonder what her baggage is and why is someone like her single? She's beautiful, kind, smart, successful. Compared to her, I'm a failure. A work in progress, as my mother says. I've been a work in progress for as long as I can remember.

THIRTY-THREE

Thursday at the café is the same as Wednesday. Both Celine and I work until ten, ten-thirty, then we walk home. David calls several times and texts everything from *You're making a mistake* to *I feel so betrayed,* and *What will I tell my friends and my family?* Celine asks me if I want to talk about it, but I don't. There's nothing to talk about. Although, obviously, David disagrees. His last text message, late at night, has a different tone. He's asking me nicely to answer. He says he wants to talk to me, and he won't give up. I don't reply.

I haven't seen the Lift driver today. He didn't come to the café and although I kept my eye on the street, there was no sign of him.

I did meet a few more of the regulars today though. One of them is Alan, in his mid, maybe late thirties, he's a lawyer in Monterey, who apparently comes to Café Azure every day after the gym. He has a latte, a three-cheese croissant and a small chocolate bar. He smiles from the door as he enters, comes over to say hi and pay for his order, asks Celine how she is and now me too. Celine asks him how his training went

—he wants to do a marathon in the fall—and he says it's hard, but he won't give up, then he sits at the window bar and waits for his breakfast.

He also comes back in the evening; at least he did today. "I lost a case," he said as he walked in, his morning smile replaced by a deep frown, and Celine nodded knowingly.

"A glass of wine instead of coffee then?" she asked him.

He's handsome, in a classic way, seems to be in good shape and obviously has a good job. I'd expect he'd be great with the ladies, but he seems rather lonely. If this was the same time last year, by now I'd have a handful of ideas for Alan stories. Now, my mind just goes blank. And it's such a pity because he looks like he deserves a good, happy story.

* * *

When we get back to the cottage, Celine orders pizza. After we eat, we sit on the terrace, listening to the ocean, drinking freshly made lemonade and talking.

It's a good night. I haven't been this comfortable and relaxed in a long time. Celine and I got close fast, which is unusual for me, but not uncommon for anything Carmel-related. She has a way about her that is inviting and comforting. She doesn't pry into my personal life and doesn't offer too many details about hers, but we talk about all sorts of things. Small things. Carmel, funny customers, annoying customers, movies, music. I hope we'll talk about books too and her brother and I keep trying to push the conversation that way, without seeming too obvious.

"Did you always want to run the café?" I ask.

"When I was seven, I wanted to be a ballerina." She

laughs. "I was *not* good at it. No grace, that's what my teachers said. Then I wanted to be a race car mechanic."

"Really?"

"I love cars. And there are a bunch of races in the Monterey area. I've been surrounded by exotic and fast cars all my life. My father had a passion for them."

"Why didn't you?"

"Who would've taken care of the family business? I had to make a choice. Besides, there aren't that many women mechanics and I had my fair share of raised eyebrows and comments when I was learning how to fix cars and went with my father to the races. I can't tell you how many times I was told that's not where a woman belongs, so—"

"That's not OK," I say. "You shouldn't let other people tell you what you can and can't do. If you want something, you should go after it," I say and then realize what a hypocrite I am and how patronizing that sounds. What gives me the right to preach? It took me forever to leave David although I was unhappy. Just like it took me forever to leave my job, and I don't even know if I was brave or I had simply reached my limit. Brave is making a decision when you have multiple options and although the one you choose might be the riskiest, it's what you know deep down in your heart is the right thing. Doing what I did and when I did it, is a feeble attempt at redemption. Pretty pathetic that someone like me would point the finger at someone like Celine.

"I know. I should've stood my ground, but I didn't have support, except for Ethan, but he had his own problems to deal with. And now it's too late. I'm too old. I guess being part of Laguna Seca and getting my hands dirty with those beauties will just be a dream."

Too late? I'm twenty-eight this month—which is basically

thirty—and I'm starting over. How easy it is to see what needs to be done when it's not your life.

"When you're not working at Café Azure, what do you do?" asks Celine. "In New York," she says and smiles. "I saw it on your driver's license."

"In that life, I was a writer for a magazine."

"Nice. Did you always want to be a magazine writer?"

Good question.

"I've always loved writing. I used to dream of writing books, rather than—"

"Journalism? You can do both—write books and write for magazines. Ethan does it too."

In theory, she's right; nothing is stopping me. Except with this manuscript where her brother and his new book—stolen book—stop me. But what prevented me from submitting it before? My fear of failure, undoubtedly. Getting an agent, a publishing deal and seeing my novel in bookstores is the last dream I hold on to and the most important. If I fail, there's nothing left to look forward to. But now's not the time to think about that. This could be my shot to find out more about Ethan Delphy. I finally got our conversation where I wanted it.

"So, your brother is a writer?"

"Yes."

"What kind of books does he write?"

Jeez. When she finds out I knew all this, she'll feel so betrayed.

She smiles. "Love stories. They're in the library if you want to read them," she says.

"The town library?"

She laughs. "No. Our library, I mean. Follow me."

What if she has the new one? Here's hoping.

We walk into a room filled with hundreds of books nicely organized by genre and author. Heaven! In the center of the room an antique desk and two worn-out red leather armchairs.

"Is this yours?" I ask.

"The library? Ethan's. And it's only a part of it; he has books everywhere. I love books too and reading, but I don't always have the time. Been listening to a lot of audiobooks lately."

On the wall by the window, six shelves of books all have Ethan Delphy's name on them.

I thought he only had three novels out. There must be a hundred here.

"Wow," I say, not even trying to hide my surprise. "Your brother wrote all these?"

She chuckles. "Yes and no. He wrote five books. A semi-biography and three novels. Wait, four. There's a new one, which I don't think is here." She stops and looks. "Nope. Not yet. It's going to be published—" She goes to the desk. On it, there's a large monthly planner. "June 17. Correct. Hmm, I wonder if he's coming the day of. That's what he usually does."

THIRTY-FOUR

June 17? That's eleven more agonizing days of not knowing. And she doesn't have a copy of the book. Great. Just great. I should've just stayed in New York. Then I realize it's pointless to think that way. I wouldn't have stayed in New York anyway. Right now, I'd be in my mother's kitchen, alone, while she's in the next room sleeping. So, what am I complaining about? It is what it is. I just hope I didn't make the trip for nothing, and when Ethan Delphy comes, he'll tell me where Max is and who he is.

"They're all the translations," she says, pointing at the books. "Like thirty or so for every book. What kind of books do you write?"

"Love stories."

"You too? That's awesome. You and Ethan will have a lot to talk about then."

I doubt it. Well, except for him telling me who Max is.

"And they're not books. Just manuscripts nobody wants," I say, realizing I sound bitter.

"How come?"

"They got rejected by agents. I have a new one I never submitted, but—"

"Do you know how many times Ethan was rejected before he found his agent?"

I stare.

"I'd say over a hundred times."

Because he's a sucky writer who steals other people's stories. Does his agent know?

"You should try again," she says. "Why don't you?"

I don't have an answer to that question. At least not an answer I can give now.

"It's complicated," I say.

"Fear of failure, maybe?" she asks. "I know about that all too well."

Maybe we're more alike than I thought. Although Celine seems to have it all together, there's regret in her voice. I recognize regret. It's my thing.

"Talking about my famously annoying brother, I should give him a call," she says.

"Now? Isn't it late in Florida?"

"Ethan is a night owl. He writes at night and edits during the day. Don't ask me why."

I wasn't planning to. I couldn't care less how he lives his life. Who was it that said they write drunk and edit sober? Maybe this is his own interpretation.

"I promised I'd tell him when there's news, so I have to call him."

"What's the news?" I ask.

"You," she says with a smile. "Plus, I need to ask him something."

She dials his number and puts him on speakerphone.

"Hey, bro, what are you doing?"

"Writing. How's everything back home?"

"Good. Great. I won't keep you long. Just wanted you to say hi to my savior."

"Don't tell me the miracle happened? You finally found someone for the café?"

"She came all the way from New York to help me," says Celine and winks at me.

"Heh," I say. "Well—"

Celine nudges me forward.

"Maya, say hi."

The plan is for me to be over-the-top friendly and get him to tell me what I need to know.

"Hi," I say. "It's so nice to meet you, Ethan. I've heard a lot about you."

Silence.

"Hey, Ethan, are you still there?" asks Celine.

"Yes, sorry, you broke up a bit."

"Ugh," she says. "Maya just said hello."

"H—Hello," he says.

"For a writer, you sure are bad with words. Say welcome and thank you for helping my chaotic sister."

"Welcome, and thank you for helping my chaotic sister," he says, and I can't tell if he's serious or joking. Either way, his voice is getting on my nerves already. Not as much his voice as his tone. Like he can't be bothered. It perfectly matches the face in the photo.

"OK, enough chitchat," says Celine. "I called because I wanted to know when you're coming back."

There's a crackling noise, and we hear half of a word that I don't even understand.

"Stop mumbling," she says and laughs.

"I said this week."

She looks at me and makes funny faces. "This week? Did Mom and Dad kick you out?"

"Aren't you the one who has been pestering me to return to California for months?"

Celine laughs. "That must've been some other sister. So, when's your flight?"

"Soon."

"OK, that sounds vague enough. So it might be this week, but it might be June 17, right?"

She covers the phone with her hand and says to me, "Typical Ethan", then uncovers it. "Will you let me know in advance? I'll come to the airport, do a banner and everything."

"No thanks," he answers dryly. "I'll see you soon."

Thank God. This might work out after all.

THIRTY-FIVE

JUNE 7

The first thing I did when I went to my room last night was to call Alisa.

"Delphy's coming back from Florida. Don't exactly know when but sooner than the 17th."

"I didn't know he was supposed to come back on the 17th," she says.

"I didn't tell you? Sorry. Must've had a conversation with you in my mind."

She chuckled.

"I have good news too. Heard back from one of the girls I asked for the book and she promised she'll send me one this week. Not a PDF, though, so it'll come in the mail."

"Great! Today's been a good day after all."

* * *

I'm a bit off this morning. Couldn't sleep last night. I don't know if it was the excitement of getting closer to answers, getting closer to meeting Max. Whatever it was, it made me toss and turn for hours. After a cup of strong, black coffee, I feel I'm starting to come back to 'human form' and I'm capable of smiling back at customers without looking like I'm in pain.

I like the smell of coffee. I think I've always liked it, but in the last few days, it's become something of a comforting, familiar presence. When you work in a café, the smell of coffee is on everything. Your clothes, your hair, your hands. No point trying to wash it off; it's there to stay.

I also notice I'm beginning to appreciate the routine more and more. Getting to know the regulars is the highlight of my day. Saying hi to them and even making small talk. That's big for me.

Today I chatted with Brienne. I know from Celine she's a single mother of three small boys and an advanced math professor at Stanford. Every morning—at least since I've been here—she barges in at seven, her hair disheveled, her clothes mismatched and her eyes puffy.

"Long night?" I asked this morning as I was making her triple espresso.

She nodded and barely said a word until she took a few sips of coffee. "I can't stay long. The boys are coming back home from a sleepover soon," she said.

I smiled. It must be hard to take care of three boys on your own, with nobody to help.

She then grabbed her quarter baguette with cheese, lettuce and tomatoes, the three pastrami sandwiches for the boys and left just as fast as she came in. Yesterday afternoon she brought the boys too, and kept them busy with tablets, while she graded papers.

Brienne is a beautiful woman, or better said, I think she

used to be. She doesn't take as much care of herself as she could.

"I never have time for anything," she complained yesterday afternoon to Celine who asked what the rush was. She must be in her mid-thirties, no more, with a naturally flattering complexion and round brown eyes, big and inquisitive. Celine calls her 'Bambi'.

A bit later in the day, I meet Hugo, yet another member of our 'Blue Valentines' Club', as Celine calls them. She told me that when he first came in three years ago, he was happily married, about to buy a house with his new wife and planning a trip around the world. He dreamed of having a child and said they were trying. Six months later, she had gone on the expensive trip together with all of his savings and the few jewelry pieces he had from his mother. There was never going to be a child because she admitted to being on the pill all that time. He was left with half of what he had, no house and obviously no wife. He has sworn off dating or even getting close to a woman and said two divorces were enough for him. I think it's too bad. He has salt and pepper hair and deep brown eyes, is charming and can hold a conversation like no other, is in good shape, plus he has a good job, working for the Mayorship of Monterey as their head communication expert.

"Where did you park your car, Maya?" he asks this morning.

"I don't have a car, Hugo."

"Oh, good. Good. There's this British delegation coming to Monterey today and they're going to pass through Carmel. They're closing all streets in the area. You wouldn't want it to be blocked," he says.

Hugo knows everything happening in Monterey Bay.

He's like an encyclopedia. The only thing he doesn't know is how to tell a good woman from a gold digger.

I have no missed calls from David yet today, which I hope is a sign he's stopped and moved on.

The first part of the day passes so fast, I don't even realize when it's eleven o'clock, the tables empty out and the crowd calms down a bit. We're in between breakfast and lunch and it should be this quiet until one or so. A breather both Celine and I need.

It's afternoon, late afternoon, in fact, when Celine asks me if it's OK for her to leave me alone for an hour or so, because she needs to get some supplies from Monterey.

"I have a feeling that what we already have in stock won't last us through the weekend and my regular deliveries won't get here until next Tuesday."

"Go," I say. "Don't worry. I'll do my best not to mess anything up."

"You'll be fine," she says. "And I'll be back quickly."

THIRTY-SIX

I think I'm doing OK, but when more and more people come in and a long line forms, I begin to panic. When is she coming back? I get my cell out of my pocket and start typing a message to her, then change my mind. I don't want her to think I can't handle this.

"Hi," says a man who's been waiting patiently in line for a while.

"Hello," I say, looking at him and putting my phone down, almost missing the counter. His eyes are mind-blowing. And just, his face... in general. He's one of those men who capture everyone's attention because they have a certain something. Black, wavy hair, tousled, too long for my liking, but not that long that it needs to be kept in a ponytail, a clean-shaved face with a strong, almost square jawline, and I'm back to those eyes. Green—and when I say green, I mean really green, like contacts. He's wearing a white T-shirt and has a big tattoo of something I can't identify on his muscular arms. I gulp and look away. Why am I staring like I haven't seen a man before? *Get a hold of yourself, Maya.*

"I'll just be a minute. Thank you for your patience," I say as I make the last order for a group.

Even as I prepare the coffee, I keep looking to my right at him. He's looking at me too and I realize I must be so obviously staring. I try to look away.

What was it? Macchiato, I think. Maybe. OK. I take the drink to the table and come back to the green-eyed god. "Sorry about that." My cheeks are on fire. "What can I get for you?" I ask, still staring. There's something about him. The way he handles himself, a particular look in his eyes.

"I'm—" he says, but a voice interrupts him.

"Excuse me, miss," says the woman I just made the caramel macchiato for.

"Excuse me for a second," I say to him and go over to see what's going on.

"We asked for an almond milk macchiato, and I believe this is regular," says the woman.

"I apologize," I say. I'm usually good at remembering orders, not sure why I'm so flustered. "I'll make a new one and bring you our pastry of the day. On the house, of course."

"This will be just a few more minutes. I need to redo this," I say to the man. "Sorry," I add, for the tenth time in five minutes.

"It's OK," he says.

I make a new macchiato. "I'll be right back," I say as I pass him on my way to the table.

When I hear the sonar ringtone, I close my eyes and clench my jaw, and I know I'm turning red. I can't believe I forgot to switch my phone to silent.

Everyone's head snaps toward the counter. A man rolls his eyes, a woman gives me the stink eye, and the green-eyed man turns around and leaves.

I reach the counter in one move and reject the call. It was David. It figures!

* * *

Celine returns soon, and the rest of the day is thankfully uneventful.

"Any word from your brother?" I ask Celine as we're closing for the night.

She shrugs. "I called him a few times and left voicemails, but no word."

We decide to skip dinner and jump straight to wine and the pretzels Celine kept telling me about, but we're out of both, so Celine goes to the store while I jump in the shower.

It's maybe ten minutes or so later when I hear the doorbell. She must've forgotten her key. It happened the other night too, when she went to the front gate to get the pizza; that's when I found out our door locks from the inside when you close it behind you.

I wrap myself in a towel and rush to open the door.

With one hand holding the towel and the other on the doorknob, I freeze.

THIRTY-SEVEN

My mind is feverously working at three hundred miles a second, processing. Why is he here? How does he know where I live? Did he follow me? Is he some nutcase?

"Hello," he says, and I open my mouth and close it like a fish. No words come out.

"I'm Ethan," he says. "Celine's brother."

"Ethan," I say and feel my face is burning up. "You're— you're Ethan."

I can't believe it. The customer from earlier is Ethan. Oh my God!

How can this be him? He doesn't look like his author photo at all; except for the shape of his eyes and the jawline. His hair is wavy, and down to his cheeks, he has no beard, no glasses, and his arms look like he's spending all of his time in a gym, not writing books. Plus, the massive tattoo. Where's the Steve Jobs look I expected?

"Hi," I say, mortified.

"H—hi," he says, sounding embarrassed for me. Which is

precisely what I needed right now. "I didn't know you lived here," he says.

"I do. I am. Sorry, come in," I say and pull vigorously at my towel, making sure nothing is showing. Water is dripping from my hair onto the floor. Could this be more awkward?

He walks behind me and I feel so self-conscious, I wish there was a hole in the floor that would eat me up now and spit me somewhere else. Anywhere else.

"I didn't know you live here either," I say. "And we didn't know you were coming tonight," I add, as an excuse for him finding me like this. And for earlier, at the café. I don't even know anymore what I feel bad about.

"I'm sorry. I thought Celine told you we both live here. When I'm around, that is."

"She didn't," I mumble, mostly for myself.

"I managed to catch an early flight. But I forgot my keys in Florida," he says.

"Good. That's good. Not the keys, I mean. The earlier flight."

Maya, get a grip of yourself. You're all over the place. He's making an effort not to stare at me; I can see it. He's looking around the room, at the window, anywhere but at me.

"Can you excuse me for a minute? Just need to—"

You know. Get dressed. Punch myself in the face. Scream into a pillow—normal stuff.

"I'll be right back," I say.

"Take your time. Didn't mean to barge in like this."

"It's your family's house. Your house. Not mine. You didn't barge in. I'm just a guest here. I'm the one who—" I stop. "Celine should be here any moment. She went to the store."

He nods but still looks away from me.

"Be right back," I say again, sounding completely dumb.

I can't believe he's the guy from the café. Why didn't he say anything? I thought he was just a customer. He saw my almost meltdown; he saw me making the wrong order for that woman. What is he going to think of me now? That I'm incapable, that's what. That his sister made a mistake hiring me. I replay our interaction from the café in my head. He could've said who he was, but he didn't. Was he having fun at my expense? Watching me make a fool of myself? And now he's seen me almost naked. This day is complete. A complete disaster.

I try to calm down. I couldn't have known it was him, could I? What threw me off, apart from his face not matching his photo, is that he also looks nothing like Celine. She has light brown hair and amber eyes, he has black hair and green eyes. What kind of twins are they? Ugh, does it even matter? He looks what he looks like. More importantly, I embarrassed myself in front of him and as far as first impressions go, his of me must be disastrous. This is not a good start. I bet the first thing he'll do when he finds out who I am is tell Max what a hot mess Maya is. He seems like the kind of person who would do that.

* * *

I'm done getting dressed and I hear Celine's voice in the living room.

"You're here," she says, sounding so happy it almost makes me happy. "What a surprise!"

"The Delphy twins back together again," he jokes and lifts her up just as I walk into the room.

Celine laughs and when she sees me, she comes over.

"Ethan, this is Maya," she says.

"We've met," we both say. He's smiling while he says it; I look away.

"That was fast," she says, chuckling. "Great. How tired are you? Wine and Karina's famous pretzels?"

"You have them? For sure. And wine sounds good too," he says.

"Red?" she asks, looking at us both.

"I'm sure you have a lot of catching up to do. I'll let you chat and go get some sleep."

I want to remove myself, go to my room, and basically never come out. Ever.

"No way! Come on, Ethan just got here. Let's all go on the terrace and pop open the bottle," she says, looking at me.

He opens his suitcase and takes out a black T-shirt. "Do I have ten minutes?" he asks Celine. "I want to take a shower and change out of these gross clothes."

"Sure," she says. "Go to Mom and Dad's bathroom, though. We took over your room."

He smiles. "That's fine."

THIRTY-EIGHT

Alone with Celine, I'm still reeling from my first failed meeting, or meetings, with Ethan.

"Did I take Ethan's room?" I ask, wondering when the embarrassments will stop tonight.

"Yes, but he's fine."

"You don't think we should switch? I can take the other one."

"Neh. Our parents' bedroom has a bigger bed. He'll like it."

"Are you sure?"

"I'm sure."

"Why didn't you tell me he lives here too?"

"Sorry. I thought you knew," she says. "No worries. He'll be back on the road soon."

I want to remind her I won't be here long either, but I don't.

We take the food and wine outside. Ethan joins us and pours wine into three glasses.

"Here's to us. All of us," says Celine.

We all take a sip and then quietly nibble at pretzels for a while. They are good!

It's awkward, and I feel like the third wheel; besides, I'm having a hard time looking at him without imagining what's going through his mind. He, on the other hand, seems relaxed.

"How's the new book coming?" asks Celine.

"It's coming. I'm done with the first draft, going into revisions," he says.

"Are you happy with it?"

"Am I ever?" he asks and laughs. "First drafts are not meant to make you happy."

She turns to me. "My brother, the perfectionist. You know, Maya is also a writer."

"You are?" he asks.

I gulp. "Journalist. It's easier to commit to two thousand words than ninety thousand."

"I always found short fiction much harder to write," he says, and although what he says seems nice, it doesn't come off that way. It comes off as patronizing.

"It's not the same with non-fiction."

He doesn't insist.

"Maya also writes books but doesn't have an agent yet," says Celine.

I blush. Here he is, this successful author and I'm a nobody. And then I remember I don't like this guy. So why would I feel embarrassed? *He* should be. He stole my story. I shouldn't envy him; I should be pissed. On the inside. Because on the outside, I need to be all warm and friendly. I plaster a smile on my face.

"Maybe you can give Maya some pointers on how to go

about finding the right agent," says Celine. "You've been there."

He nods. "All writers go through the same process," he says. "You write, you edit, you write some more, you submit, you try again."

Still fake smiling. *Easy for you to say,* I think.

"I don't always have time for writing," I say. The lamest of excuses. Everyone who's not writing says the same thing.

"I saw a laptop on the kitchen counter. Is that yours?" he asks.

I nod.

"Why don't you take it with you to Café Azure and when you have dead times, sit down and write? Even if it's a hundred words. They add up."

He turns to Celine. "Remember that's what I did when we both worked at the café?"

"I remember," she says. "I ended up doing most of the work, while you stared at an empty screen and said you were plotting."

They both laugh.

"I'm more of a pen and paper type of girl," I say.

"I see," he says. "Even better. You can sneak that in pretty much everywhere."

That seemed like a nice, helpful thing to say, but it almost feels like he's doing it in a patronizing way. It's like he's trying too hard, instead of showing his true colors and being the difficult, uptight, and grumpy man I imagined. In reality, I bet he's one of those people who looks down on everyone, convinced he's better than all of us because he's successful and thinks he's some literary genius. Before I get my story from Alisa, which I'm sure he butchered, I should read one of his earlier books, since I paid for them, just to see how 'genius' they are.

"There's this cool store on Ocean that sells fancy note-books and pens," says Celine.

"I saw it, it's amazing but so expensive. I could never afford anything there," I say.

He stares without a word and I'm so much in my head, I can't even hide it.

I think it's a mix of envy and hate, what I feel for Ethan Delphy. I hate him because he stole my story and had no business writing about me or that day, and envy because he knows Max, he knows what Max was thinking about that day, what he felt. I imagine them talking late into the night like I did with Alisa. And I suddenly feel exposed. He doesn't yet know that I'm the woman in the book, but he's going to find out, and when he does it'll be embarrassing. He must know all about David, what he did to me; he must know about my insecurities, my feelings. I don't like this and I don't like him. Being this exposed in front of someone like him is the worst part because he strikes me as judgmental and I can only imagine the things he told Max. Maybe he advised him not to look for me. Oh, no, if I think that, I'll jump at his throat right now.

I stare at him, trying to control my emotions. The silence is awkward.

"I heard you have a book coming out soon," I say.

I wanted to say Celine told me, but if I can avoid lying, I'll do it.

"I do, yes."

That's it. That's all he says. Not offering any details. Getting information from him about Max is going to be even more challenging than I thought.

I have a feeling he doesn't like me. He smiles and he's accommodating, but there's just something about him that makes me want to retreat in my shell like a turtle.

"Are you enjoying Carmel?" he asks.

"I love it," I say. "It's my kind of town."

He smiles politely.

"Maya came here last year; she loved it so much, she returned," says Celine.

"Is that true?" he asks, his tone still flat, polite, semi-uninterested.

I force a smile.

"You keep coming back and Ethan keeps running away from it."

"That's not true," he says.

Celine rolls her eyes and starts laughing. "If you say so."

Eventually, we all go to sleep. It's late and tomorrow Celine and I have to be at Café Azure bright and early.

THIRTY-NINE

JUNE 8

I wake up feeling anxious about seeing Ethan again. I wasn't expecting him yesterday and haven't properly planned how I will ask him about Max. The way I see it, I have three options:

1. Ask him directly.
2. Trick him into telling me
3. Trick Celine into asking him, which I should've thought of before he got here

If I ask him, he can say no, and that's that; I'm stuck. If I trick him, that's all fine and dandy, but how do I even go about doing that? I have no idea. I can pretend I'm curious and what? Hope he'll just say, 'Oh, yes, it's my friend Max from two houses down the road. Let me introduce you to him.' That sounds stupid, and I'm not manipulative enough to get that out of him. Even considering how I sneaked my way into her life under false pretenses, using Celine is too low.

It sounded simple when I flew here, but now that I'm faced with two actual people...

I don't even leave my room and risk waking them up. Instead, I call Alisa.

"He's here," I whisper.

"What?" she asks so loudly, I'm afraid they'll hear from the other rooms.

"Don't yell. They're still asleep."

"Who?"

"Celine and Ethan."

"Oh, the maestro. How is he? Just like you imagined? What's the plan?"

"Easy on the interrogation. And no, he's definitely not how I imagined."

"Give me details. I'm dying here."

"Remember the photo we saw online?"

"Yes."

"Well, there's no beard, no glasses, longish black hair, and these eyes that stare you down no matter where you are—"

Alisa laughs hysterically. "Like Mona Lisa?"

I laugh too. "Yes. Like that."

"OK, what else?"

"A massive tattoo of a bird of some sort, with large wings on both his arms. And by the way, he looks like a gym buff. He's all muscle."

"Give me an actor, something to work with here. Because right now, I'm picturing that tattooed guy that keeps popping up on Instagram. The one with the beard and the tattoos."

"I told you, no beard. Actor? I don't know. Gerard Butler?"

She laughs again. "What you're basically saying is that the frog is actually a hot prince?"

"No! And he's married, for God's sake. I don't think of him in those terms."

"What terms? Gerard Butler, hello. Are you from another planet?"

As much as Alisa amuses me, it bothers me that I thought he was handsome before I knew who he was. Very handsome. I'm doing my best not to think about it.

"Let's not talk about it anymore. He's Max's married friend, and he's a thief. We don't like him, remember?"

"Sure, we don't like him. So when are you asking Mr. Butler about Max?"

"Stop calling him that. And I don't know. Soon. I just met him last night. Plus, I'm living in his house and working for his sister. When she finds out I did all this just to talk to him, I'll be without a place to live or source of income."

"Maybe. Unless you come clean. It's not like you wanted to hurt her or lie to her."

"But why did I go through all this charade only to tell her the truth after three days?"

Silence. "You're asking me? That was your crazy idea."

That's true. It was. I could've just come to the café every day. And maybe today I would've met him and there would've been no need for all the lies. Patience. When will I learn?

"I could talk to him and ask him not to tell her," I say.

"You're digging yourself a hole you won't be able to climb out of."

"Then I don't tell him the truth either and just get Max's details some other way."

"What other way? Using a psychic?" asks Alisa.

"No, funny girl, still from him, but not just straight-out asking for Max's real name."

"Complicating things again."

"I don't want to. I'm just afraid he'll say no, and then what do I do?"

"But he could say yes."

"Would you say yes? And remember that girl's email? He doesn't divulge his sources."

Alisa sighs. "You're in a pickle."

"I'm at the bottom of a massive jar of pickles," I say.

"Why don't you wait to read the book then, maybe you'll get some clues, and in the meantime, I guess, get to know Ethan? Maybe Max is still in his group of friends and one thing will lead to another, and you'll meet him."

"That'd be nice. Too wrapped up with a pretty bow, but nice. Any news on the book?"

"I should be getting it today or tomorrow. I'll ship it overnight to you. Don't do anything rash. Don't do anything you'll regret, promise?"

"Promise."

FORTY

I take a shower, get dressed and when I go into the living room, Celine is already putting on her pumps. Ethan is nowhere to be seen.

"Good morning," she whispers. "Mr. Writer is still asleep."

I smile and nod and we quietly get out of the house and head over to the café.

"You're quiet," she says when we're making the first coffee pots and about to open.

"I am?" I ask.

I'm dying to tell her. Dying. I hate lying to Celine because I've come to like her in the short time since I started working here. I remember Alisa's words and calm down. I can't just tell her what's going on. It's too risky. I have to think things through.

I wonder when I'll be seeing Ethan again. Tonight? I hope he's not so uncomfortable with me in the house that he decides to move out or something. If I don't have access to him, this will be much harder. And it's already hard.

Our morning regulars come in and I spend a few minutes talking to Gaby. Gabrielle is her actual name. In her early forties, she recently went through a trial separation that turned into a divorce. Every morning she seems to be on the verge of either crying or having a meltdown and yelling at us. Both instances happened in the last two days. After each outburst, she apologized profusely to both Celine and me, and told us she's under a lot of pressure. Her soon-to-be ex-husband is trying to take their daughter away, accusing Gaby of working too much and not being a good mother, and she might also lose the apartment. The apartment she paid for and made a home for the three of them.

"He cheated on me. He cheated on me and he still finds a way to make me feel guilty about everything," she complains when I ask how things are going. "Hit me up," she says as she props herself up on the counter and I know it's time for a triple espresso with ice and lots of sugar. "Nothing to eat today?" I ask, still trying to convince her to have something. She looks like a ghost, skinny, with dark circles under her eyes. "I'm not hungry, thanks, Maya." Gaby is a smart, educated, well-traveled woman with a good job and a lot of bad luck. Celine told me this will be her third divorce and if it wasn't for the child, she doesn't think Gaby would take it so bad. The house, the money, she'll recover. But now she has a three-year-old daughter and things are different than they used to be.

"She loves that little girl and dotes on her," said Celine to me. "Her name is Annalise and she's adorable and so well behaved. I have no doubt her husband is a leech who married her for money and now he's using the child as leverage to get as much as possible of it."

"That's so sad," I say.

Celine nods. "Gaby owns a couple of fashion stores in the Bay Area and is doing excellently. She just makes bad decisions when it comes to her love life."

"Don't we all?" I say and judging by the look on Celine's face, I know I've hit a sore spot.

"Divorces are nasty," she says. "Ethan was lucky to get out unscathed. Isabella just signed the papers, got her check and left. I, on the other hand, wasn't so lucky..."

I don't know what I'm shocked most about. That she's divorced or that he's divorced. Wikipedia said he was still married. You can't trust anything anymore.

"I'm sorry," I say. "I didn't know."

"Not something I want to remember," she says.

I don't know what happened, but it obviously still hurts.

* * *

It's maybe ten o'clock when I see Ethan coming in. I feel nervous. He's here and I can talk to him, but how? How do I do this?

He smiles from the door and waves before going behind the counter and making his own coffee. Then he heads straight for a small table by the window, takes out a laptop, and starts typing.

I look at Celine, she looks at me, and she bursts out into laughter.

"Good morning to you too. By that ruffled hair of yours, I'd say you just woke up," she says to her brother.

He groans and plasters a barely visible smile on his sleepy face.

His face changes when he smiles. It's not a full-blown smile; it's more of a shadow. Just like in the photo. It makes him look less like a manly man and more human. Pleasant, almost.

"He's not a morning person," says Celine. "I usually give him a couple of hours before I ask anything that needs an answer longer than one syllable."

Two hours later, the line isn't getting shorter, and Ethan hasn't looked up once. I know, because I watched him. He's wearing headphones and seems absorbed in whatever he's writing. Unless it's solitaire. As long as it's not another story about me, I couldn't care less.

I'm cleaning a table next to him—on purpose or not—and looking at him. He must've felt my gaze because he raises his eyes from the computer and looks straight at me.

He takes his headphones off with a sudden movement and accidentally pushes the coffee mug with his elbow to the edge of the table. He tries to stop it from falling, fails, but I manage to catch it at the last possible second. Luckily, it's empty, otherwise, this would've been messy. Our hands touch for the briefest of moments; a second, less than that, and he pulls his hand back like I threw boiling water on it. I wish I'd pulled my hand away first. Instead, I just stood there like a rag doll.

What's with the awkwardness on my part? *Just act normal,* I tell myself.

"Nice catch," he says, straight-faced.

"Thanks," I respond with a smile. "How's the writing going?"

He stares and doesn't even answer. OK. Here we go again with the staring.

"Do you want a refill?" I ask.

"No, I'm good," he says. "I have to make it myself. I have

to earn it, you see, otherwise Celine will make me pay for it or throw me out."

"Oh, yes, she's pretty scary," I say.

I hope he got the joke. Straight face. Nope, he didn't get it. Awkward.

"If she sees you talking to me, you'll get in trouble," he says. "Relationships with the staff are strictly prohibited."

My face is on fire. I feel embarrassed as if I'm doing something wrong.

"Just kidding," he says.

Alright. We have a sense of humor mismatch here, ladies and gentlemen. That'll be fun.

* * *

When we get back home, at the end of the night, Celine takes me aside.

"Can I ask you for a big favor?"

"Of course."

"Could you possibly open the café tomorrow morning?"

"Sure. All good?"

"I need to go to San Francisco for a meeting."

"Everything OK?"

"Yes. Of course. I won't be long. Just a few hours."

"No worries. I'll make sure everything runs smoothly. Take your time."

In the morning, my mother calls and I apologize a hundred times for missing our weekly Saturday call. I act in my most casual, relaxed, 'vacationing' kind of way, and don't tell her I quit my job because I know she'll worry. I also don't bring up Max and except for an 'any news?' question, she doesn't either. Instead, I focus the conversation on Carmel, and how pretty everything is here and what a good time I'm having.

"David keeps calling my cell," she says.

"Just ignore him, Mom. Don't answer."

It's funny. Now that she mentions it, I realize David didn't call or text me yesterday. Good. Maybe he got the message.

"Is that man worth all of this, Maya?"

There. She brought him up.

"He is worth it," I say firmly.

"When are you coming back?" she asks.

"Not for another week or so."

I think. Maybe. I honestly don't know anything right now.

* * *

I'm a couple of hours into my solo adventure at Café Azure, and besides the fact that Ethan just arrived, barely said two words to me and hasn't even offered to help, it's all good.

I pass by his table, juggling a tray of coffee cups, glasses of lemonade, and orange juice.

"Good morning. Can I get you anything?"

He's writing something on a piece of paper and seems startled to hear my voice. He lifts his eyes to look at me and makes a jerky move with his arms, like he's about to push his chair back or to get up. Or get further away from me. Surprised by his reaction, I jump to the side. I don't know why I do that. I'm startled by him being startled and worried I might've gotten too much in his space. I honestly don't know. It all happens so fast. What I do know is that a second later, all the glasses and cups on my tray come flying down. Broken glass everywhere, dripping coffee and sticky juice on the table. On his clothes. On his laptop.

I'm mortified. Oh my God. Two days in a row. "I'm sorry, so sorry," I keep saying.

I'm waiting for him to swear or have an aggressive reaction. Instead, he gets up with a swift move and just stands there, staring at me, not saying a word. I run to the bar and bring paper towels, to help him wipe his clothes but when I'm about to clean his sweater, he mumbles something I don't understand as he backs off. He doesn't want me touching him. I have to keep that in mind. People don't like strangers touching them, especially strangers who live in their house and who just ruined their clothes, quite possibly their laptop, and definitely their day. Not that I want to touch him.

Ethan takes his things, dripping as they are, shoves them

in his backpack and goes into the kitchen. Everyone in the coffee shop is staring at me and I wish the earth would swallow me. I see myself going deeper and deeper into the stone floor, until there's no trace of me.

That won't solve my problem. Quickly, I remake the orders I've just ruined and take them to the people who have been waiting, apologizing profusely for the delay and the mess.

"Sorry," I say again.

He's never ever going to tell me anything if I continue like this. I'm a mess.

The shop is suddenly quiet, making me feel even more humiliated.

After searching for it for five minutes in the back, I find the broom and use it to get rid of the broken glass. I'm drying the chairs with paper towels and at the same time, cleaning the table. I'm like a juggler. The table is a mess and the liquid has gone under so I'm wiping the floor too when I see a piece of paper.

It's drenched in coffee and juice. I grab it and throw it in the direction of the trash.

Finally managing to clean everything, I go back to the counter to wash the dirty dishes.

From the corner of my eye, I see the paper I tried to throw in the trash landed next to the basket, so I pick it up when I see something written on it.

I don't think anything of it as I unfold it.

It's written in pen and it's now all smudged.

Dear past me,

You're not crazy. It's not all in your mind. What's the worst that can happen? Act like a fool. Be brave. Go to her.

Stop her from leaving. Hug her, kiss her and tell her how you feel!

If you don't...

The next time she sees you, you'll be nothing but a long-lost memory to her.

The next time you see her, you'll know letting her go was the biggest mistake of your life.

Someone yanks the piece of paper out of my hand before I get a chance to finish reading.

"This is mine. Thanks," says Ethan and stuffs the piece of paper in his pocket.

I didn't even hear him coming up behind me and he's wearing a different T-shirt—I guess he had one in his backpack? He's fast and stealthy.

"It's for the book I'm working on," he says, although I didn't ask.

"I thought as much," I say. "It's sweet."

"You mean sappy."

"No. No, I think it really is very touching. At least the part I read."

He raises an eyebrow as if he's doubting what I'm saying. "Yeah, sorry about that; I don't like people reading my work."

"I'm the same way. In fact, I don't like people reading anything I write, at any point," I say and chuckle, trying to lighten the mood and make him forget what I just did.

He asks if he can help clean up. "I'm good. Thank you, and sorry again. I didn't mean—"

"It's OK," he says. "Not a big deal. It was my fault. I'm a bit of a klutz."

Without a doubt, I'm prone to disasters whenever he's around.

I should ask. I have to ask.

"Is this for a new book or the one being published later this month?"

He stares at me with a questioning look before answering.

"No, that's been done for a long time. It's a new one."

"What's it about?" I ask.

"This one?"

I gulp. This conversation is so obviously forced. "No. The one publishing this month."

"A chance encounter that goes—" He stops. "Well, unexpectedly."

He sits back at his table and starts wiping his laptop with a paper towel while I'm standing awkwardly next to him. Lingering for much longer than I should.

"I'd love to read it," I say.

He smiles. "It's a tale as old as time," he says and chuckles.

"Is it?"

"Boy meets girl. Boy falls in love with girl. Girl breaks boy's heart."

"That's sad," I say.

And not true. How is that true? My tongue is itching.

He lifts his eyes and looks at me. "Everything worth something is always a little bit sad."

"How did she break his heart?" I ask, my jaw clenched.

He doesn't answer. Instead, he looks at me with an absentminded expression on his face.

"I'm sorry for your friend," I say.

I'm annoyed. This is not the truth. *He* broke my heart. *My* heart.

"My friend?"

Ooops. Quick, quick. What do I say? BIG MOUTH!

"Celine told me you get inspiration for your stories from real life. From your friends."

A lie. Not so white. Hopefully, he doesn't mention it to Celine.

"Did she?"

Come on. Give me something. I'm already enduring this painful account of what happened, which is so far from reality. Make it not be in vain.

"So, what happened to your friend? Did he get his heart fixed? Did he find love again?"

He types something. A sign that his computer still works, despite taking a juice bath. Also a sign that I'm overstaying my welcome.

"Maybe."

What does that even mean? Tell me he doesn't have a girlfriend. Tell me he didn't fall in love with someone else. I didn't fly thousands of miles to find out he's married with kids now. Wait. Is that why I came? No. No! I came to talk to him face to face and ask why. This is not some desperate attempt at chasing a man who doesn't want me. I'm not that pathetic. Am I?

"I would love to meet him," I say.

"Why?"

"I don't know."

That's a stupid answer. I guess I didn't expect his question.

"When you know... let me know. I might introduce you to him."

I'm so shocked; I don't even try to hide it. "You would?"

"Why not?"

"What's his name?" I ask. I'm on a roll. I got this.

"Max Meridian."

Pfft. Come on. "Not in the book. In real life."

"How do you know his name is Max Meridian in the book?"

OK. Twice in a row. I should put duct tape on my mouth. What now?

I look down. "I googled you. Last night." Right.

"Aha. Did you find anything interesting?" The slight smile is back.

"I was just—"

"Yes?"

"Looking for details about your books. You know, writer's curiosity."

I feel bad about admitting I googled him. But, at the same time, this is the first bit of truth I've told him. So, in a way, it's good to have something out there that's not a complete fabrication.

"Don't believe everything you read on the internet," he says. "I think someone's waiting for you," he says and points at a man fidgeting at the counter and looking around. I nod and go behind the counter. From the corner of my eye I see Ethan putting his laptop in his backpack and leaving.

This conversation is not over. I was so close to finding out who Max is. And I will. I also need to read the book ASAP. I don't like what I hear about the story. Because it's a lie.

FORTY-TWO

It's past nine at night. We're still putting out orders every few minutes when Ethan walks in, with a sly smile on his face. He struts around like a peacock.

Celine, who's usually a ball of energy, seems exhausted, and while I am too, I'm making an effort to be the one who lifts up her spirit.

"What are you so happy about?" she asks Ethan when he comes behind the counter. She's not snappy per se, but there's a hint of crankiness in her voice.

"Just had a good afternoon, that's all," he says. "Need help?" he asks.

"What do you think?" she asks.

"It looks like you're doing great." He snickers, pushing her down on a chair next to the coffee machine in the corner. "There, sit for a moment. You look like you're about to faint."

She doesn't fight back, which confirms she is beyond tired.

Ethan snaps into action mode. "Any more food orders?" he asks, looking at his sister.

Celine shakes her head. "All done, just drinks. Tables 3, 8, 9, 12."

He starts making the drinks and I hear him mumble, "Who drinks coffee at ten at night?"

Our interaction is silent. No words are being exchanged between us. He puts each order, together with the printed receipt, on a tray, I take them to the table and again and again.

* * *

"I'm so hungry," says Celine a couple of hours later, "and we have nothing in the fridge. I should've prepared something earlier, when I still had the energy."

"I can go grab something," I offer.

"Pasticcio is open late. We can have dinner there when we're done," says Ethan.

"Are you crazy? You can't get a table at Pasticcio tonight. Let's do Taquitos on Ocean. Eliza will find us something. She owes me for the Porsche."

I give her a questioning look. "I fixed her car a few months ago for a fraction of what everyone else asked and in half the time. Of course she didn't tell her dad it was me, because he would've had the Porsche checked and double-checked to make sure I didn't break anything."

So she does fix cars; it's not just a distant dream. She just does it off the record in a way. She just can't get herself to commit to it, just like I can't with my writing. And she lacks confidence in her skills, in herself, just like me. Who would've thought?

Ethan raises an eyebrow. "Taquitos is loud and suffocating, but if you insist—"

"I do. We'd waste time with your fancy Italian place and end up eating fast food."

He shrugs.

It's past midnight when we finally close Café Azure and walk the three streets that separate us from the Mexican restaurant.

As much as I don't like to admit it, Ethan was right about the restaurant. The music is loud, and with over seventy or eighty people in one room, the constant noise of chatter and forks hitting the plates is mind-numbing.

We order, and the food takes forever to arrive. We all get margaritas, which are 99.9 percent water and lime juice, and 0.1 percent tequila and orange liqueur. I feel I would've needed the exact opposite proportions after today. It's been a long day.

There's an awkward silence, which I wasn't expecting. Celine seems too tired to be her usual self and compensate for me staring at my glass and Ethan is zoning out. I don't know why it's so hard to talk to him. It's like I feel awkward because I admitted interest in his work. And he's not saying anything either. Does he think I'm some sort of groupie?

Celine takes another sip of her margarita. "My God, we should've brought our own tequila bottle," she says and starts laughing.

"I was thinking the same," I say. "A bit more would've been nice."

Ethan looks up from his glass. "Tough day?" he asks her.

"Kind of. My meeting in San Francisco was pretty unpleasant."

I look at her and realize what a crappy person I am. That's why she was in such a bad mood, and I didn't even ask her about it.

"I'm sorry," he says. "Do you want me to talk to him?"

"I doubt it would help," she says, taking yet another sip from her drink.

"What's going on?" I ask.

"Remember I told you about my divorce?" she asks.

I nod.

"Well, my ex is suing me for alimony."

"Alimony? Do you have kids?"

She shakes her head.

"Then how can he ask for alimony?"

"Apparently, he can. I heard his lawyer is excellent at impossible claims, so—"

"I'll make some phone calls. We'll fix this," Ethan says and puts his hand on hers.

The side of Ethan that's capable of such feelings is not something I can easily imagine. However, he does write love stories for a living. Come think of it, I'm not sure that's relevant; thriller writers are not murderers in real life. The truth is, Ethan is a bit of an unknown to me.

"I might have just the thing to take your mind off it. Earlier today I was sent two tickets for a show tomorrow morning. In the city," he says to Celine. "An off-Broadway premiere."

"An obligation," she says and stares at him.

"Yes, sort of, but it might be fun."

"Appreciate the thought, but musicals are not my thing. Anyway, I have to work, Ethan."

"I can hold the fort at Café Azure," I offer. "I think you'd enjoy it. I went to a few, back in New York, and they were pretty good," I say.

"Why don't you go then, Maya? You'll probably appreciate it much more than I would. And truth be told, the thing that's keeping my mind off things is work."

"Oh, no. I didn't mean—"

Ethan looks at me. "That's a great idea and you'd be doing me a huge favor. It was a last-minute thing that I have to go to, and I don't know if I'd survive it alone."

I'd be doing him a favor. That means he will owe me. Oh my, how the tables have turned.

"It'll be painless. And I can be quiet all the way there."

I raise an eyebrow.

"Or talk all the time. Whatever you wish."

Celine starts laughing. "That's how he talks me into all sorts of things. Remember when we ran from home because you wanted to learn how to ride a horse?"

He chuckles. "And wasn't it fun?"

"It was. Until we got caught."

"I didn't know there were shows in the morning. Except for kids' stuff," I say to him.

"Me neither," he says. "It's a closed-door, early premiere for a small group. I think."

"Do I need to wear anything fancy?"

He smiled. "As long as it's not flip-flops, you're good."

"Converse it is," I say and laugh.

FORTY-THREE

When we get back to the cottage, I call Alisa, who texted me before lunch.

"Are you awake?" I ask.

"I am. The question is what are you doing up? It's what? One in the morning?"

"Just came back from dinner."

"I have a feeling Mr. Butler is part of the story. Oh, and by the way, your research skills are not what they used to be, Miss Journalist. Ethan Delphy is not married anymore."

"Old news," I say. "I found out this morning from Celine."

"Fine. Ruin my moment. Let's move on. Tell me about this dinner."

"Not much to tell. We went out to eat."

"We who?"

"The three of us. Me, Ethan and Celine."

"OK. OK. So he's not Ethan Delphy anymore. We're on a first-name basis."

"We have to be. Did you forget why I'm here?"

"Judging by the excitement in your voice, I wonder if you forgot why you're there."

"That's not funny. I'll admit he's not as bad as I thought he was, but nothing's really changed. He's still a means to an end. He's my ticket to Max," I say. I think my tone must be a bit edgy because Alisa immediately says she was just teasing me.

"I know you are. It's just that this thing is hard enough as it is. It's complicated and I'm doing a lot of lying and pretending. I don't like it, and I hope it will be over soon."

"I know."

"He asked me to go with him to an off-Broadway show in San Francisco tomorrow. I guess he needs to go, and it will look weird if he shows up alone. Either way, I'm doing it as a favor and hope he will return it. We did talk about Max today."

"You did? Why did you wait so long to tell me? What did he say?"

"He offered to introduce us."

"Wow. Problem solved then. When?"

"He didn't say; I plan on pushing him on it tomorrow. I'm very close, Alisa, I know it."

"Good for you. Going for what you want. I've always wanted to see this side of you."

Her words make me both sad and happy. I am feeling a change in myself lately, and she confirmed it. But it's sad also because I'm almost thirty; Alisa has known me since I was nineteen, and it's only now that she's seeing me as someone who fights for what she wants.

"You have to call me tomorrow and let me know how it went, OK? By the way, I got the book and already mailed it.

And guess what? She sent me two copies, so tonight I'm reading it."

After we hang up, I try to sleep, but I can't. I'm thinking about tomorrow, how the conversation will go. I keep hearing about me breaking Max's heart, making me question how much of this book is fiction. Or worse, how much of what Max told him is true.

I see Ethan's books by the window. I can't quite figure him out. The sarcasm, the occasional raised eyebrow, and the slight smile, plus a certain kind of snob-like tone he picks up from time to time annoy me. At the same time, he's friendly, funny, and down to earth. There are moments when he looks into my eyes, and I feel confused about everything he just said.

I get out of bed, grab his first book, *Need No Words*, and start reading. If his writing is in any way similar to him in real life, it'll confuse me no end. But maybe it'll help me understand why he is the way he is. Or why I am the way I am around him.

The moment I wake up, I know three things for sure.

One is that sleeping only four hours is never a good idea if you're approaching thirty.

Two is that Ethan is a gifted writer. Although some things in the novel were far-fetched, they didn't take away from the beauty of the story or from hoping the characters would find a way to get past their heartbreaks and fears and just take a chance on each other. It's hard to imagine all the twists and turns, drama, betrayal, and tragedy came from Ethan, but at the same time, it isn't. A complicated, complex book. Just like him.

And three, which is strongly related to one... I overslept, missed my alarm, and now have only fifteen minutes to get ready. Ethan said eight-thirty.

I take a quick shower, put on my black pencil skirt and a light lavender shirt, grab my shoes—not Converse, although it's tempting—and walk into the living room. The house is quiet. The door to Ethan's bedroom is open, and he's not there.

I hear something behind me and when I turn, Ethan is standing there, all dressed up. He bursts into laughter when he looks at me. Did I put my clothes backward or something? Then I realize what he's looking at. We're matching to a T like we're one of those couples who go to weddings wearing coordinated clothes: black pants—black skirt, lavender shirt—lavender shirt.

I start laughing too. I've only seen him in short pants and basic tees until now. Except for that photo in the paper, but he looked like a completely different person there anyway, so I can't even associate that image with this Ethan I know.

"Interesting choice of clothes," he says with a snicker.

"Is lavender your color?" I ask.

"I hope not," he says, smiling.

He grabs a set of car keys—they have a custom-made Mustang and a Porsche in the garage. Celine showed them to me and said she tinkered with both for years after getting the Mustang for almost nothing from its first owner and the Porsche at a car cemetery auction.

"Ready?" he asks.

Ethan gets in the shiny red Mustang. It seems brand new, although it's from 1964.

"I wanted to thank you for doing this. I know I basically forced you, but you could've said no, and I appreciate you didn't," he says.

"Say no? Do you know Celine?" I ask and we both laugh. "By the way, she did a great job with this car. I heard it was a ruin when she got it."

"She's amazing. I wish she'd focus on this more. My sister is better than most mechanics I know. It's because she's technical but also creative and she does it with passion. She likes working at the café, but cars will always be her soft spot."

"Why isn't she doing it full time then?"

He shrugs. "A sense of duty, I guess. I told her I could take over Café Azure. I could hire a cook if she's afraid I'll mess up her recipes."

I laugh.

"It's true though. I'm no Bobby Flay," he says.

"You can't be worse than me. I did notice that most customers want either drinks or super simple food. Sandwiches, salads. I think if you took the complex meals off the menu, we could definitely do it."

He turns to me for a moment, then back to the road.

"I read your book," I say out of nowhere.

"Which one?"

"*Need No Words.*"

"Good. Don't bother with the second. Not my best work."

"You should've told me that before I bought it," I say jokingly.

He snickers.

I feel like he wants to ask me what I think about it, but maybe he's too proud.

"I really liked it," I say.

"But—" he says.

"No buts. OK, fine. But that whole instalove is not something that happens in real life."

"Instalove?" he asks, sounding amused.

"You know. That slow-motion, from across the room, the street, the bus station, the whatever. No words needed, just like your title. Just head over heels, forever and—"

"Ever," he adds. "Yeah, I thought that's what you meant. So, you don't think people can fall in love just by looking into each other's eyes, is that it?"

We're waiting in line to take an exit and the traffic comes to a full stop.

I shake my head. "Not in my experience. And whatever it is they call love is just chemistry. There's no such thing as looking into someone's eyes and falling in love."

He looks at me; I look at him. If the tension between people would be like auras, I'd be blind right now. I have a weird feeling in my stomach, my chest, and my heart is thumping.

"Hmm," he says and looks back at the road when the line starts moving. "Are you sure?"

I shrug. "Anyway, I think you're a talented writer," I say.

I see a small smile in the corner of his mouth. "That's quite the compliment when it's coming from a fellow writer."

"Oh, I wouldn't call myself a writer."

"Do you not write?"

"I used to. Haven't really, in a while. Anyhow, I haven't published anything."

"Not being published doesn't make you less of a writer," he says.

I shrug. "Tell me more about your new book," I say.

"This is still professional interest?" he asks, looking over again, then back at the road.

"What else?"

He smiles. "Actually, I wanted to talk to you about that too—" He stops.

"Yes?" I say and hold my breath. Jeez, I hope he's not onto me.

"Can I ask you something first?"

"Sure," I say, all too eager.

"You said you'd like to meet Max Meridian."

I gulp and nod.

"Why?" he asks.

"Why what?"

"Why do you want to meet him?"

This would be my chance to come clean. It's on the tip of my tongue. I want to. The lies are killing me because it's not who I am. But before I get the chance to, we arrive at the Orpheum Theater. It's about twenty minutes before the show starts.

I didn't expect the theater would be this full and it takes us a few minutes to get to our seats, which are front and center.

Ethan lies back in his seat and closes his eyes.

"Are you going to fall asleep?" I ask.

"I hope so," he says and snickers.

It's about fifteen minutes in when I shuffle in my seat, and my leg accidentally touches his. He opens his eyes and looks at me. I look back and mouth, 'Sorry.'

The next time I look to my left, Ethan is paying attention to the stage.

I lean over and whisper, "The chair not comfortable enough for your nap?"

I don't know what makes me come up with these quips, but I must say, I enjoy teasing him. It's not fun playing ping-pong with a wall, but it's quite entertaining if you have a partner.

"We have over two hours back to Carmel. Thought I might as well have an opinion since judging by how into it you are, you'll talk my ears off about it," he whispers.

I wasn't planning on discussing the show on our way back. We have far more important things to talk about. Like Max. But I like that he's watching it with me; it gives me a good feeling. Not that I'm some musical aficionado; it's just the idea of sharing this with someone. And to think that a few days ago I wanted to strangle him and hated the mere idea of him.

After the intermission, he's doing something on his phone during the second act of the play and drops it. He's trying to get it back, and by accident, our hands touch. I turn and look at him and for a moment we stay like that, eyes locked, then he mouths, 'Sorry.'

That feeling I had the night I met him, and a couple— more like a couple of dozen—other times since then, I have it again. I don't know what it is or how to describe it. I don't know if it's my guilty conscience or something else but being next to Ethan is both comfortable and nerve-racking at the same time. And I'm not used to confusing feelings. For me, things are either black or white. I don't do well with grays and shades thereof.

FORTY-FIVE

When the show is over, we walk toward the exit, but we pass through a wide hallway before we can get there. It's more like a grandiose foyer with red walls, gigantic chandeliers and one of those arched marble staircases like in the movies.

"This is impressive," I say to Ethan.

He turns to me and smiles.

I look around. There are perhaps a hundred, maybe more, people squeezed in here, and nobody seems to be in a rush to leave. They're standing around, in small and large groups, chatting and drinking champagne.

I look at my watch.

"This is your crowd? The 'one o'clock champagne and theater' cool kids group?"

He laughs quietly.

Ethan nods a few times, left and right, smiles and shakes a man's hand.

"If we move fast enough, we can survive this without any major scars," he says quietly.

But it's pretty crowded and it's not like you can make a

run for it. We have to go from one side to the other of the room.

"Ethan," I hear a woman's voice behind us.

He stops short. "There might be some scars after all," he whispers in my ear, his mouth so close to my face, I instinctively pull back.

"Dinah," he says and hugs a woman in her sixties, with silver-white hair up in a fancy bun, long dangling earrings that sparkle in the chandeliers' pale lights, and a long black dress.

"I'm so glad you could make it. Cameron will be so happy you came to his premiere. He's somewhere around. You know, doing the rounds."

Ethan smiles. A different kind of smile than his usual. It reminds me of his expression in that photo at the awards ceremony, with his ex. It's stiff, pained a bit.

"Of course. I wouldn't have missed it. Thank you for inviting—" He stops. "Us."

"Oh, yes," she says, and now her attention is on me, her dark eyes drilling through me like I'm in an X-ray machine. "Who's your lovely friend?"

"This is Maya," he says.

"Maya? The famous Maya? I'm so glad to finally meet you. What an absolute pleasure. I didn't know you two—"

Ethan squeezes my arm and looks me in the eye, as if saying, 'just go with it. Play along.'

I don't know what I'm playing at, but I'll do it.

"I have to tell Cameron about this," she says. "I'll be right back. Don't move."

Ethan lets out a loud sigh when she leaves. "I'm sorry, I didn't realize. It's my fault."

"What was that all about? Did she think I was someone else?"

"Yes. No. It's a long story. I'll tell you on our way back, but for now, please, just be—"

"Maya?"

He smiles. "Yes."

"I think I can do that."

"And, whatever I say or do, just, you know, it's part of this—"

"Charade you're pulling?"

"Sort of."

He barely finishes his words when Dinah returns with a man, about her age, equally elegant. Behind them is a guy with a camera and a long lens, the ones Mason used for sporting events rather than social gatherings.

Cameron, who is two heads taller than Ethan and much more solid, lunges at Ethan and squeezes him in a bear hug.

"Ethan, son," he says, his baritone voice attracting curious glances.

I pull at Ethan's sleeve. "He's your father?"

I'm surprised—shocked—and I sound like it.

He turns to me and whispers, "He just calls me that. Another long story."

"Thank you for coming and bringing along your beautiful lady. We've heard so much about you, Maya," the man says to me and grins.

I smile. It's a fake, forced smile, but I'm doing the best that I can with the little I know.

I might've told a couple of lies, but I wonder how those compare to what Ethan has been doing with these people, whoever they are.

"Let's all take a photo," says Dinah, and without waiting

for an answer, comes over to my left, while Cameron moves over to Ethan's right.

The photographer snaps a few photos and both Ethan and I are frozen, probably with the same kind of plastic smiles on our faces.

"And one just with you two," says Cameron, sounding all excited.

Ethan and I are left alone now, while Dinah and Cameron stand in front of us, next to the photographer and stare.

"Don't be shy. It's alright. Just ignore the camera," says Cameron.

Cameron and Dinah continue to stare. The photographer isn't taking any pictures.

I turn to Ethan, trying to ask him, without words, now what? What do they want from us?

I think he understood because he takes my hand in his and pulls me to him.

I let him do it. The same feeling from earlier. This time though, I also have goose bumps all over my body. I'm fine. This is not real. It's just... whatever it is.

"Just smile," he says through his teeth.

"Can you look at each other?" asks the photographer.

We listen, and both turn and look at each other, still holding hands. I have looked into his eyes before. That very first day at the café, that first night on the terrace, and the last few days. Countless times. OK, not countless, but plenty. Now, it's different somehow.

"Beautiful," says the photographer, and I hear his voice as if it's coming from far away.

We're still looking into each other's eyes and I'm losing

track of time. Is it a second? A minute? I almost forget there are people around.

I hear, as if from another dimension, "A kiss?" but I can't be sure anyone said that or if my mind fabricated it. I can't be sure of anything right now. At this very moment, there's only one thing for certain. My lips are inches away from his lips. Or are his lips inches away from mine? Who's doing this? Him or me? His hand caresses my face. And then, just like that, our lips touch and I can't remember the last time I felt like this. It's dizzying and overpowering, and I'm out of breath.

I pull back, my legs feeling wobbly, and stare at him. He holds my gaze.

"Perfect, got it," I hear the photographer say and I'm immediately brought back to reality.

A feeling of panic comes over me. What's going on? What am I doing? Why did I kiss this man? He is Max's friend. What did I do?

I take a step back and he lets go of my hand.

"I have to go," I say and neither Cameron, Dinah nor the photographer even mind me, as I'm making my way through the crowds and outside. I need air.

At the door, Ethan is right behind me.

"What was that all about, Ethan? We shouldn't have—" I am all out of words.

"Maya, I— Look, there's something I've been meaning to tell you. I was hoping for a better moment, but I didn't foresee this. Today. I guess now's as good a time as any though."

He takes a step toward me and without thinking, I just blabber, "Ethan, I can't have those photos posted online. I don't know who those people are or what they were going to do with them. They can keep them for themselves, but they can't share them or put them on social or anywhere else. Nowhere public, OK?" I hear myself sounding hysterical. "He can't see this, no matter what. What just happened isn't even real. You know that; I know that. It meant nothing. But people seeing the photos will think it was real. This was a mistake and whatever you were trying to do with that fake Maya relationship setup, I shouldn't have gone along with it."

My phone rings and I grab it nervously.

"Not now, David," I mutter under my breath and reject his call.

Ethan looks at me, without saying a word. I don't think I've ever seen that look on someone's face before. I don't even know how to interpret it. Hurt? Shock? Anger? Annoyance?

"I get it," he says. "I'm sorry. It was a mistake. My mistake. I didn't know—"

"I'll get a taxi back or a bus or something," I say.

He stares, silent.

"If you want to fix this and you're genuinely sorry, then make sure the photos won't be posted anywhere," I say and walk off with no sense of direction. Just away from him.

FORTY-SIX

How could I have been so stupid?

David calls again. I reject his call and instead call Alisa.

"What's up? I didn't expect to hear from you so soon. Thought you wouldn't be back in Carmel until after three."

I try to stop the tears from coming, but I can't.

"Hey, hey, what's wrong? What happened?"

I can't speak.

"Maya, you're scaring me. Talk to me!"

"I did something stupid. Something idiotic."

"What?"

"I—"

"Maya, what?"

"I kissed Ethan. Or he kissed me. I don't know. And it wasn't even real. It was for some sort of publicity stunt or something. I'm not even sure. And then I left him and didn't let him take me back to Carmel and I don't know where he is and I'm taking a bus."

"Maya, slow down. I don't understand anything. You and Ethan kissed?"

"Yes."

"Wow. OK. It's OK. If that's how you both felt, it's fine. These things happen. I don't see why it's such a tragedy. I know it wasn't in the plan, but plans change."

"No! It's not that. It wasn't real. I had to pretend we were together for some snobbish woman who I think mistook me for someone else. And then they took photos and now the whole thing might be all over the internet. Who knows? Ethan is a well-known writer after all."

"I need you to take a deep breath and tell me everything."

I sit on the curb, in a back alley, and take her through everything that happened.

Alisa always knows what to do or say, but this time, when I'm done, she's silent.

"I'm so confused," she finally says.

"Me too."

"Do you have feelings for this guy, Maya?"

"What feelings? I don't have any feelings for Ethan. No, I'm lying. I do feel something. Hate. I hate him, OK? I HATE HIM," I bellow. "I can't stand him. He's the most annoying man I've ever met! You know why I'm here. Ethan is just a means to an end." I blow my nose into a paper tissue. "And now he ruined everything for me."

I hear a noise behind me, and I turn slowly. I have a bad feeling about this.

"I'll call you back," I say to Alisa.

Ethan stands there, frozen like a statue. If looks could kill, I'd be dead now.

FORTY-SEVEN

"You hate me? Good to know," he says eventually. "That's fine with me, but I brought you here so I still have to get you back to Carmel." Can this day get any worse?

"Let's go," he says, his tone curt. He starts walking toward the parking lot, and I follow. I messed up big time, and honestly, I don't know if there's any way to recover from this.

I look out the car window and don't say a word. What could I possibly say anyway?

We're halfway back when he turns his eyes to me for a moment, then back to the road.

"I'm sorry. What happened was a mistake. I understand there's someone else—"

He continues driving in silence for a few minutes.

I don't know what to say.

"Why did you do that, Ethan? Who were those people?"

"The main character in my upcoming novel is Maya June," he says. "Cameron is a senior VP at my publishing house. They've been trying to get me to reveal who Max and Maya are for months, to use it as a publicity play because my stories are inspired by real life. When they saw us together, and I introduced you as Maya, they just assumed—"

"What? What did they assume?" I gasp. "That I'm Maya from the book. Wait, but we kissed; what will they think?"

He shrugs. "Who cares?"

"I care," I bellow. "This will be all over the internet, won't it? I should go back and find the photographer. I'll pay him to not give anyone the pictures. Let's just go back."

"I already talked to Cameron," he says. "I told him I didn't want him to publish them."

"And?"

"He said he'll see what he can do but gave me no guarantees."

My mind is racing.

"Who is he? You have to tell me who I need to talk to. I need to explain."

"Who's who?"

"Max!"

"Why? Why do you want to know?"

"Because *I am* Maya from your story. Isn't that why you named her that? Because he told you my real name?"

He stares ahead.

"Ethan, you don't seem surprised. Why are you not surprised?"

I feel a chill all over my body. "Did you already know it was me?"

"How could I?" he asks, eyes on the road.

"If you knew, that makes you the worst friend in the history of mankind. I feel sorry for Max. And if you didn't, you just used a random person who happened to have the same name as your character... for what? To sell more books? You asked me to go with you today, so they'd see us together. You kissed me in front of them to give them 'material'. Are you kidding me? Who gives you the right? Isn't it enough that you wrote my story without asking if I wanted it out there? I wrote it first and my manuscript will never see the light of day because of you."

"I didn't steal anything," he says. "And who's stopping you from submitting yours?"

"What's the point? Who would want to read the same thing all over again?" I ask.

"There are always two sides to every story."

"This is not even about my manuscript. And, yes, there are two sides to every story. Two, not three. Yours wasn't one of them. It was mine and his. But that wasn't enough for you, was it? You had to up it and drag me into this mess. Lie to me. Use me."

"Isn't that what you've been doing too, Maya? Using people? Celine, me?"

Tears roll down my cheeks. "Just tell me who he is. Have the decency to at least do that."

"I don't understand why you want to know who Max is. Why you keep insisting. If you hadn't heard about my novel, you wouldn't have returned to Carmel. You obviously didn't come back for him, or you would've done it a long time ago, or better yet... never left in the first place. You've obviously moved on, if you ever even stopped. If that day even meant anything to you. Well, it meant something to him. A lot. Why do this and put him through it again?"

His nostrils are flaring, and I'm staring in shock at him. He's so angry.

"*I'm* putting him through stuff? Look in the mirror. You are the reason photos of us kissing might be all over the media soon. I'm putting him through stuff? You have the nerve."

"I know him better than you do. He's moved on from you. He wouldn't care."

I feel tears pooling in my eyes.

"What is it that you want? Why are you even here? You want royalties too? I gave you publicity. Isn't that what you were after? All you seem interested in is your writing. This should help. So why put on this 'I'm a victim' show? It's not like anyone forced you to kiss me; you did it, and you did it on camera. What did you expect?" he asks.

"I'm not even going to dignify that with an answer."

"Of course not, because you have no answer. That's what this was all about, wasn't it? Fame. There, you have it. Enjoy! Just keep him out of it. He deserves better."

"Why are you so cruel? You don't even know me. Just because you wrote the story, you don't get to pass judgments on what he or I deserve. And any reasons I have to find Max are mine and mine alone. I'm not discussing them with a middleman who's set on ruining my life."

"Ruining your life? I never meant to ruin anything," he says, his voice calmer now.

"I find that hard to believe. So you're not going to tell me his name? This is it?"

"Even if I did, I doubt he'd want to talk to you."

"It's not your decision to make."

He shakes his head. "It's not yours either."

"Fine. Ask him then. See what he says. Does he even know I'm here?"

Ethan stares at the road, a frown on his face.

"Does he?" I push. "Ask him. After everything that happened, you owe me this much."

"Do I?" His tone is mocking now. Sarcastic.

Pushing my buttons. Driving me crazy. He's the most frustrating person I've ever met.

"Stop the car," I demand.

"We're on the highway; I can't stop the car."

"I want to get out."

I'm boiling inside. Boiling.

"I'll shut up if the sound of my voice is getting you this worked up."

"I need to be by myself, and I don't want to fight anymore. I don't like fighting."

"You're very good at it. You could've fooled me."

He takes an exit for San Jose and drops me off in front of a Starbucks.

I get out without a word. Why is he not leaving? I want him to leave. But he doesn't.

FORTY-EIGHT

I go in, my head spinning. Get a Caramel Macchiato and sit on a barstool by the window, watching people pass by. Trying to calm down, avoiding looking in his direction and trying to think of what I should do next.

I thought I was so smart, playing Celine and Ethan, and it all came back to bite me in the behind. I knew I wasn't cut out for this. I'm a lousy liar and manipulator.

All good? Can you talk now?

It's a text from Alisa.

I call her.

"This is turning out to be the worst day. Ethan was behind me. He heard everything."

"That's not good. What did he say?"

"What didn't he say? By the way, among other things, I think he knew who I was."

"How could he have known?"

"You sound like him," I say bitterly. "Well, guess what? The main character's name is Maya. He used my freaking real name."

"No way! Wait."

I hear the rustling of pages.

"Wait. I'm on page 50, and there's no mention of you or that day. It's his life before. Wait." More pages rustling. "OK, I didn't read, just scanned for names. Yes. Maya June from New York. And her description is the spitting image of you."

"How did he know what I look like? I don't get it. He didn't see me."

Pages. More pages. Rustling. And 'oh', 'ah'.

"You'd better read it yourself. Let me check the tracking."

I wait. A minute. Two. "So?"

"About that. You're going to kill me. I'm so sorry. I made a mistake."

"What?"

"I accidentally sent it to the inn. I don't know why. I must've had both addresses written next to each other. Can you get it from there? It says it was delivered this morning."

"I will, no worries; now I'm scared to even read it."

"Don't be. It's just different from what we thought, I guess."

"Almost forgot the other shocking thing. He asked me to go today on purpose."

"What do you mean on purpose?"

"He used me to get publicity. He knew there would be photographers there and some senior executive from his publishing house. When they heard my name, you should've seen their faces. It's like I was Madonna or something."

"I don't get it. What are you talking about? Did they know about you?"

"Maya in the book. Maya in real life. Ethan kept the identity of Max and Maya a secret, and when they saw us together, they might've thought—"

"Thought what?"

"That Max is Ethan, I guess. Why else would 'the Maya' be with him?"

"That's ridiculous. Ethan already said Max is a friend of his," says Alisa. "Maybe they thought you're cheating on Max with his friend. That gets more publicity."

"I don't know what to tell you and I don't care. What I care about is that there are photos of us kissing and I need to talk to Max before he sees them. I doubt Ethan will tell him the truth."

"What kind of friend is he? This whole thing is making my head spin, honestly. I never imagined it would turn into this complicated affair."

"Don't use the word affair or I'll vomit."

"Sorry."

"And David keeps calling and I'm just at the end of my rope here."

"I'm sorry. If there's anything I can do to help, I'll do it. I don't like to see you like this."

"You're already doing a lot. I'd go insane without you."

"Why don't you take it easy today? Go get the book, avoid Ethan, and let's hope he at least has the decency to give you Max's contact details. He's much sneakier than I thought. I guess you were right about him after all. Your intuition was spot on."

"What good did that do if I didn't listen to it?"

"It's OK. We'll figure it out. It's not the end of this story."

I wish I could hug her. If she only knew how much her friendship means to me. How lost I'd be without her.

FORTY-NINE

I search on maps and there's no train or bus station around. I guess I'm too close to Carmel for a bus and too far to walk. As much as I don't want to spend the money, because Celine hasn't paid me yet—I get a weekly paycheck on Mondays, so I'm living on fumes right now—I still have to get back.

I request a Lift to take me to the inn and it gives me a five-minute wait.

* * *

When I look out the window, I see the car and immediately feel queasy and unsteady. It's *the* car. The car I've seen around town. It's the man I've been running into. I'm sure of it.

The walk to the car seems to take forever. When I finally reach it, my hand clutches on the door's handle and I can't move. I'm about to meet him and I'm beyond nervous. Deep breaths. Deep breaths. This is actually happening.

Ethan is still in the parking lot. He watches me get in, then drives away.

I open the car door.

"Maya?" asks the man as I sit in the back. Is he Max? Is this Max's voice?

"Aaa—how did you know?"

He smiles. "It says in the app. Though I did know a Maya once."

I feel like an idiot. Obviously, it says in the app. I open it; his name is Aaron.

"How's your day going so far?" he asks. "So glad I got this trip. I was looking for a ride to take me back to the inn."

I just listen to his voice, trying to match it with Max from my imagination.

"Are you staying with us?" he asks.

"Sorry?"

"At the inn."

"You work at the inn?" I ask, confused.

"My mother owns it. Susan. Did you meet her?"

"Susan is your mother?"

Wow. The inn is his family's? The inn where Max sent me last year to change? Odds?

He nods. "I'm sorry, did we meet before?" he asks, looking at me in the mirror.

My breath catches in my throat. I know I should be looking for words instead of staring at him, mute, but I can't. I've been so focused on this whole thing with Ethan and finding out from him who Max is, that I missed exploring this on my own. I should've looked for him earlier, ever since I saw him for the first time, instead of spending all my time with Ethan. Then that fiasco from earlier today would've never happened. I stare. *Are you him? Are you Max?*

"I did stay at the inn but moved in with... a friend in town."

"That's nice. Hope you liked The Lantern."

"I did. It's a charming inn and your mother is wonderful."

He smiles. "Are you coming over for karaoke?"

"Sorry?"

He laughs. He has a nice laugh. Not like I imagined Max's laugh, but nice.

"I thought you might be in the singing competition this afternoon."

"No, I just need to pick up a package that was accidentally delivered there."

He goes on to tell me about some of the things we're passing by and asking me what, if anything, of Carmel I've visited yet and offers to give me pointers and I have a feeling of déjà vu. The more he talks, the more I convince myself it has to be him. And I know I'm not the only one named Maya, but... does he know it's me? Does he suspect?

"I came here from New York," I say, hoping to get a reaction.

"You did? Business or pleasure?"

I gulp. "Not business, no."

He has ice-blue eyes—my mom would call them husky eyes—and bushy, sandy eyebrows. He has an attractive face and I wish I'd feel more looking at him. Like that crazy, instantaneous attraction. Should I feel something right away? Maybe not. This is not like in the movies or books. In real life, these things build up. Maybe it's one of those emotional connections that will take a while to catch up in real life, to get to the physical stuff.

"We're here," he says as he pulls in front of the inn.

We both get out of the car. I'm not leaving before asking him if he's Max.

Susan's not here, and Aaron gets behind the front desk. "You said you have a package? Let's see," he says. "Maya, Maya...."

"Maya Maas?"

"Yes. Here it is," he says and hands me a thick yellow envelope. Finally, I have it and I'll get some answers soon. But all my answers could be standing in front of me now.

"Can I ask you something?"

"Of course."

"Are there many Lift drivers in Carmel?"

"A few. Me, Candace, Mr. Harris and I think there's one more. Maybe. It'll just be me soon, because Mr. Harris is in his eighties and his sight is not so good lately and Candace is moving to Canada. But there are plenty of drivers in Monterey and surrounding towns. Why?"

I gulp. Why. Good question.

"Just wondering. I might consider doing Lift. Wanted to see if there's competition."

He laughs. "Not much, no."

"Is Lifting all you do or—"

"You're asking if this is my full-time job? No. I'm only doing it to help my mother. Taking people to and from the inn, when I can. I'm an artist. Trying to be."

My heart is beating like crazy. "You are? What kind of artist?"

"I'm a sculptor."

"Oh, wow, that's so nice."

I stare. Every piece of the puzzle coming together.

"Can I ask you one more thing?"

"Sure. Ask away."

"Do you know Ethan Delphy?"

He raises an eyebrow before nodding.

"We grew up together, sure. We've been buddies for over twenty years."

Deep breaths. Deep breaths. "And one more thing."

He smiles.

"You said you knew a Maya. Did you by any chance meet her last year?"

He lifts his eyes and stares at me as if he's debating whether to answer or no.

"Maya, you're back." I hear Susan's voice and turn.

"Susan, so nice to see you," I say.

"So glad you stopped by. Just saying hello or are you staying for the karaoke?"

"Just hello," I say smiling and as I'm saying this, I see Aaron making his way out into the hallway. "Have a great day, Maya. I hope I'll see you again soon," he says.

He didn't answer my question. Why? Is it him? It must be. Everything matches.

FIFTY

On my way to the cottage to change into work clothes, I call Alisa again.

"I know I've been driving you insane today. But guess what? I think I found him. And I didn't need Mister Fancy Pants Writer to help me. Ha. In his face!"

"You found Max? No way! Who is he? Tell me, tell me."

"He's a Lift driver."

"Obviously," she says.

"He's a sculptor."

"OK. OK. So an artist like in the book."

"He lives in Carmel."

"We weren't sure about that one, were we?"

"We are now," I say. "And he's been friends with Ethan since they were kids."

"Then yes, it has to be him. What's his name? Is he hot?"

"His name is Aaron and he's definitely good-looking. I wouldn't say I fell over backward when I saw him, but it's just that I'm so guarded now because of this Ethan thing."

"What do you mean?"

"I don't know. I had such a strong reaction when I first saw Ethan and that reaction... you know led to chaos and—"

"I see."

"And check this out. The first thing Aaron told me was that he knew a Maya once."

"He had to throw it out there, I see."

"And then when I asked him if he met her last year, he kind of dodged the question."

"It has to be him. You found him! You're awesome! Wait. But—now I'm confused."

"Why?"

"Because if it's him, he should've recognized you."

"Why would he?"

"You have to read the book. Unless Ethan made up that part, which wouldn't be surprising. He couldn't have just told the events as they happened. Not that they weren't exciting enough, but he's a fiction writer. It's what he does."

"You're not going to tell me what you're talking about, are you?"

"Honestly, I haven't read it yet either. I skimmed when I was looking for her name, your name, but I saw some things that made me believe his version of events is different than yours. The thing is, I don't want to tell you just bits and pieces that don't make sense."

"Fair. I just got your package so as soon as I can, I'll read it. Today, for sure."

* * *

I walk into Café Azure, wondering if Ethan is back already, if he's here and if he told Celine what happened. He's not inside and judging by Celine's wide smile when she sees me, she has no idea what went down between us earlier in San Francisco.

I know I'll have to tell her. I'll also have to move out. And I need to come up with a plan to talk to Aaron and get him to confirm he's Max.

"You're back," says Celine and hugs me. "Did you have fun? Tell me everything."

Where would I even start?

From the corner of my eye I see Ethan in front of the café. He's about to come in when he sees me and turns around. I don't know where he's going, but I'm glad I don't have to see him or be near him right now. I feel like punching him in the eye.

FIFTY-ONE

The rest of the day passes incredibly slowly, and I keep watching the door more often than I care to admit even to myself. It's not that I want him here, but at the same time it feels weird not having him around. Now that I've somewhat calmed down, I'm more confused than mad. I want to talk to him and tell him I'm almost one hundred percent sure Aaron is Max and get him to confirm.

I look over at Celine, who's serving a customer. It makes me sad knowing I have to move out. I'd gotten used to having her around and I like our evenings—out movie nights and dinners. But I'll have to leave once she finds out the truth. Plus, I can't continue living in the same house with Ethan. It would be beyond awkward. Where would I move to though? The inn, to be close to Aaron?

It's late afternoon now and still no sign of Ethan.

Evening.

"Where is Ethan anyway?" I ask as casually as I can.

"On his way to Lake Tahoe, if he's not there already," she says.

"I didn't know he was going to be away."

"He texted me earlier. Said he needed some air."

"When is he coming back?"

"Not sure. Last time he went to Tahoe, he stayed a week or so."

I nod dumbly, because I don't know what else to say.

She tilts her head and looks at me. "I know. I'm sad too. I was hoping he'd stick around longer this time," she says. "Especially since—"

I hear her talking, but I'm not listening anymore.

Sad? Is that what my face is showing? Sadness? Hah. I'm anything but sad. I'm pissed off he left without a word. Like a five year old. He stomped his feet, took his toys and left.

He can't just leave. He owes me. I need answers. About Aaron, about the photos.

* * *

Back at the cottage at night, I almost expect Ethan to be here, although I know he can't be.

"Hey," says Celine, "Ethan left something for you."

"What is this?" I ask, as she gives me a small package, wrapped in matte yellow paper.

"Open it. Let's see."

I rip the paper open and inside, there are two boxes. I open the first. It's a beautiful, leather-wrapped notebook. The smaller second box holds a silver pen, just like the one I saw at the fancy writing store.

There's also a card.

I wanted to give this to you on our return from San Francisco, but things didn't work out the way I planned. So...

I stare at the notebook and pen and I have no idea how to

react or feel about it. What is the point of all this? Does he think he can buy me with gifts? Wait, buy what? What am I talking about? Maybe he was trying to ease his conscience then? Knowing SF was about to happen. I don't know.

Celine just looks at me and smiles but doesn't say a word.

"Do you mind giving me his phone number? I want to text him and thank him."

"Sure," she says.

It's not true. I mean, it is, in a way. I want to thank him, because I'm not a barbarian, but I also want to ask him about Aaron. Just because he's not here, it doesn't mean my plans change.

Ethan, thank you for the gift. You shouldn't have.

I hit send and wait. I hope he answers. He does, five minutes later.

You're welcome. I hope you will write many amazing stories in it. Maybe your next novel.

I wish we could've talked about this face to face, but since you'll be away for a while, I was wondering if you have news about Max. I also wanted to see if I'm right about this: Is Max's name Aaron?

Five minutes. Ten. Twenty. I haven't heard from him yet. He didn't confirm it's Aaron but he didn't deny it either. And my thoughts go back to today. The whole thing. How Ethan left, what happened in San Francisco, our conversation. A few minutes later I text him again.

I hope you didn't leave your house because of me. If anyone should go, it's me.

Don't read too much into this. Any of it. My departure has nothing to do with you. I'm not the runaway type, even when things get complicated. Just need to take care of some stuff.

That felt like a slap on the face. *Way to go, Maya,*

assuming the world revolves around you. He basically put me in my place. Ouch!

I tell Celine I'm tired and I'll head straight to bed, then say good night and go to my room where the first thing I do is to tear open the envelope and take out the book.

The cover is amazing! Eerie almost. Two silhouettes, a man and a woman, with their backs to each other and holding their phones.

It's us. Oh, my heart!

I open the book, breeze through the chapters Alisa said were about his life before that day, our day, and get to that morning.

June After Midnight
By Ethan Delphy
CHAPTER 15

I snicker when she says what she's wearing. I thought I was the only one still into Guns N' Roses.

I don't like Lift pool. There are too many stops, and they all cram in like sardines, but it's the most popular option, it seems. It was after I dropped off the third person at Embarcadero in San Francisco, and I was getting ready for the final stop of the trip, that I started hearing that nagging sound, like a sonar. On and on and on. I just assumed it was the client's phone.

"Is that your phone?" the guy in the back asked, sounding annoyed, and that's when I realized it wasn't his. It wasn't mine either, because mine was on the dashboard. The ringing stopped. But just as he got out, it started again, so I pulled to the side of the road and following the sound, I eventually found it in between the back seat and the door.

I wasn't planning on answering and definitely not texting back. My first reaction was to file a report with Lift, but then I saw the texts and I just felt I had to say something.

I drive to the airport. When I get there, it's madness, as always, but it doesn't take me long before I see her. I park right across from her.

She's beautiful in such a natural way. And so innocent-looking. What would a girl like her be doing with a meathead like him? The guy's neck was almost as big as his head.

Just as I'm about to get out of the car, she texts me.

You know what? I don't want his phone. You can keep it. Throw it away for all I care. I have more important things to worry about now.

I get out and just stand there, looking at her.

Like what? I reply.

Like sleeping in the airport tonight and eating vending machine food. My return ticket isn't for another day. God, this is the worst birthday ever!

She puts the phone on the bench next to her and wipes her cheek with her hand. She's crying. It breaks my heart and I feel so guilty. If only I hadn't texted her back, she wouldn't even know. She'd be oblivious to what he was doing. But then again, wouldn't I want to know? If this was happening to me, wouldn't I want someone to say something?

It's your birthday?

Unfortunately, yes, and I've had some depressing ones, but this is the worst by far.

Instead of cutting short the conversation, getting in the car and driving away, I let myself be swept away in this chance encounter. It's hard not to; she's gorgeous. And now she's all alone here. And I'm in a way to blame for this, right?

You shouldn't stay at the airport on your birthday. Why

don't you just go somewhere for the day? There are so many nice places in the Bay Area.

The only thing I wanted to do here was to see the ocean and spend five minutes on a beach. Anyway, my funds are very limited so it's not like I can afford to get around or stay in a hotel. I heard everything is super expensive in California.

I can give you some money and you'll Venmo me back some other time.

I'm afraid you'd have to wait a long time. I just lost my job and without Dan, I also lost the apartment. So I'm jobless, penniless, and homeless.

That sounds like a lot. I'm sorry. I don't mind if I have to wait. I just want to help.

That's very nice of you to offer. Thanks, but no, thanks. Don't take this the wrong way, but I don't even know you.

It's true. She doesn't. A minute later, she texts back.

Maybe I shouldn't even go back. What would I go back for?

Then don't. Stay here, I text back. It's just a thing I say. I don't even know why.

The moment I hit send, I realize it makes me sound like an ass, so I text again.

Anyway, wherever you go, you can get a new job, apartment. As for the boyfriend, I'm sure a woman like you will have no problem finding one. A better one.

Judging by the way she looks, getting interest from men is the least of her concerns.

A woman like me? Thanks, I guess, but you don't know me.

What am I doing? She's right. I know nothing about this girl, and here I am, getting all friendly. Yes, she's gorgeous, but I'm not looking for anything and let's not forget the only reason she's talking to me is because I told her about her douchey boyfriend, so she's definitely not looking for anything either. And even if she were, it wouldn't be with me.

Sorry, I didn't mean to imply anything. Just trying to boost your morale.

Is that part of the Lift services?

Sometimes.

OK, well, I've kept you long enough. Thanks for your help, I appreciate it. It's nice to know there are still kind people in this world. I'll go back to the airport. Have a nice day.

I start to type, 'OK. You too', then delete it. I start the text a couple more times only to delete it. She's sad and I feel crappy about the whole thing. Just seeing her there and thinking that she'll spend all day at the airport. What an awful way to celebrate your birthday.

Nobody deserves to be stranded in an airport on their birthday. I have an idea. If you want, of course.

I watch her read my text, wanting to reply, then changing her mind. No answer.

I know a place, a hundred miles from here and it's just like you said you imagined California. Ocean, beach. If that's what you dreamed for your birthday, you should totally do it.

What's the name of the place?

Carmel by the Sea. You probably never heard of it. It's small.

I haven't. And while this is a nice idea, I just don't know. I'm not used to being by myself. I don't know anyone here. What would I do the whole day?

I can pick you up and go with you if you want.

This is beyond forward and I'm not sure what's gotten into me. I think I've been spending too much time being serious, and following a routine, and now I'm overcompensating.

I see her reading the message, but she's not texting back. I freaked her out. Great job!

No offense, but I don't know you. Sorry, I know you're trying to be nice, but...

I just offered because you said you didn't want to be alone. I think you should go... even if you're by yourself. What's the alternative? Sitting on a plastic chair for twenty-four hours?

She gets up, and paces and paces. *OK. I'll go.*

I can't believe it. She said OK. This is by far the craziest thing I've ever done.

OK. Great. You need to take a shuttle to Carmel. It's $40. Just follow the signs to the bus station and you'll see it there. By the time you get to Carmel, I'll have sent you an itinerary.

She puts the phone to her forehead then texts.

Why are you being so nice to me?

Because nobody deserves to be alone and unhappy on their birthday.

Thank you! And sorry if I seemed a bit antisocial. I'm not pretending to be, that's just how I am ha-ha. I'm a bit of a mess. Don't like being alone, but I'm not great with people either.

Don't worry, you're doing great. And, you're very welcome.

FIFTY-TWO

It is absolutely surreal to see things from Max's perspective. It's like being in his mind.

Now I know what Alisa meant when she said his version of events is different than mine. He saw me. He knows what I look like. I never imagined he made it all the way to the airport that day. I wish I knew. I wish I'd have lifted my eyes and looked on. Maybe I would've spotted him.

It makes me laugh seeing he also thought what we did was crazy. It was. The craziest thing I've ever done in my life. And it's interesting that so far, only my name is true to what happened. He changed David's name, although he kept it close.

I read on. I'm dying to know more.

June After Midnight

Chapter 20

Would she freak out if she knew I boarded the Carmel bus with her? Would she think I'm a weirdo who follows women under the pretext that he's trying to be nice and helpful? Probably. Is it too far from the truth? For one thing, I've never done this before, so there's that for an excuse.

My intention was definitely not to scare her. I just want to make sure she's alright. Just want to keep an eye on her. I do feel responsible. Typical me. I do something out of character, and then spend an eternity trying to fix it. It's only for one day though. Not even a full day. A few hours. Tomorrow she'll be on a plane to New York and that will be it. She'll get back to her life and I'll get back to mine. No harm done. But, if I do my job right, perhaps she will always remember this day. And not for being cheated on, but for having a great adventure.

I sat in the back of the bus and made sure I put Daniel's phone on silent. Who doesn't have a password on their phone in this day and age? A stupid guy. I didn't mean to go through his photos and messages, or maybe I did, I don't know. I wanted to find something more to justify my actions, I guess. There are tons of women's numbers in here, so, even if I had any doubts—which I didn't—now they're gone. He's a big douche. He's on Tinder too, wow! Why would he be on Tinder if he's in a serious relationship?

There are some text messages between what I think is a friend and Daniel. The guy says Daniel could do much better and then goes on to describe Maya physically in not so flattering terms. My immediate reaction is to feel even worse for her, then I feel rage against him when I see he's agreed with the friend. Is he blind? She is beautiful. To me, she is beautiful. I don't know what that guy is talking about. There is nothing wrong with her hair, her face or the way she dresses. I think she's quite special.

FIFTY-THREE

I stop reading, unsure what is more shocking. That Max was on the bus with me all the way to Carmel, that he thought I was beautiful, or that David was a hundred times worse than I ever imagined.

Maybe I should be freaked out finding out Max was a few rows behind me on the bus, but reading his thoughts, I realize it was coming from a good place. He wanted to make sure I was alright. He wasn't trying to be creepy. It's still a bit unsettling. He was there. Just like with the airport, I wish I'd known. If I'm honest though, I think I would've taken it the wrong way if I did know. I wouldn't have allowed him to explain and we wouldn't have gotten to know each other the way we did. I would've never felt what I ended up feeling for him.

As for David, I wish I could say that it's all a huge shock. It's not. It hurts that it was that bad for so long and I had no idea, but it's not a big surprise. Once a cheater, always a cheater, I guess. I'm just glad that's over with, but I regret now more than ever the time I lost on him; so much time on a man who never deserved me. To think he dares to still call and text me after all this, is just mind-blowing.

The truly terrible thing about what I just read is that soon, the whole world will read it too. Thankfully—or hopefully—they won't know it's my story. To them, it's just going to be fiction.

June After Midnight

Chapter 21

She gets off the bus first and I follow.

Her reaction when she sees the town is endearing. That innocence, the first thing I noticed about her, is evident and the joy is heartwarming. I'm so happy I did this.

At the café, I don't want to risk it, so I go across the street to the small eatery on the corner. Thankfully she decides to sit outside, so I can still see her from where I am.

The most interesting is when we get the bikes. I'm the last one to join the group and I almost give myself away when she doesn't brake enough on a curve and almost falls over. My first instinct is to catch her, so I rush and get to her and just as I'm catching her elbow and straighten her, the older couple catch up to me and then her and ask her. "Are you alright?" She never turns around to see if there was anyone else there and no doubt she thinks one of them helped because she excuses herself and says she's a klutz.

I sit far from her on the beach with my own bottle of soda and pastries that I bought a few minutes after she did from the bakery on Ocean Avenue.

I look at the ocean and at her and can't help but smile. We aren't sitting together, haven't even said hello, but I feel closer to her than I've felt to anyone in years.

When she texts me *If you have other things to do, you can just tell me the names of the places in advance, so I don't bother you all the time,* there's a moment of panic. It comes out of nowhere and it's a terrible feeling. I immediately respond and assure her she's not bothering me.

There are only a few hours left of this unexpected adventure we're sharing, and I'm not ready for it to be over.

But what I'm definitely not ready for is what I feel when I text her:

Are you trying to get rid of me?

My heart beats fast. Faster and faster as the seconds pass.

She says no and I let out a sigh of relief and immediately look her way as if I'm afraid she heard me, which is impossible, I know.

I reply and then sit there, my feet in the warm sand, the wind whipping my face, and I start smiling. And I can't stop smiling. I'm giddy. The kind of excitement one wouldn't expect to feel in this situation.

But I feel it and I don't try to stop it. I ride it out. I know everything is happening on borrowed time, and the clock is ticking faster and faster now, but I'll take it. I'll take every moment of this day. Because I haven't smiled like this in forever and it feels amazing.

June After Midnight

Chapter 22

We're doing the cottage tour and everything is going so well. I love seeing her reaction, the smile on her face, and how she takes photos and then texts them to me. Hansel and Gretel, the Grant Wallace House, The Woods, the Hugh Comstock Residence and Studio.

They seem so tiny, almost as if they're built for storybook characters, she texts.

Some are incredibly small. That one is less than 400 square feet, I message back.

The moment I press send, I realize how stupid that was. I have to think fast and see a woman walking a dog. Isn't she the librarian's daughter? Cora? Kara?

"How's it going? I haven't seen you in a while," I say.

She looks a bit confused for a moment, then there's a look of recognition.

I haven't seen her in years. Last I heard she moved to Los Angeles.

"How are you? I'm here for the weekend, to see my father."

"You know how it is," I say, looking over her shoulder to see what Maya's doing.

I excuse myself to text her back. *The one I just told you about. The Woods.*

She immediately texts back. *I passed it already. I'm at the heart-shaped one.*

Our House, I say.

Our House, she replies. *Funny name.*

That was close. Dangerously close. But why am I so afraid she'll see me and know I'm here? Because it's not OK what I'm doing, right? She's vulnerable and lonely and doesn't need someone following her around. She would misunderstand. She'd get back on the first bus out of here or call the police. And this amazing day would turn into a nightmare.

FIFTY-FOUR

Ha! I knew it. I KNEW IT! I felt it. In that moment, I felt his presence. Oh, if he only knew how much I wanted to meet him. If he'd only admitted he was there. By that point, I would've said yes to meeting him.

June After Midnight

Chapter 28

I stay away from the fire, at a considerable distance. No way she can see me. It's too dark out.

It's risky what I'm doing and I know it. Yet, I'm still here. I don't know if I should continue this; it's gone so well so far. She's had a blast, a birthday she will surely remember. But she's still leaving in a few hours. I'm not sure why I'm here. I just couldn't stay away, I guess. Wanted to see her again. I've been watching her all day, but from a distance. It would be amazing to sit together by the fire, to see her smile. I'm curious what her voice sounds like. I only heard it for a few seconds when we were doing the bike tour, but I was in such a state of panic that she'd discover me, I didn't truly pay attention. I'm curious what color her eyes are.

The more I think about it, my rational side is nagging me with the same question: why am I still here? Will I tell her who I am? Will I just go over there and introduce myself?

'Hey, Maya. I'm the Lift guy. I'm sorry I told you about your boyfriend because it hurt you. And now I don't even know if I'm sorry anymore, because you're here and I'm here. Do you believe in signs? Or fate? Or whatever it is? I didn't, until today. And, sorry, hope this is not freaking you out that I'm here and all. I just wanted to meet you. What am I doing here? Aaaa, I just happened to be in the neighborhood.'

Yes, not creepy at all. Perfectly normal. That's how people meet.

And here she is; walking down the path, then onto the beach, going toward the fire, and I have that strange feeling again. Like nervousness but mixed with excitement.

She smiles at people and they all seem welcoming. As they always are.

She sits by the fire, right next to Remy. He plays his guitar all over Carmel and Monterey, does weddings and parties. He's got some talent and is very good with the ladies. It only takes him ten seconds to start a conversation with Maya. She talks to him but seems to keep a distance. I can't hear what they're saying, but I hope I'm reading her right. It's not that she's not friendly, but she's not responding to his flirting.

He gets up, grabs his guitar and, looking at her intently, sits back down.

"This song is for the lovely Maya whose eyes are like the ocean."

I try not to gag. Never liked the guy.

She smiles but is obviously embarrassed.

He starts playing 'Can't Help Falling In Love'—terribly cliché but that's what he does for a living after all. She doesn't seem impressed, which is all I care about.

As he's singing, she lifts her eyes and looks at the fire.

I can't help... looking at her.

My God, she's beautiful.

What am I doing? What am I doing? I should just leave.

If she needs a place to stay for the night, I will give her the inn's address. She knows it already; it's where she changed earlier.

I should just go.

Daniel's phone vibrates. I didn't even realize she was texting, I was so in my head.

Please don't take this the wrong way... Is it strange if I say I wish you were here? I don't know you, but you are the reason for this wonderful day and although I'm not alone and I'm not even lonely—surprisingly for me—I would've loved to share all these amazing things with... with the person who made it all possible.

I stare at the text and instead of making me go to her and tell her the truth, it freezes me in place. I don't know what to do or how to answer that. 'I am here.' That's what I want to say, but I don't.

I don't know if it's seconds or minutes, but I keep looking at her and she keeps looking at the phone. Her expression changes gradually to a serious, almost sad one.

I'm sorry. I didn't mean to make you feel awkward. It's just that nobody has ever done anything this nice for me and I'm a bit woozy from all this wine and beer. Been drinking quite a lot at the bonfire. I just meant that I'm grateful, that's all. It would be totally strange if you were here. We don't even know each other. Please ignore what I said.

And I ruined it. Of course I did. It's a talent.

I continue watching her. She's sad and disappointed. I bet she's beating herself up for her text. And I know very well she hasn't been drinking anything except for hot cocoa.

It's not strange at all and I don't feel awkward. I wish I was there with you too.

I almost hit send. It's a lie, isn't it? I am lying to her.

I delete and restart. I don't want to lie to her.

Not strange or awkward. I wish I was next to you at the bonfire too.

That's not a lie. I do wish I could be next to her. I'm close, but not as close as I want to be.

I see her checking her phone a few times. Has she not read my text? The expression on her face doesn't change. I blew it, like an idiot.

The fire is getting smaller. Some people leave; others lie in the sand and fall asleep covering their faces with their hoods or small blankets. I'm not chilly or warm and I don't feel tired. I just stare at her. She's talked to a few people. A couple of men approached her, but she didn't entertain them. Remy got tired of trying and moved on to more receptive pastures.

It's getting darker as the fire is not as strong. Should I text her again and apologize? I look at the phone and that's when I see it. My text message to her. I wrote it but, in my chaos and rush, never sent it. I manically press send.

Seconds later, Maya checks her phone and smiles. The way I smile when I look at her.

I see her texting something, but I don't get any message. She puts the phone down, then she picks it up and again it looks like she's typing something. What is she trying to say? What am I hoping she will say? 'Why don't you come then? I'm still here. I would love to meet you and spend the last hours of my birthday with you.'

No message. She does the same thing a few times and I can see the angst in her eyes. She's struggling. She's not that kind of woman; I know it. I've known it ever since I saw her at the airport. I should say it. I should be a man and not a chicken and say it. Spare her the humiliation of making the first step. We both want the same thing. I think. I hope.

If you're not too tired and can make it a little longer, the sunrise on Carmel Beach is a once-in-a-lifetime sight. It's at six. I could... if it's OK with you, meet you there. There are some large rocks—you can't miss them—and right next to them, an old green bench.

I don't stop to analyze. I don't think about the consequences. About the last hours before she leaves. Just press send. I see her reading and covering her mouth with her hand. Her eyes sparkle in the last flickering lights of the fire.

I look away for a few moments, trying to calm my nerves, and when I look again, she's gone. She's not by the fire anymore. Where did she go? What did I do? I said too much. I scared her. Jesus! If this is the right thing, there will be signs. She will say yes and everything will work out.

FIFTY-FIVE

I have tears in my eyes. He felt the same way. He actually did.

It wasn't just me who fell in love that day. It was both of us...

What happened, Max? What changed your mind?

I desperately turn the pages.

June After Midnight

Chapter 29

The phone vibrates. Someone's calling and it's not her, so I don't answer. Let's not forget this is not my phone. It rings again. Then a text message.

Whoever you are, you have my phone. I want it back.

My brain stops working for a second. It's three-thirty in the morning. This was bound to happen.

Panic. And no text from Maya.

I decide to stall and play dumb. *Who is this?*

I'm Daniel Woodward. You have my phone. Who is this?

It rings again and I answer.

"You left your phone in my Lift today," I say.

"Man, I thought someone stole it. I'm coming. Where are you?"

"It's the middle of the night. Can't this wait until the morning?"

"I'll get you a beer or something. Don't Lift drivers wake up early anyway?"

"Not this one," I say.

"Come on, man. My flight back to New York is in a few hours. Just give me an address."

I groan. He can accuse me of theft if I don't give it back. I know I have to.

The phone vibrates as I'm giving him the bus stop's address; it's a message from Maya.

Sorry it took me a while to answer. I've been thinking. I don't usually do this; I want you to know that. But there's something about today that's different—I don't know what—but I'd love to spend the last few hours of my birthday watching the sunrise... with you. I'll be there at six.

The worst of timings. Absolute worst. The most perfect day, the most perfect girl and here I am, about to meet her boyfriend to give him back his phone. And this is how it ends.

I could still go and meet her, talk to her. Explain. Ask her to understand. Say that it started as a joke, but it soon turned into something I never expected. Ask her to forgive me.

I keep looking for reasons why I should and why I'd be stupid not to, but a voice is telling me this isn't right, and it doesn't make any sense. I could've done it earlier, at the fire. Or at dinner. Had so many opportunities, but something held me back. The same something that's stopping me now. All the signs are pointing me in the opposite direction. That's why Daniel called now. That's why she hesitated. Because it's not meant to be.

I walk on the beach and plan to take a left where it meets Ocean Avenue, when I see something in the sand, in the spot where Maya and I sat earlier today, ate our snacks and drank our juices. Together but separate. It makes me sad thinking I missed the opportunity to get to know her better, to spend this day with her, not just watching her and watching out for her, but looking into her eyes and hearing her voice. I wish I had been bolder. But it's too late for regrets.

At first, I think I imagine it and get closer. It *is* Maya. She fell asleep on the beach. I approach as slowly as I can, afraid I will wake her up and then stand there looking at her, wondering what it could've been had we met under different circumstances.

Maya moves a bit, and in a panic, I rush away from her and to my meeting point with Daniel—I don't want to call him her boyfriend because I'm still holding on to the hope.

He calls again; he'll be here in fifteen minutes. As I sit on the sidewalk waiting, I realize what I'm about to do. I didn't realize it was going to be this hard. The worst idea I've ever had. I delete all my texts with Maya from his phone and check twice to make sure they're gone.

Daniel shows up in a Lift. Of course!

"Here's your phone," I say and hand it to him.

"Thanks, man. This is for your trouble," he says and hands me a twenty.

I don't take it. "Thanks, it's fine."

"No, no. Take it."

"I said it's fine," I say and push his hand away.

He puts his phone to his ear and listens to something. "Damn, I hate surprises. My woman is here. Did she call when you had my phone?"

I stare. I don't want to be anywhere near this guy. He makes my stomach turn. I'm about to turn around and leave but this is irking me. "Why string her along?"

"Come on, man. You sound like my mother. You know what I always tell her?"

This should be good.

"Why choose when you can have both? Or all three?" he says and winks and I'm this close to punching him in the face.

"It's not OK," I say, trying to calm down. "You should tell her the truth."

He winks. "Why? You know what they say. What you don't know can't hurt you, right?"

"I don't know who says that."

"What's it to you anyway?"

"I just think she deserves better."

"Pffft. You don't even know her. Or me. Mind your own!"

He mutters something under his breath and gets back in the car. What an ass.

June after Midnight

Chapter 30

It's almost six o'clock and I'm going back to the beach to wait for her.

I have a bad feeling about Daniel. He'll call her for sure. What if he tells her he didn't do anything? Will she take him back? Why would she trust me? If he says he wasn't with someone else, she has no reason to doubt, except for what I told her.

What did I get myself into? I should've known better; I'm not a child. This stupid thing I did backfired and now I'm paying the price.

It's five minutes before six and I see her coming down Scenic Road and my heart is in my throat. I'm at one end of the street and she's at the other and we're both walking, not toward each other, but toward the bench.

She didn't leave. And more importantly, she didn't leave with him. She's still here and she's coming to meet me. I wished for it to happen, but I still can't believe it. I feel like pinching myself.

She's getting closer. I'll just go to her and tell her who I am. Ask her to stay. At least for one more day. Or more. Why would she go back? She said there's nothing left for her in New York.

I take a few deep breaths, trying to find the courage to do this absolutely crazy thing.

One step closer.

I will do it. I don't want to regret not being brave enough. What I've felt for her in these last twenty-four hours, I've never felt for anyone.

I stop. My heart is pounding like crazy. I feel it in my throat. I'll just go and talk to her. How hard can it be? I don't want to rehearse it. Just be natural. Me.

One more step.

I don't hear the car, and I see it at the last possible minute. It's a Lift, the same one from earlier. He's here. Daniel gets out and he doesn't seem to notice me or if he does, there's no shred of recognition in his eyes.

I was wrong. I was so wrong. They didn't break up. He came to get her.

That heart-thumping leads to my temples thumping and a slight queasiness.

He walks over to Maya and hugs her, and I know I should be looking elsewhere, I shouldn't do this to myself, but I do.

Don't kiss him. Just don't kiss him. It's crazy and it happened fast, but these are not feelings you can ignore. I can't. Push him away. Choose me.

I close my eyes for a moment and when I open them, I see

them kissing and now the queasiness is all I feel. I'm frozen in place, staring at them.

I feel so ridiculous, betrayed and walked all over like a used carpet. Was this all just a game to her? A game I joined willingly, like the fool I am. She saw an opportunity to kill time and not be alone on her birthday, and she took it. Who's to blame for believing it was more than that? Who made this day happen? Who pushed boundaries? Who wanted more? Me. It's my fault.

I can't believe I let myself be swept up in this impossible fantasy. I allowed myself to hope and dream ridiculous, unrealistic things. It was nothing but a fleeting moment to her. How ironic that of all the things I've been through, this one managed to crush me in ways I didn't even know were possible. No face, no name, no number. No importance. That's me to her.

I walk away, head down, heart in pieces and that ridiculous song from the Nineties keeps popping in my head. Shut up! Now I'll never be able to listen to it ever again without remembering this moment.

FIFTY-SIX

It's four in the morning when I read that last page of Ethan's book and I'm crying.

He saw me with David. He saw us kissing. I did break his heart and I didn't mean to.

But he didn't give me a chance to explain. If only I'd known he was there, watching us, I would've stayed. I would've never gone back with David.

I'm left with so many questions and a feeling of incredible loss.

"He saw me. He was there, all the time. At the airport, on the bus, when I did the bike ride. All day. He was there. How did I not see him? How did I not know he was there? Aren't you supposed to feel these things? How could I have been so blind?" I say when Alisa picks up.

"I know. I read it too last night. Maya, you didn't know you were supposed to be on the lookout for him. You were alone in a new town. Everyone was a stranger."

"Did you read the part about David?" I ask.

"Daniel, you mean? Ethan changed everyone's name but

yours. I wonder if Max asked him to keep yours as-is hoping you'll read the book and recognize yourself in it."

"Hah. He could've named me Princess Leia; I still would've known."

"As for David, the whole thing made me so angry. Not only that he cheated on you, but also that he was so casual about it. I loved how Max wanted to punch him. I wish he had."

"I wish Max showed up," I say with a sigh. "I wish he told me the truth. I wish—" Tears pool in my eyes. "I can't get this image out of my mind, of him standing there, wherever he was, having to watch me with David. That's the worst part. He saw us kissing. He probably saw us leaving together. He thought he meant nothing to me. I hurt him. I hurt him, Alisa," I say, desperately trying to stop the tears. "And I didn't mean to."

"I know," she says.

"He thought I chose David over him and that day meant nothing to me."

"Well, you did choose David and I'm not judging you; you picked the long-term 'secure' relationship over a day's worth of messages from a stranger—"

"That's not true. I would've stayed. If only I knew he was there somewhere. If only I knew he felt the same, I would've broken up with David then and there."

"There are no guarantees in life, Maya. You should know that."

"I didn't want any guarantees." I stop. "That's a lie, isn't it?" I ask, mostly myself.

"Yes, it is," she says. Kindly.

"If I was sure of what I felt, I should've done it anyway. Risked it. Not give up so easily."

"It doesn't matter now. What's done is done," says Alisa.

"It does matter. He must hate me. All the things he felt for me that day must've transformed into hatred. I broke his heart. Ethan was right."

"Maybe. Maybe not. You don't hate him, and you haven't hated him for the past year when you thought he stood you up. When you fall in love, you can't easily let go of that feeling."

"I hope you're right."

"Aren't I always?"

I laugh and wipe my tears. "Almost always."

"What are you going to do?"

"Get some sleep first and then try to fix what I've broken."

"It's easy. Go to Aaron, tell him what happened and see what he says. How he reacts."

"Yes, that's what I'm going to do."

"Good luck. Can't wait to hear the good news."

I wake up with a major headache, jump in the shower, but neither that nor the first coffee of the day help me feel any better.

As Celine and I walk together to the café, all I can think of is how early I can go to the inn. Would eight be too early? And what will I say? I should start with an apology. I think. Then an explanation. Imagining the scene makes me feel so nervous, my mouth goes dry.

"Celine," I say. "Would it be OK if I left for an hour or two this morning? I have something to take care of."

"Oh—" she says, and I can tell it wouldn't be OK at all for some reason. "Sure. It's just that I have my annual checkup at nine. I was about to ask you the same thing," she adds with a faint smile. "But it's fine. I'll reschedule it."

In a way, I feel relieved, as strange as that sounds. Celine is buying me some time to gather my thoughts before talking to Aaron. I've waited a year to talk to him, and now that the moment has arrived, I'm literally chickening out.

"Don't. My thing can wait."

"Are you sure?"

"Absolutely."

"Thank you. I should've told you last night. I'm sorry."

"Don't be sorry. Please!"

I barely talk to Celine before she leaves for her doctor's appointment. It's not because I hold a grudge—not at all—but I just can't get my thoughts together. Aaron, Ethan, what happened yesterday in San Francisco, the book. Everything. Everything is moving in fast circles in my mind. I made a mistake. A huge mistake and no matter how many times I've thought about it, I have no acceptable explanation and no excuse for the kiss. It shouldn't have happened. Under any circumstances. It's like something took over my brain when Ethan was staring at me with those eyes of his you feel go right through your soul. It's not as if Aaron didn't have enough reasons to resent me and to want nothing to do with me.

I can explain, or try to, what happened last year. Why I left, why I didn't wait for him at the bench like we said. Why I kissed David. But how can I explain why I kissed Ethan?

My only hope is that nobody will use those photos and they'll be forgotten and then erased from that guy's camera. Maybe Cameron will just keep them as souvenirs. I couldn't care less. As long as they don't make it public.

* * *

I'm in a foul mood, but I make a huge effort to smile at customers and not let them see through my pathetic poker face. They've done nothing wrong and don't deserve my crappy attitude. It's hard though, because I feel bad for being called out by Ethan on lying and manipulating both Celine and him. I'm judging Ethan for what he did, but I'm no better. I just don't feel like a good person right now, so that makes me want to try even harder. Smile more, make jokes, be extra friendly. I scrub the kitchen, make it sparkly clean. I give a customer a free drink. I search through a magazine to help a customer with a recommendation for a one-day tour in the Monterey area. Anything that can make me feel like I'm getting something right today. *Look, I am nice and helpful and I'm kind.* But it doesn't work. I still feel bad.

Hugo comes in, as usual, for his dark coffee and veggie sandwich. He's scanning a newspaper, while waiting for his order.

"What are you looking for, Hugo?"

"I don't know. A miracle. I've decided to quit my job and start my own public relations company and my lease is up in Monterey, so I need both a place to live and space for an office."

"Congratulations! A new start. That's great," I say.

"Only I can't afford any of these places and still have enough to start the business."

"You want me to look in the paper, maybe I'll find something?" I offer.

"It's alright, Maya. You're busy. There's nothing in there anyway. Thank you though."

"I'll keep my eyes open then," I say, putting the coffee cup and sandwich in front of him.

As he leaves, I see Brienne in line and a few people behind her, Alan.

I look from Brienne to Alan and from Alan to Brienne and the more I watch them, the more I feel like this guilt I carry around would feel less suffocating if only I could do a nice thing for someone else. Last year, when Max—Aaron—

was kind to me, I promised myself I'd pay it forward. And I broke my promise. When he broke my heart, I even stopped the one thing that I felt was my contribution to making the world a better place. I stopped writing my happily ever after stories and the world has felt gray ever since.

I grab the notebook from Ethan and the pen, and while the customer who is first in line is busy going through each and every menu item—thank God for undecided clients—I jot down, 'Alan and Brienne have known each other for a long time, but it's not until one summer day at their favorite café that their romance begins. Unexpectedly. It was a busy morning—'

"I'll have the latte," says the customer and I close the notebook.

The exhilaration of writing. The joy. It's back and I can't help smiling.

FIFTY-EIGHT

Brienne reaches the front of the line, and when she does, I wonder if I can give fate a little help. I've never taken my stories off the page, but maybe it's time. I've been so bitter this past year, letting that impact the one thing I loved the most—writing—and also changing the core of who I am. I'm a believer in love making the world go round and I will not apologize for it. I should've never let anything change that. Now that I know what went wrong, I feel like I got it all back.

It would've worked out. He did fall in love with me, just like I fell in love with him. Oh, no, I think, and I chuckle to myself. Is this the instalove Ethan and I talked about? No, it's not, and I don't want to think about Ethan. What Max... Aaron and I shared was not about staring into each other's eyes across the room. I have to remind myself it's Aaron now. It's not Max anymore. It has to be. What *Aaron* and I shared was months of getting to know each other, all in one day. It's like drinking concentrate syrup versus pouring water over it.

"Can I also have orange juice?" Brienne asks, and I realize I missed the rest of her order.

"Concentrate or with water?" I ask and she stares. "Sorry. Thinking out loud. It's freshly squeezed, of course. Don't mind me."

I scan the café for a solution—Ethan's table. There's another table, but it won't do.

I take her order and then lead the way to Ethan's table.

She stops in front of it. "Are you sure? This is usually Ethan's."

"I'm sure," I say, not before rolling my eyes. I don't see a 'reserved' sign on it.

I take care of the next customers and make sure there's no empty table when Alan orders.

"I think I'll take it to go," he says, looking around.

"Nonsense. I know how much you enjoy your breakfast here. I'll find a solution," I say as I pretend to scan the room.

"Follow me," I say when I have his order.

I stop at Ethan's table, where Brienne is with her back to us, facing the window.

"Brienne, do you mind if Alan sits with you? It's packed in here this morning," I say, sounding innocent and casual.

She seems startled at first and barely looks at Alan. He has the same reaction. These two are made for each other, I think, and I see the story playing out in my mind.

"I don't want to bother you," says Alan, his cheeks turning red.

"No—no bother," she says. "Please, sit down."

I turn around and hear Alan say, "I've seen you here almost every morning."

Brienne says something, but I can't hear. They both laugh.

"If you need anything else, just let me know," I say.

"We will," they both say and then they look at each other. And I see the smiles.

Maybe I haven't been a good person since I came here. Maybe I've made mistakes and I manipulated people and I was selfish, but right now, in this very moment, I feel better about myself. I think I did a good thing. I look at them. He's leaning forward; she's giggling. Yes, this is a good thing. And it can work. It *will* work.

* * *

As the crowd calms down a bit and I'm still watching Alan and Brienne who have been here for hours, I reach for my bag, take out the notebook for a second time and continue writing their love story. The irony of me starting to write again in Ethan's notebook is not lost on me.

Celine returns before noon, apologizing a hundred times for the delay.

"The doctor went into an emergency surgery, so I had to wait."

I smile and tell her it's perfectly fine. I'm still in the Alan and Brienne mood. I think it was a good thing that I didn't go to the inn first thing this morning. I should first find out what's going on with the photos to know what to say and how to approach this.

"Glad to see you in a good mood. I was worried a bit this morning," she says.

"Sorry," I say. "I'm good now."

"Don't apologize. I guess what I was trying to say is that if you need to talk about anything, I make a mean coffee and I'm a good listener."

"I know," I say, the smile still on my face.

I wish I could talk to her. I do have Alisa and she's been amazing, but she's not here with me. And Alisa doesn't personally know Ethan or Aaron or anyone in this small town.

"Maybe tonight, over dinner? I plan on finally cooking something decent for us."

I don't know if I'm ready to tell the truth. Ethan didn't say anything to her and I can't help but wonder why. If he wanted to get rid of me, all he had to do was tell his sister who I am. Or he could've asked me to leave. But maybe it's on purpose. This way, he's letting me stew in my own 'manipulating' juice.

* * *

I googled my name on and off all morning on my phone. I googled Ethan's name. Nothing for me and nothing new for him. If the photos were headed online, they would've been published by now. I think I'm in the clear; I think I'm OK. I should go; talk to Aaron.

One of the customers who's sitting at a table in the corner is reading the local newspaper—which I assume he brought in because we didn't have it on the shelf earlier—and raises his eyes, giving me a questioning look.

"Can I bring you something else?" I ask.

He shakes his head and goes back to reading.

As I'm scouring the place for Celine, planning to tell her I'm leaving, I see her at one of the tables outside, taking someone's order. A customer from the table next to it turns the newspaper he's holding toward her and shows her something in it.

Celine and the man exchange awkward glances. The look on her face. On his face.

My blood freezes. The customer... the customer is Aaron. This isn't happening!

My hands start to shake. It can't be. I rush to the man by the window.

"Can I have the newspaper for a second?" I ask. "Just want to see something."

"Are you looking for this?" he asks. "I thought it might be you but wasn't sure."

I try not to panic. The paper is open at the entertainment section. Half a page and a photo.

This story has a happily ever after... after all is the title and I can't read any more.

My eyes are stuck on the photo. Ethan and I. Kissing. But all I can see is Aaron's face. Celine's face. My eyes get blurry. If I don't hold on to something, anything, I'll lose my balance. I grab the man's chair and try to regain composure, but I feel I'm going to be sick.

"It is you," he says, sounding amused.

"It's not," I say. "It's not."

I see Celine coming back in, and I know I can't face her right now. I'm at the counter in two steps, grab my bag from behind it, and rush to the kitchen. I see her recipe notepad on the table and scribble, barely readable, '*I'm sorry. Maya*' before I run out.

FIFTY-NINE

All is lost. It's too late. I shouldn't have waited. I should've talked to him at six in the morning. Or yesterday when I first suspected who he was.

I'm not crying, although I feel like crying. I think I'm too much in shock and my body is numb and my brain is numb too. I can't feel anything but desperation. I have failed.

I walk through Carmel, not knowing where I'm going or what I'm going to do.

My cell rings. I have to do this once and for all. "Hello, David," I say.

"Finally! I've been trying to reach you for ten days. I'm still in denial; can't believe you left. I'm sure we can fix whatever is wrong. Just come back and let's talk it through."

"I'm not coming back, David. I thought I made that clear in my note."

"Where are you? I know you're not in Hartford. Your mother told me."

Ugh, Mom. I told her not to answer his calls.

"It doesn't matter where I am."

"Why don't you want me to know where you are?"

"What is that saying? What you don't know can't hurt you?"

"Wha—?"

"Don't call me again. Don't call my mother. We're done."

"Maya, I—"

"Goodbye, David," I say and hang up.

A few minutes later, my cell rings again. I'm about to block David's number when I see it's not him. It's a local number and although I haven't saved it on my phone, I recognize it. It's Ethan. If I answer, hell shall be released on him. My fury knows no limits now. I reject his call.

It's maybe a couple of hours since I started walking. My feet hurt, my head hurts and I still have no solutions. I don't think there's any way out of this. I call Alisa, but her phone is turned off and when I look at the time, I realize it's been way more than two hours. More like four. It's almost five o'clock, which is one in the morning in London. I have no one to talk to and I don't know what to do. I should get my things and go back home. It's done. I'm done.

Ethan calls again. I'm about to reject his call again, when I hear footsteps behind me.

I turn and it's Ethan. My jaw drops. The nerve! "What are you doing here?"

"I just came back to Carmel."

"No, what are you doing *here*?"

"Celine told me you left the café, so I came looking for you."

He sounds calm. Of course he's calm. Why wouldn't he be calm?

"Why would you look for me?"

He clenches his jaw. "She was worried about you."

"Please, go. I don't want to talk to you right now."

"Maya, look—"

"Don't *Maya, look* me. I saw the newspaper. Celine saw the newspaper. And what's worse, Aaron saw the newspaper. Are you happy now? I assume you're happy."

He smiles and I feel like punching him. Again. "Don't worry about Aaron."

"Don't worry about Aaron? Stop patronizing me. Who do you think you are?"

"All I meant is that it's not Aaron. Max is not Aaron."

"Max lives in Carmel and there are only a handful of Lift drivers here. It has to be him."

"You're wrong. Max doesn't live in Carmel anymore. He moved out last year."

"W—what? Why would I believe you? Why would I believe anything you say?"

He shrugs. "For one, because Aaron's been in love with the same woman for years."

If Aaron is not Max and Max doesn't live here, how could I possibly find him? Is there any other way that doesn't involve Ethan? There's none. None.

I take a deep breath. "OK. Let's say I do believe you; Max is not Aaron. Then who is he? Why won't you tell me? Why are you so against me talking to him?"

He stares into my eyes and although I'm furious at him and a minute ago I would've physically taken him on, I find myself calming down. And that same feeling I had the other day in San Francisco, when we were looking at each other, wraps around me like a warm blanket. What is it about this man? I've never been so conflicted, so torn in my feelings for someone. Ever. One minute I could just stare into his eyes and get lost in them like a teenager, the next I'm attacking him. I have all the reasons in the world to hate him right now. He stands between me and the man I fell in love with a year ago. He stands in the way of my happiness.

"I will tell you who he is if you tell me why you came back to Carmel. You said I was wrong thinking it was to advance your writing career. Prove me wrong. Tell me why you came back. But I want the truth."

"I don't have to tell you anything, Ethan. Why are you getting in between us? We're not kids who need a chaperone. He's a grown man who can take care of himself."

"I already said. Because I don't want him to get hurt again. He's been hurt enough."

"Has he? By me? I read your novel and that's not what happened."

"I'm not even going to ask what strings you pulled to get an advanced copy."

"I wouldn't tell you anyway."

"So what is the lie in my story?"

"Everything about how it ended."

SIXTY

"Really? Let's see then. Did you and your boyfriend hug?" Ethan asks.

"Yes, but—"

"Did you and your boyfriend kiss?"

I stare.

"Did you go to meet Max like you said?"

"I was on my way."

"You were on your way. I see. And a hurricane came and took you away and back to New York. I read this story, the Kansas version. I expect more from a writer. Anything else?"

"You're twisting it all."

"How? It's what happened. He followed you around all day, watched out for you, fell for you, and when he got the courage to ask you to meet him, you chose your boyfriend."

"There's an explanation for that."

"Keep it for someone who cares," he says snappily.

"I thought he changed his mind. He wasn't where we agreed we'd meet."

"Was he supposed to show up, shake your boyfriend's

hand and then walk with you... into the sunrise? Of course he wasn't there. He'd just watched you two kissing."

"This is not fair."

"No, it's not. When is love fair, Maya?"

My eyes are brimming with tears.

"You didn't care enough to take a chance on him and now you're back. So let me ask again. Why?"

"To explain."

He makes a noise like a buzzer. "Wrong answer! You already tried to explain to me and look how that went."

"He's not going to have the same reaction. Max is not like you. He'll understand."

"You're wrong," he snaps back.

"I'm not wrong. I know him better than I know most people in my life."

Ethan starts laughing. "You never even saw him that day. You don't know his name. What makes you think you know anything about him?"

"Because I do. Because—you don't have to see someone to fall in love with them."

"Love? We're talking about love now? If you loved him, you wouldn't have left like you did. That's not love. You were not here after that. I had to pick up the pieces."

"I did love him. I still do, a year later. I never forgot him or our day together."

I wipe a tear with the back of my hand. Ethan is so cruel.

"Does your boyfriend know you love another man then?"

"What boyfriend?"

"The one who keeps calling you. The same one you left Carmel with last year."

My nostrils are flaring. His words spin around in my head.

"How do you know it's the same guy who's calling me now?"

He stares for a moment. "Because I saw his name on your phone. I'm not dumb."

"Not that you'd care, but my 'boyfriend' and I are over."

"Weren't you over before and then you weren't?" he says coldly. "I expect this David fella will show up here, promise you the moon and the stars or whatever he does to change your mind, and you'll be back on the boyfriend express; direction: New York."

"You're wrong," I say.

He shrugs. "Sure. If you say so."

I take a deep breath. "You're not going to tell me his name, are you?"

"I'm still waiting for the answer to my question. If I tell you or not, it's up to you."

"I don't know what you want me to say."

"The truth."

"I already told you the truth. I want to explain."

Ethan puts his hands in his jeans' pockets. "If all you want to do is explain why you left, you're wasting your time. And mine. How will that help? You broke his heart once and I think you'll do it again. Nothing has changed. The only difference is that a year has passed."

"You're only saying this because you don't know me," I say, feeling hurt.

He sighs. There is hurt in his eyes and sadness. Alisa is just as protective over me, like he is with Max. This side of Ethan, just like his strong feelings for Celine, erases some of his negatives. He's not a bad man. He's a caring friend, a protective brother, a talented writer, has a quirky sense of humor and he cleans up nicely. And he's an excellent kisser. I can't believe I thought about that now, of all times. What's wrong with me? Something's definitely wrong.

"Maybe you're right, although I doubt it. I think I know you."

"How could you possibly know me? You haven't even tried to get to know the real me. You never gave me a chance. You think you have me all figured out, but you don't." I'm all out of ideas. "How about this? A pact. A temporary truce of some sort."

"I thought you hated me. Why would you want to make a pact with me?" he asks.

"That's how much that day means to me. I'm willing to do whatever it takes and because I think that once you get to know me, the real me, you'll feel better about my relationship with him. So, whether I hate you or not is irrelevant—"

"So you do hate me," he says with a straight face.

"Yes!" I say. "Are you happy now?"

"Ecstatic. So, what's the pact?"

I open my mouth to say the words, but I can't. The magnitude of what I'm about to do hits me. Can I go through with this? Nothing terrifies me more than sharing my work with someone. Sharing my work with a bestselling author is excruciating. But I have to do it so I can find Max. I don't know what else would convince Ethan of what's in my heart.

"I'll let you read—" I stop. I'm about to hyperventilate.

"Yes?" he asks and I'm already feeling a tinge of mockery in his tone.

Deep breaths, Maya. You can do this. "My manuscript. You said you don't know what my intentions are, and you don't believe I'm telling the truth about that day and what I felt. Read it and you'll know the truth."

No muscles move on his face. "I hear an ask is coming," he says.

"After you finish reading and you get to know the real me, you'll tell me his name."

"That's if I believe you."

"I'm convinced you will."

"And if I don't?"

"I'll be out of your life and never bother you or your friend again."

I stretch out my hand. "Deal?"

He hesitates. Then he shakes my hand. "Deal."

SIXTY-ONE

"What now?" he asks. "What does this temporary truce entail? Are we going to be civil while I read your book, or what's the plan?"

"Civil would be nice," I say. "A truce is a truce."

He smirks. "The Maya in my book is far less feisty. And stubborn," he says.

"The Maya in your book is a fictional character. As much as you based her on me, she's not me. I'm me. And there are a lot more unpleasant surprises where that came from."

"That sounded like a threat."

"Just the truth. The real me... this is it. And yes, stubbornness is part of the package."

"Can you stand walking with me? Not sure on what hate level we're at," he says.

I scoff. "Are you always this dramatic?"

"No. Only with you."

"Lucky me!"

* * *

We walk side by side on Scenic Road and after a while, when we take a break from picking on each other, and start talking like normal people, it's actually quite enjoyable.

I can't help but feel like for the first time since I came back here, I'm where I'm meant to be. In my quest to find Max, in my inner quest to find myself. My relationship with Ethan has gone in a week through more ups and downs than I've ever experienced in any relationship, even the ones that lasted years. I've hated him, I've liked him, I've admired him, envied him, despised him, I've felt confused by him, I was amused by him, I was for a brief moment—or two—swept off my feet by him. And now, we're suddenly friendly, walking together and exchanging small jokes about the guy wearing tight sweats and the tourist snapping selfies in front of trees.

"What about Celine?" I ask as we're getting close to Café Azure.

"I told her the truth," he says. "Just now, before I came looking for you."

"The truth?"

"That it was a publicity thing for Cameron. I suggest we leave it at that."

"How did she react?"

"She was worried about you and how you took it. I said you agreed to it, to help me."

"Don't you feel bad about lying to her?"

"I don't want to mix her up in this. She has enough on her mind. If she thinks we're friends and this was a friendly favor, she'll sleep better at night."

I nod. "What about Max? Are you sure he didn't see the paper and he doesn't know about this?"

He smiles. "Don't worry."

"Again with the 'don't worry'."

"Yes, don't worry," he repeats.

"Is he on an island in the middle of the Pacific? Or in a non-English-speaking country?"

"Nice try. But you won't get me to tell you anything. You're not the first one to try. I'm a master at dodging Max-related questions."

I groan.

"You know, there are a few things in my book that didn't make it into the final draft. Things you should know... before meeting—"

"Max?"

He nods. "Maybe I'll show them to you; these missing pages. Someday. After I read yours and if—"

"If you believe me. I know," I interrupt.

"I wanted to say if I get to know the true you. And the true you is not someone who's going to hurt him again."

I smile. "Someone much wiser than me told me there are no guarantees in life."

He nods absentmindedly. "So, is the real you the one who was yelling at me earlier or this one, right now?" he asks.

I shrug. "Both."

"And the one who rolled her eyes during the musical?" he asks.

"You saw that?"

"Yeah. Not a fan?"

"Meh. It was OK," I say.

"I won't tell Cameron that. That show is his baby."

"Let's not talk about Cameron anymore."

"OK."

"And I'm also the one who spilled coffee on you," I say a minute later.

"Oh, yeah." He laughs.

"I also snort when I laugh really hard and I cry at romantic movies. I'm picky about what I eat, and I drink too much coffee. I have too many books on my to-be-read list, but I keep buying more and more."

"That sounds familiar," he says.

"Which part?"

"All of it. Except for the snorting."

I smile. We both do.

Back at Café Azure, Celine asks me if I'm OK and I assure her I'm fine. 'Great.' While I don't exactly feel great, I'm not sad or mad or upset either, quite unexpectedly.

The rest of the evening, Ethan and I interact a few times; mostly accidental looks or polite smiles. When we're next to each other, we don't talk much.

At night, we all walk home together and talk about what we'll do for dinner.

"How about I keep my promise and cook something for us?" asks Celine. "And you guys are in charge of the movie."

"Sure," says Ethan. "Maya?"

I nod. "If you choose what we're going to watch," I say.

"Are you sure?" he asks jokingly. "I have pretty eclectic tastes."

"I'll risk it."

Celine laughs. "You asked for it."

We quickly decide on the 'quickest spaghetti dish Celine can make'—all of us famished, none of us very fancy when it comes to food, it seems. Half an hour or so later, we're sitting at the kitchen table, enjoying the most delicious chicken parmesan I've ever tasted.

Right before we start watching the movie, the landline rings and Celine asks me to pick up. It's their mother. I know she calls them every couple of days, but it's the first time I've spoken to her. She sounds like a lovely woman and we hit it off straight away.

"I don't want to interrupt if you're getting ready for a movie," she says kindly. "Just let Celine and Ethan know we're leaving for Kauai, so if they call, they should use my cell number."

"Are you sure you don't want to talk to them?" I ask.

"No, darling," she says. "It sounds like you're all having fun. That's nice," she says as Celine and Ethan laugh in the background.

When I tell them about Hawaii, they're not surprised. "They go there for a month, every year. Our godparents live in Kauai. They've been asking us to go for a long time—it's just that we're both so busy, it never happens."

"You guys should definitely do it. I wish I had someone asking me to go. I'd drop everything and hop on a plane. I've never been to Hawaii, but it's definitely on my list."

"We should," says Celine, half-joking, half-serious. "And take you with us."

"I doubt Maya would go," says Ethan.

"Don't I seem like the adventurous, impulsive type?" I ask teasingly.

Ethan, who's sitting at the end of the couch—Celine between us—leans forward. "If I asked you to drop everything and go, would you go? Right now?"

I hesitate. "Not right now," I say and laugh it out because I know he's joking.

"Tomorrow then?" he asks.

"I can't tomorrow. I have to work and—"

He interrupts. "See? Case closed. Let's watch the movie."

Monty Python's And Now For Something Completely Different. That's what we watch.

We all laugh until we can't breathe anymore and when we eventually go to sleep, my stomach and jaws hurt. Poor Celine, stuck between us on the couch, had to listen to the same bits on repeat because apparently both Ethan and I know the movie by heart.

It was a good night. An excellent night.

SIXTY-TWO

JUNE 12

I couldn't sleep. The thought of Ethan reading my manuscript terrified me and even more so, the idea that he'd read an unfinished novel. After hours of tossing and turning, I got up, opened the envelope with my manuscript and started writing that ending I haven't been able to even get close to until now. Longhand, on white paper, without stopping for a second, without overthinking it. Ten thousand words about how we end up finding each other after I return to Carmel. How magical it all is and how love wins. This feels like the perfect ending to this story. Our story. Ten thousand words led me to the final two. The ones I never thought I'd write. 'The End'. And now my untitled manuscript also has a title. *Our Perfect Day*. It's personal, raw and I adore everything about it. It should be easier now to show it to him. Should be.

* * *

"I'll be right there," I say to Celine who's waiting in front of the cottage.

THE MEETING POINT   281

I get the envelope with my manuscript, put it on the kitchen counter and leave a short message for Ethan.

It still needs editing and it's not perfect, so don't focus on that. Just the story.

I hesitate again before leaving the house, but I know I have to do it. That was the deal and it's the only way I can make him understand my intentions and feelings.

Celine is waiting for me by the gate, smiling as usual.

"I had the cutest dream last night," she says. "And you were in it."

"I was? Tell me."

I rarely recollect my dreams, if I even dream at all.

"I was sitting on a bench on the side of a big green field covered in daffodils. Tens, hundreds of them. You were standing among them, plucking them out of the ground and making a bouquet. I tried to tell you they'll all blow away at the first gust of wind, but you were too excited, so I didn't want to make you sad."

"And then?" I ask.

"And then the wind started blowing, and with it your daffodils went up in the air. And you were jumping to catch them and get them back. It was almost like you were flying."

"That's nice," I say. "And?"

She smiles at me. "That's it."

I laugh. "Still nice."

"Yes," she says and scoffs lightly. "My mother called to let me know they arrived in Kauai. I guess she forgot again about the time difference."

I do the same to poor Alisa all the time.

We get to the café and follow our usual morning routine when a man checks the door and rattles the knob. He looks like he needs coffee and fast! We're still closed, but Celine opens the door, and lets him in.

We have a little bit of time before customers trickle in. Still, I like to be prepared, so I start arranging the chairs, checking the tablecloths, the napkin holders, the menus.

After she serves the customer, Celine comes over to help.

The breakfast crowd starts coming in and Celine and I split responsibilities, going through the line like a well-oiled machine. Before long, all the tables are full, both inside and in front. I'm not surprised. It's a beautiful day, the sun is up, and Carmel is living its best life. I feel lucky today to be part of it. Not sure why, I just have a smile on my face.

And then I look over at Celine. When she doesn't realize anyone is looking at her, the corners of her mouth face downward. There's a sad, almost melancholic look in her eyes.

She notices I'm struggling to arrange today's papers—I checked and I'm not in any of them, thankfully—on the shelf and gives me a hand. She would do anything to keep everyone happy. Me, the customers, Ethan, her parents, even random people on the street. Celine is one of those rare people who are genuinely and profoundly good. I wonder what went wrong in her marriage; for some reason I don't think it was her fault. She probably tried her best, but there's only so much you can do. She's precisely the type of person you imagine will have a happily ever after, a perfect family, a beautiful life filled with love. And she should. She should have all that. She says she's OK being single, that she's had enough of men to last her two lifetimes, but that sadness in her eyes is saying something else. I think she'd want someone by her side, but she's too afraid to risk her heart again. And I can't say that I blame her.

I would love to write a story for her. Even more than that,

I wish my stories were magical and words on paper would come true. I look around the café. This is the most significant part of her world. Maybe someone here then. I don't see anyone worthy, though, but I'll keep looking. She definitely has to have her own story.

"Putting the second batch of croissants in the oven. Keep an eye on the front of the house for me, please?" she says.

"Yes, boss," I say and salute jokingly.

Since no new customers have come in for ten minutes, I grab my bag and pull out the notebook and the pen Ethan gifted me and start her story. I might not have a 'him' in mind for Celine just yet, but I have to start somewhere.

It's funny. I haven't found inspiration in anything in the last year—if we exclude my one day with Max—but now it's like I got my mojo back. I feel like writing nonstop. I'm inspired by this place, the people, my experiences.

A couple of pages in, I hear the bell and I'm ready to close the notebook and serve a customer. I do a double take. And that feeling in my stomach, and my chest is back.

"Good morning," I say, smiling and unable to stop myself from sounding peppy.

"You're writing," Ethan says, returning the smile.

I awkwardly point at the notebook and pen. "T—thank you again."

"You're welcome; glad they're useful. Thanks for the manuscript," he says and winks.

"Bored with it already?" I ask. I'm afraid my insecurities come through. It sounds like I'm fishing for compliments, but I'm not. I need reassurance, especially from someone like him.

"Not at all. I started it and I think it's fabulous."

I nod and smile.

"And I was planning to read more this morning, but—" he stops "—I changed my mind."

"Why?"

He doesn't respond, instead stares at me. I don't know what it is about looking into Ethan's eyes that makes me feel this tension between us. I swallow nervously.

"You said you want me to get to know the true you. Since I'm a slow reader, I thought we should try and speed up the 'getting to know you' process," he says with a smile.

"Where should I start? A list of all my likes and dislikes? I could give you a résumé too," I say and chuckle.

"Why not?" He laughs. "But no, I have something else in mind. If you're up for it."

I purse my lips. "It depends. Is it dangerous?"

He shakes his head.

"Embarrassing?"

He shrugs, then laughs. "No and no more questions. You'll spoil it. In or out?"

I don't like not knowing what comes next, but this time I'm tempted. "In."

"Good," he says and the mischievous smile on his face makes me question my decision. "What time can you leave? It has to be at or before four."

"Four then," I say caught in the moment. Then I reflect on it. "Wait, I have to talk to Celine first. See if it's OK with her."

He nods and continues to stand in front of the counter as if he can't decide what to do.

"Can I bring you anything? Are you staying or—" I ask.

"Yes, I'm staying. Why don't you go back to writing? I've kept you long enough and I'm sure the next wave of customers is coming soon. I can make my own coffee. Do you want one?"

I want to say no, but change my mind. "Celine said you have a secret recipe that involves chili and dark chocolate."

He's all smug. "Maybe," he says and goes to the espresso machine.

A few minutes later, he brings me the coffee and a hazelnut croissant on a small plate.

"Thought you might want to eat something too," he says.

"Thank you. It's my favorite," I say in a low voice.

"Sit. Eat," he says and walks toward the window table.

I want to stop him and ask if he wants to sit with me, but I don't. Because I'm not used to it. This pact of ours. This temporary peace or whatever it is. I'm not sure exactly how I should act around him. I'm mostly playing it by ear, but it's not as simple as it might seem.

SIXTY-THREE

"Where are we going?" I ask as we leave Café Azure at four. Celine basically had to force us out, after I told her about some afternoon plans, but then kept finding things to do.

I'm a bit nervous; not sure why. As much as I'm trying not to think about it, the last time we went somewhere alone, it didn't go as planned at all.

"Not telling you," he says.

He looks at me, as if he's sizing me up. "Good, you're dressed properly," he says.

I'm in jeans, a regular, boring white T-shirt—which miraculously doesn't have coffee stains—and blue Converse. At least I know it can't be anything fancy. Good!

"I thought for the first outing we'd start somewhere close. Just in case you want to leave again," he says, a hint of bitterness in his voice. "It's only twenty-five miles from here."

"If it doesn't involve me being on the front page of a newspaper, you're safe," I say.

"Touché," he says.

The convertible Mustang is parked in front. I didn't even see it.

"Jump in," he says.

Alisa texts and I realize I forgot to call her last night. I promise myself I'll call her tonight. She doesn't know anything about what happened. She doesn't know Aaron is not Max and she definitely doesn't suspect where I am now.

We head east on Ocean Avenue toward San Carlos Street and then California 1 South.

At first, all I see is the highway, but all that changes quickly. On the right side, I see the ocean below and a sprawling beach with beautiful, perfectly white sand. I let out an excited squeak.

"I thought you might like it," he says.

"How?" I want to ask how he knew about my fascination with beaches—aka obsession.

"You only mentioned the Pacific and the 'dreamy beaches' five times in the first five pages of your manuscript," he says, turning to me before focusing back on the road.

And what an amazing road. It follows the ocean, and the views are breathtaking.

"You work every day at the café, so I assume you haven't done much sightseeing."

Now that he mentions it, I realize he's right. I haven't. How many times I dreamed of being back on the beach, my toes in the warm sand, feeling that incredible sense of freedom? Reliving that day from a year ago? Why didn't I go back? Why did I only limit myself to the café and back to the cottage? I don't know. I don't have an answer to that question, just like I don't have an answer to many questions lately. Mostly when it comes to my behavior and my feelings. Is it too late to discover yourself when you're almost thirty? Is it normal to be this confused about what you want and who you are? I hope I'm not the only one.

The sun is on my face, the wind in my hair, making a mess of it, but I don't care.

Ethan is singing along with the radio, 'You make me a believer'. I turn the volume up and then we look at each other and we belt out at the same time, 'believeeeeeer,' and laugh.

I close my eyes and take it all in—every single second of it. And when I open them, the reality is even better. Who would've thought?

If it wasn't for the occasional cars from the opposite direction, I'd swear we're the only people on this coastline; it feels cut off from civilization but in a good way. The landscape is wild. The deep blue ocean is truly magnificent seen from up here, and the narrow winding road bordered by the mountains on one side and the ocean on the other is spectacular. I don't know if I've ever seen something so awe-inspiring.

When we get to an uncovered bridge above the ocean, Ethan slows the car.

"What's this called?" I ask. It's amazing.

"Bixby Canyon."

I stare with my mouth open. I think I must've seen it on a postcard, but a postcard can't do it justice. I've taken a hundred photos at least by the time we got here, and now I'm snapping shots of the bridge from all angles as Ethan's car picks up speed again.

"You know, you don't have to use up all your battery. We can always—" He stops. "You can always come back. It's not far."

"There's no day like today. Who knows where life will take me?"

"Wherever you want it to take you," he says. "You're not a feather in the wind."

It's funny he would say that. I've felt like a feather in the wind most of my life. Almost like a character in a story. Just not one I'd write because obviously, I would've only given myself great experiences. The only two times I broke out and changed the pre-written storyline was one day last year and two weeks ago when I packed my bags, quit my job, and returned here. I might not be doing an excellent job at writing this story of mine, but you know what? With all the ups and downs, and everything I've gone through since I arrived in Carmel, I feel more in charge of my destiny than I've ever felt. I'm taking the reins, albeit awkwardly, but I am. Truth be told, I've never wanted anything that strongly or passionately to fight for it. Coming back to Carmel is the first time. And now that I'm here, I feel this is where I belong. It's strange.

"I guess we'll see what happens," I say.

"Whatever happens, the decision should be yours. Stay, if you want to stay and go if you want to go. But don't stay and definitely don't go because of someone else," he says, and I suspect we're both thinking about the same thing. What happens if Max got over his feelings for me? Old me wouldn't hesitate to pack and go back to the East Coast if that's the case. The new me, I hope will at least hesitate. Which would be huge progress.

I smile, but don't say anything. It would be too much to explain, and I don't want to overthink now. I just want to enjoy myself and the views, the music, the weather, this afternoon. Everything is too perfect for me to spoil it with my overanalyzing!

"We're almost there," he says.

"I thought the drive was the whole thing," I say. "It's incredible, by the way!"

"It is the whole thing," he says. "We just have a couple of stops along the way."

I don't ask for details; he won't tell me anyway. I'm just excited to see what's next.

A few minutes later we stop on the side of the road, Ethan gets out and I follow. "Here it is," he says, leading the way to where the pavement ends on the right side.

"Look," he says, pointing down.

My jaw drops. Below us is an idyllic cove with turquoise waters and perfectly white sand and the tiniest of waterfalls, as thin as a thread.

"Wow! This is beautiful."

He looks at me for a moment, as if wanting to say something, then turns to the waterfall.

"Yes, yes, it is," he finally says.

I feel a fluttering in my stomach, and I have the strangest of sensations for a moment.

Ethan brings a blanket from the car, puts it on the ground and we sit, nobody around, watching the waves crashing on the shore and that dreamlike waterfall. So peaceful.

"Alright," he says after a while. "We should get going or else we're going to be late."

"Let's go," I say, not without feeling a small regret we have to leave this place.

He turns the car around and I feel disappointed. I thought we had one more stop. I don't want this to be over; I'm enjoying this unexpected adventure too much. But I don't want to say anything because I don't want to seem ungrateful. He said he doesn't want to be late, so maybe he has plans back in Carmel. Why not, right? It's totally possible.

We drive for about fifteen minutes when Ethan turns left on a country road, then right and then takes a sharp left, pulls over and tells me we've reached the last stop.

"I thought we're going back to Carmel," I say, this time admitting what I'd been feeling.

"That's why you were so quiet?" he asks, smiling.

I shrug. How easy I am to read.

He opens the car door for me and we take a set of stairs until we're on what looks like a terrace. To my left, the mountains and to my right, the ocean.

"This has got to be the coolest restaurant I've ever seen," I say excited. "Let's take photos quickly before they throw us out."

He chuckles. "Aren't you hungry?" he asks.

"I am, but judging by this long line, we'll never get a table."

The restaurant, with sun umbrellas on the patio and three levels inside, is packed. There are dozens of people waiting—patiently or not—for their turn to sit and eat and gawk.

"That's where a little planning comes in handy," he says and after he chats for a minute with a waiter, he tells me to follow him. Not only do we have a table, but we have a table on the outer edge of the patio, with almost a 360-degree view. A breathtaking view.

"This place might not look like much and it's far from being fancy, but you can't beat the views," says Ethan. "The food is not bad either. I know you said you're a picky eater."

"I changed my mind," I say and laugh.

We enjoy a super-tasty meal with wine for me and sparkling water for Ethan. The sun is setting. "You are right. You can't beat this."

"Happy you like it."

We continue looking at the sunset and from time to time, I glance at him. He is one good-looking man. As much as I try not to think about it, it's hard not to. Very hard.

"Today was very—" I think of a word that could sum it up. "Unexpected."

The lopsided smile. "I got to know you when you were mad at me, so I know that side. Thought I'd try your happy, sunny side for a change."

And what a spectacular try it is. Don't know if anything can beat this day.

"Hmmph," he says and, turning from the ocean, looks straight into my eyes. "And you know what? I can't decide."

"Decide what?"

"Which side of you is more attractive."

SIXTY-FOUR

My eyes pop out of my head. Did he just say that?

He starts laughing; a belly laugh. "Your face," he says, still chuckling. "Just kidding, relax."

Jeez. I thought he was flirting with me. He's not. Why not? Obviously, because I'm in love with Max. And he's a good friend who's only spending time with me to make sure I'm not some sort of psycho who will hurt his friend. That's all there is to it.

"I knew you were joking," I say, and it sounds just as stupid as I feel.

He knows it and I know it. For a second there, I thought he meant it.

"This place is pretty special," he says, completely unrelated. "A bunch of famous people are part of its history."

I shake off the feeling of disappointment. We're friends, I remind myself. "Like who?"

"Rita Hayworth and Orson Welles. The legend says they were hiking or whatever they were doing, they stumbled upon this place and fell in love with it. They bought it on the spot."

"Hah," I say and I try to imagine how it must feel to be so spontaneous. So crazy. Crazy in love and just crazy and reckless in general.

"Then there's Henry Miller. He lived here for a while and wrote. Writers do sometimes come up here for inspiration, even now."

"Did you ever?" I ask.

"No. I haven't been here since I was a kid."

"Who else?" I ask.

"Let me see. Richard Burton and Liz Taylor were here back in the Sixties. They filmed, what was it called? *The Sandpiper*."

"This place is a magnet for—" I want to say lovers, but I quickly change the course. "Famous people."

"Yeah. Famous people and us," he says.

"You're famous."

"If you say so."

Before we leave, we stop by the gift shop and although Ethan insists on buying me a small painting I've been staring at for ten minutes, called *Isle of No Sorrow*, which is the exact view we had from our table, I ask him not to. I don't think he should be buying me gifts and although I would die to have that beautiful canvas, I don't even have a place of my own to hang it in. And it's too expensive anyway.

* * *

We return late at night, singing along to radio tunes and telling silly jokes all the way.

At one point, Ethan takes a phone call and halfway

through, I realize what it is about. Celine's legal problems with her ex.

"Thank you for calling this late," Ethan says. "That's great news," he says at the end.

"Solved?" I ask, seeing the smile on his face.

"Yes! She's going to be so happy."

And I'm happy for her. "Is he a lawyer specialized in divorces?" I ask, thinking of Gaby.

"Yes and a very good one. Why?"

"There's this nice woman who comes by the café every day. She's going through an ugly divorce; her husband is trying to take her child away. I was wondering if this lawyer could help."

He smiles. "Gaby?"

"Yes."

"Celine told me about it. I already put them in touch and last I heard the lawyer found a loophole that will keep the husband away from her, her daughter and her money."

"I'm so glad. Please thank him for me," I say.

* * *

We're back home and after he parks the car, we walk side by side to the front door.

Before we go in, Ethan grabs my arm. "Did anything change?"

I look at him, not knowing what he means.

"Do you still hate me?"

I smile. "You think that will go away with a pretty sunset and a decent dinner?" I say and honestly, I can't believe those words comes from my mouth. I never thought I had it in me.

"Fair," he says, and lets go of my arm.

Celine is on the couch when we walk in, watching a series on Netflix and sipping wine.

I stay with them while we tell Celine about our afternoon and evening in Big Sur, before calling it a night. They stay behind and I can't help but wonder if my name will come up in their conversation and how. Does she find this sudden friendship strange? Does she know anything about Max? I think if she did, she'd force Ethan to tell me what I need to know. I should tell her. If I want to know now, this is the answer. Alright, yes, this might be the answer, but the real question is: do I want to know now?

If I do get my answers, that will mark the beginning of something new, but the end to this. This unconventional pact thing Ethan and I have going. And I'm not sure I'm ready for it to end. It just started and it's going so well...

SIXTY-FIVE

JUNE 13

Last night I slept poorly again. Kept waking up and then struggled to fall asleep.

I shouldn't have called Alisa before I went to bed.

I picked up the phone and put it back on the nightstand a few times. I wanted to call and tell her what happened, but something made me hesitate. Realizing she'd know something was off if I missed our call two nights in a row, I dialed her number.

"Finally," she said. "I was about to send MI6 after you."

I told her about the last two days but kept it to a minimum because I knew it would be hard for her to understand our arrangement.

"So, Aaron isn't Max and you're basically back to square one."

"Sort of. It's just a matter of days before I find out his name though."

"And this is the reason why you guys watched a movie and today went for a drive?" she asked casually. "So you can find out Max's real name?"

"Yes."

"Why?" she asked a bit bluntly. "I don't get it."

"What do you mean why? I told you. Before he tells me, he wants to make sure my intentions are good."

"Like in an eighteenth-century chaperone type of thing? Is Max a tween?"

She had the exact same reaction I had when Ethan refused to tell me who Max is. But, since then, things have changed, I think. I see things differently now.

"He's just looking out for his friend," I said, realizing how it sounded.

"Isn't this the same man who plastered a photo of the two of you kissing in a paper, not caring about his friend's feelings? *Now* he cares? What's going on with you, Maya?"

"Nothing is going on," I said, trying to sound convincing. "And it was his publishers who put the photo in the paper. Besides, you told me I should be more open and make friends."

"This is not what I had in mind."

"You know what? Me neither. But sometimes it doesn't work exactly as you plan."

"Hello? Is my friend still there? Who's talking? I hear the voice, but I don't recognize who's behind it," she said and I know she was trying to joke but it wasn't too far from the truth.

That was why I hadn't wanted to call her.

"I'm going to ask the obvious. Why are you not talking to Celine about this? Ask her if she knows who Max is."

Smart Alisa.

"I thought about that too, but I'd have to explain too much and hurt her feelings, probably for nothing since she doesn't seem to be that involved in his writing."

"That sounds like an excuse to me," she said.

"I'm beat," I said. "Have to get some sleep. Long day tomorrow."

"Another impromptu adventure?" she asked sarcastically.

"I doubt it. I think it was a one-time thing."

"As if. Either way, there can't be that many adventures left. He's leaving in a few days."

Her words fall like rocks on my head. It was as if I had put that part out of mind. But the reality is that, yes, there are only a few days left. I wish she hadn't reminded me just yet.

* * *

In the morning, we all get up at the same time, which is unusual. And as Celine and I are leaving, Ethan comes with us.

Celine doesn't act surprised, so I follow suit.

Ethan and I don't talk much on the way there, but from time to time we look in each other's direction and when our eyes meet, we both smile. Celine seems oblivious.

He helps us open up the café and then goes to his table and I see him taking out my manuscript and reading.

An hour passes. Two. He's still reading. He takes a break for a while and writes or edits his latest book. After lunch, he takes out the manuscript again.

I found things to do around his table way too many times today, but every time I got close to him, it's as if he had eyes in the back of his head. He'd turn the page on its back, and I couldn't see where he was and he keeps putting the pages he finishes back under the manuscript.

It's early in the afternoon and there's no line; the dishes are washed. Celine is out back on the bench, taking a break.

I've tried to write some more of her story but haven't been able to focus. I tried everything I could to keep my mind off Ethan reading my work. Everything.

"I see you prefer to get to know the quiet version of me," I say, pointing at the manuscript.

He looks up. "I didn't know if the talking version could stomach me two days in a row."

"Wasn't that bad, was it?" I giggle. What's next, batting my eyelashes? What's wrong with me?

"Not for me," he says.

Celine comes from the kitchen and I walk away from Ethan's table and as I do, I see a blond guy, sitting at one of the tables outside.

SIXTY-SIX

I immediately recognize him: Aaron. How could I not? For a few days, I was convinced he was Max. But that's not what drew my eyes to him this time. It was the way Celine reacted when she saw him. She suddenly stopped and kept staring at him.

I walk over to the counter, watching her. She keeps herself busy, but from time to time, glances his way. Sometimes customers sit outside waiting for us to bring them the menu. I look over and don't see anything on his table. Celine must've noticed that too. Why is she not going?

In three steps I'm next to Ethan. "Can I ask you something?"

He looks up. "Sure."

"But please be honest and don't ask why I'm asking."

"The suspense is killing me," he says, amused.

"You know how you told me that Aaron is for sure not Max?"

"Not that again," says Ethan, sounding exasperated.

"Relax, it's not that. I just want to know if the woman he's been in love with is Celine."

Ethan raises an eyebrow. "How did you—"

I mirror his raised eyebrow.

"Fine. Yes, sort of. Do you want the unabridged or the regular version?"

"The condensed one, please. I only have a few minutes. At most."

"They were high school sweethearts; each other's first love. He left for college; they broke up. She got married, then divorced. He came back to Carmel at about the same time she and her ex split, about two years ago. They've been awkward around each other ever since."

"That's all I need to know," I say and squeeze his hand as a sign of gratitude.

I go out to Aaron's table. "Hello there," I say, all smiles. "So nice to see you again."

I feel Celine's eyes burning the back of my head.

He smiles and seems surprised to see me. "Do you—"

"Work here? Yes," I say, not letting him finish.

"I saw you—"

"In the paper. I know. Old news. Can I ask you something? Apart from your order."

I think I'm speaking too fast, because he seems dizzy.

"I'll have a large vanilla latte and a butter croissant."

"Lovely. Are you seeing anyone right now, Aaron?"

"Aaaa. No, I'm not but I'm not—" He seems embarrassed.

"No, no," I say and laugh. I know what he must be thinking.

How easy it is talking to him now, and how tongue-tied I was a few days ago.

"I'm not asking you out. Although you're a catch, I'm

sure, but I have enough on my plate as is. It's just that an acquaintance we have in common, seems to harbor feelings for you."

I might be jumping the gun. It's possible. Maybe it's a mistake and Celine will hate me for it. But she might not and it's a risk I'm willing to take, to potentially see her happy.

"An acquaintance?" he asks and looks at me, confused.

"Let's try it this way. If you could ask anyone out, anyone at all, who would that be?"

His face turns bright red in seconds. "I—I..."

"It's OK," I say. "You don't have to say anything. I'll just throw it out there that I know someone will have the night off tomorrow. I'll do a full shift, so, if you were to take a risk and go for it..."

"Are you sure she wouldn't say no?" he asks, sounding truly terrified.

I shrug. "Are you sure you'd rather not try until it's too late?"

His embarrassment turns into a smile, and then a full-blown grin. We get each other.

When I go in, Celine pulls me aside. "What was that about?" she asks nervously.

"What was what about?" I ask, playing dumb.

"You were talking to Aaron."

"We met," I say. "A few days ago. He was my Lift driver. And he saw me in the paper, of course," I say casually, as if it means nothing. It's obviously not true, but it has to seem that way to her. She thinks, after all, that I agreed to it. But it still means a lot! The only thing I'm thankful for in this whole mess—hoping that Ethan didn't lie to me—is that Max didn't see it.

"That's it?" she asks.

I smile. "Why? Is there anything more?"

"No. I just—"

"He asked about you," I say in passing.

"What? He did? What do you mean?"

"Just if you're seeing anyone."

"He asked you if I'm seeing someone? Why you?" She then tries to control her reaction but it's so obvious. "Sorry, I didn't mean to offend you. I just didn't know you two were close."

"Well, he knows we work together, so he probably assumed *you* and *I* are close."

"And we are, aren't we?" she asks, and she's so cute, in an insecure kind of way. I know what she's trying to ask. Still, I'm not going to give her any more details and possibly let her in on my involvement in what might or might not—but hopefully might—happen tonight.

"I said you're single for now, that's all. I shouldn't have?" I ask, playing the innocent.

"No, no, that's fine. It's the truth."

"Yes, it's the truth."

SIXTY-SEVEN

I would lie if I said I didn't spend the next couple of hours watching Celine and Aaron, hoping he'd make a move, praying she'd say yes. I almost forgot my own complications for those two hours. I focused less on Ethan reading my book or why he hadn't suggested we spend another day together, or why when I look at him, I can't stop looking at him.

Instead, I took out the notebook, and wrote down Aaron and Celine's story, this time not only based on my imagination but what was right in front of my eyes. I like these new stories, much more than my old ones. I don't want to say the literary agents were right, but I will admit they're far more realistic. Not less hopelessly romantic, though.

When Aaron left the money on the table and walked away without coming in, my heart sank. Looking at Celine and seeing the same disappointed reaction on her face made things worse. I gave her hope and it backfired. I wanted to go after him but didn't know what else to say; instead, I just stood there, watching him leave.

About half an hour later, before we start dinner service, Ethan leaves to meet someone.

"I'll see you ladies later," he says from the door and waves smilingly.

"What's he so happy about?" asks Celine and I hear the hurt in her voice.

I made a mistake and I'm so sorry about it. I got overconfident after my success with Brienne and Alan. I had good intentions but didn't know anything about these two. Only what Ethan told me.

* * *

It's early in the evening when a man walks in with a large bouquet of red roses.

"Celine Delphy?" he asks, looking between Celine and me.

"That's me," she says.

"Can you please sign here?" he says and gives her a pad.

I swear I'm more excited even than she is, and I want to snatch that card out of her hand and read it. Could it be that Aaron listened to me? Is it possible it worked after all?

She reads the card, and her face turns pink. Then red. Is she happy or mad? I can't tell.

"Where are they from?"

"Aaron," she says.

"They're beautiful," I say.

"He's never sent me flowers before."

"Ever?"

She shakes her head and when I look at her, I see she has tears in her eyes.

"Celine, don't be sad. This is something to be happy about," I say.

"Now? After all these years?" she says and shows me the card.

This might surprise you. The out-of-the-blue flowers, the out-of-the-blue apologies. Except they're not out-of-the-blue. I have been thinking about it... about you for a long time. I never stopped. I feel that more than anything, what I want you to know is that what I said that last night we were together is still true. And it always will be. Aaron

"What is he referring to? What did he say that last night?" I ask.

Celine wipes a tear with the back of her hand. "That he never stopped loving me."

She's now full-blown crying, so I take her in the back, away from prying eyes.

"It's my fault. I don't even know why he's apologizing. He did nothing wrong."

"What do you mean?" I ask.

She blows her nose, and I think she'll stop crying, but the tears keep on coming.

"I was the one who broke off our relationship when he left for college. I told him I wasn't interested in a long-distance relationship. He insisted and insisted, until he forced me to say—"

She sits down and holds her head in her hands.

"What?"

"I told him that I didn't love him, and I didn't want to be with him. I thought he was going to find someone else in college, leave me and I'd have my heart broken, so I did it first."

"Oh, Celine."

"It was stupid, I know. And then I went on and did something even stupider. I married a man who never loved me and who I thought I was in love with, when in fact, all I was trying to do was forget Aaron. Look where that got me," she says with tears in her eyes.

"You were young; we all make mistakes when we're young. Some of us still do."

She attempts a smile.

"He obviously still loves you," I say. "And you love him too."

"I—"

"Don't even try it with me," I say.

"What do you think I should do? Should I message him?"

"What is your heart telling you?"

She hugs me and there's a smile on her face that makes me think she's made a decision and I couldn't be happier if this was my own love story.

SIXTY-EIGHT

It's closing time and Ethan didn't come back. I miss having him around. Even when he doesn't talk much, I still like knowing he's here. He always helps us close the place, clean, and keeps us awake and entertained with his geeky jokes. Not tonight. It's not the same without him and I find myself turning and looking at the door until my neck hurts. He's not coming; and it's a bitter preview and reminder. Alisa was right; it's a matter of days and one more just ended.

* * *

Celine and I are almost home, when she grabs my arm tight.

"What?"

"Aaron texted back," says Celine, her voice high-pitched like a mouse's squeak.

"When?" I ask.

"Just now. I messaged him right before we left Café Azure."

She's smiling from ear to ear. She's always smiling but I haven't seen her *this* happy.

"When are you seeing him?"

"Tomorrow evening," she says. "If you're OK holding the fort on your own."

"Of course," I say. "I'm so happy for you, Celine."

We get home. Ethan's not here. Celine jumps in the shower and I'm snuggled under a blanket on the couch, staring at the blank TV screen, when I hear the front door.

Ethan tiptoes over and jumps onto the couch. "Where is she?" he whispers.

"In the shower."

"Did she get the flowers?" he asks, and grins.

"How—"

I tilt my head and look at him.

"You did good. He just needed a slight, friendly push in the direction of the florist. Sorry I left you both with the coffee shop. Was it complete madness?"

"No, it was fine," I say, still stunned about this.

He sighs amused. "Reminiscing ten years with him, took longer than expected."

"So it was you who convinced him to ask her out."

"No," he says innocently. "We both did."

"Don't tell her, OK?" I say. "I don't want her to know we're involved."

"I won't. I promise. It'll be our secret."

He sits comfortably, looking at the dark screen. "What are we watching?"

"Whatever it is, it's super interesting. I'm glued to the couch."

"Want something to drink? I noticed you don't drink

much so I'm not going to spoil a full glass of wine on you, but how about this much?" he asks and shows me two fingers.

I nod.

"Two wine fingers times two coming up," he says. "And I brought you both this," he says and hands me a food tray.

In it are a few crab Rangoon, spring rolls and pot sticks.

"You can't say I'm not a provider."

"Where did you get this?"

"Picked it up on my way back. Thought I shouldn't come home empty-handed after I stood you up tonight."

"You didn't stand us up. You have things to do," I say.

"Not you and Celine. You. I thought we talked about doing something."

"We did?"

"Maybe we didn't," he says. "I might've misunderstood your question about the manuscript then."

I laugh. "How's the reading going?"

"It's going. Still fabulous. Still a slow reader."

Maybe I shouldn't ask this. Maybe I shouldn't ruin it for him too, but I do it anyway.

"Will you finish by the time you leave?"

"By the time I leave?"

"The day after your book launch, right?"

His eyes are fixated on mine as he puts the wine glasses on the table and comes back on the couch. "Correct. Yes. Almost forgot. Wow. Not much time then."

"Nope. Not much time at all," I say.

He's quiet for a moment. "Alright then. So, what are you doing tomorrow?"

"Besides working? Celine has a date tomorrow, thanks to you. So I have to be there."

"Right. That leaves only the morning. Hmm... I have something in mind."

"You do?"

He takes his phone and checks something on it.

"All set," he says. I suggest you go to bed now. We need to be out of the house at four."

I hear Celine coming out of the bathroom. He gets up and walks over to her bedroom door. "I'll let her know about tomorrow. Wear comfortable shoes and layers. How are you with heights?"

"Four? In the morning? What heights?" I ask, but he's gone already.

* * *

I text Alisa, and without waiting for an answer, I go straight to bed.

I have to go to sleep early because tomorrow I'm waking up at 3ish to go somewhere with Ethan. Not sure where but it involves heights. I'm thinking rock climbing or something. Talk tomorrow.

SIXTY-NINE
JUNE 14

When my alarm blares, I mumble something addressed to Ethan—for my ears only—and force myself to walk/crawl to the bathroom to take a shower and hopefully wake up. It doesn't help. I get dressed in layers as he said, put on a pair of sneakers and stumble out of my room.

Ethan's already in the kitchen, filling a thermos with coffee and looking like he's just been taken out of a box. No puffy eyes, no grumpy face, all smiles.

"Good morning," he says a bit too loud, and I point to Celine's room.

"Let's go," he whispers. "We have a bit of a drive."

"Are you good?" he asks, after I have my first sips of coffee.

"Getting there," I say.

"Not a morning person?"

"Are you taking notes? Does this disqualify me?" I ask half-aggressively, half-jokingly. "And I don't think three can be counted as morning."

"Mental notes," he says. "And no, you're still in the running," he says, ignoring my tone.

"Since it's too early for loud music and definitely too early for jokes—" I say.

"Especially mine."

"Especially yours, and since you're putting together this thick file on me, how about you tell me something about yourself?"

I think he's smiling, but I can barely see him. "Fair. What do you want to know?"

"How come you look like you've slept twelve hours and woke up four hours ago to get ready? I thought you weren't a morning person either."

He laughs. "I'm not. But like you said, this is not morning. I don't sleep much. In general. Four hours maybe five. I got six hours of sleep last night."

"Why don't you sleep?"

"I usually write at night. I like the quiet, the darkness. I write outside, on a patio, a terrace, something. It makes me feel free. Physical walls are like walls on my imagination."

"I like that idea. Are you writing something now? A new book?"

"I'm jotting down ideas. But I'm mostly editing. That's what I do at the café. I wrote a book a couple of months ago and now I'm basically rewriting it."

"So you can write during the day too," I say.

"It's not the same. Revising is not writing."

"Let's agree to disagree. How long did it take you to write *June After Midnight*?"

"Not long at all. Three weeks maybe. It was my fastest first draft."

"I guess you were inspired," I say, realizing I sound somewhat bitter again.

"What about you? How long did it take you to write yours?"

"Funny enough, the same."

"It is a story that writes itself," he says eventually. "It's a special story, isn't it?"

"Yes, it is."

"I'm sorry," he says.

"What for?"

"That I wrote it first, I guess. That you feel I stole it from you."

"Yeah, well," I say. "I was wondering. Why did you use my real name?"

"Because, like you said, it's your story. Your name."

"Why didn't you use Max's real name then?"

"I used it in my first draft. But it didn't get past my editor. She said calling him by the name you gave him would be more fitting."

"Is your editor the one who changed David's name to Daniel?"

He smirks. "No. I just didn't like the name David."

I try not to smile.

"Publishing is a mystery. For instance, my book has a different title in the UK."

"What is it?"

"*The Text.*"

"No! are you serious?" I ask, trying not to laugh.

"You can laugh if you want. I did."

"Which text?" I ask. "There were a few hundred back and forth."

"Maybe it was the last one," he says.

"Or the first," I say.

"That was the one that changed everything, wasn't it?" he says.

Yes, that first text changed everything. Then what am I doing here with you? At five in the morning, driving God knows where when Max is somewhere out there, hopefully waiting for me. And why am I thinking about him less and less when I'm with you? I would ask all these things, perhaps, if I was a different person.

SEVENTY

"We're here," he finally says after two hours of driving.

I'm awake now. A bit apprehensive about what we're going to do, a bit confused about this fight going on inside my mind, but I try not to let it show.

We get out of the car and walk toward a field and into a tent, where a man and a woman ask us all sorts of questions and make us sign a waiver. I barely see what I'm signing.

"Did I just give away all my possessions? Are we joining a cult?" I ask, snickering.

"Sort of. Do you want a full surprise or it's enough of a surprise as it is?"

"Is it a nice surprise?"

"I hope so, otherwise it's going to be a long drive back."

"Full surprise then," I say, feeling suddenly risqué.

"OK. I don't have a blindfold, so—"

He puts his hands on my eyes. I feel my eyes burning under his touch and shiver.

"Sorry. Too cold?" he asks and rubs his hands together, then puts them back on.

No. Not too cold. My eyes burn even more and that hot sensation is going through my body all the way to my toes. Is it normal to react like this when he innocently touches me?

He leads me forward and helps me climb over something. As soon as my feet touch a marshmallow-like surface, I a man's voice asking if we're ready.

"I'm not sure," I say laughing.

"We're ready," says Ethan.

Although I have no idea where we are or what we're doing (hopefully not bungee jumping), I feel strangely calm. He's here with me, his hands on my eyes. Everything's fine.

I feel a movement, then hear a hiss, and I put my hands on his to make him let go.

"Not yet," he says. "Just a bit longer," and I pull my hands back.

Movement again, this time stronger, and an actual physical pit in my stomach. We're lifting. I'm not imagining, we're... are we floating?

I don't know if it's seconds or minutes, but he takes off his hands and when I open my eyes, I'm so shocked I genuinely feel like crying.

We're up in the air, the sun is rising. We're in a hot air balloon above fields and vineyards and a beautiful lake. And I'm completely and utterly speechless. I don't even try to say something because I know it will not come out intelligible.

"Good morning again," he says. "This time, properly."

"Wha—this is—we are—"

I can't even make a sentence.

The balloon swishes to the side, I lose my balance and Ethan grabs my hand to prop me back up. I'm up, I'm fine now, but he doesn't let go and I don't pull my hand either. The thing is, I don't want him to let go. It's scary and confusing and it doesn't make sense, but I don't want him to let go. I want him to hold my hand and cover my eyes again with his hands and... kiss me. I look away, ashamed of these thoughts. I shouldn't have them. But I do.

The man piloting the balloon stands away from us, on the other side of the basket, giving us privacy. The other night was picture-perfect, but this moment is a hundred times that.

"Don't tell me you picked this idea from my book as well," I say.

"Actually, I did. You said you have a thing for sunrises. And it's something I picked up from my book too. I know you missed a sunrise, which would've been very special for you."

Don't bring that up now. Don't. Don't pop the bubble and ruin the magic.

"I wanted to give you another one in return."

He didn't ruin the magic. He just created it and if I was a different kind of woman, I would kiss him right now. But being as I am, all I can do is stare into his eyes and together we stare at the most beautiful sunrise I've ever seen. I'm overwhelmed by all these feelings, the beauty of this moment, and the big heart of this man. A man who, I'm discovering day by day and hour by hour is so different from what I thought he was.

* * *

I'm quiet on our way back; just have a lot on my mind. Not sure if he feels it or our quiet times align, but Ethan doesn't force a conversation. Back at the cottage, he parks the car and tells me he's not coming straight to Café Azure because he has some things to take care of first.

"Thank you," I say. "This was a once-in-a-lifetime experience."

"It was a first for me, too. Just thought we'd try it together."

What and how he's saying it makes my heart grow and grow, like it's about to explode. I wish I could react differently, but this is what it has to be under these particular circumstances.

He tilts his head. "How are we on the hate front?"

"On the wha—"

And then I remember. "Same-o, same-o. Nice try with the cute sunrise though."

He chuckles, I smile and thank him again, turn around and leave. I leave this man standing there, a man I'm painfully attracted to, both physically and mentally, and a man I connect to on all possible and impossible levels. But I leave him like that and I'm incapable of saying what I wish I could, because somewhere there's this other man I've been looking for. A man I've never seen, I've never held hands with, kissed, laughed with, watched a sunrise or sunset with. Alisa is right; I have a talent for complicating my life like it's nobody's business.

SEVENTY-ONE

I get to Café Azure a little before lunch, and the moment I see Celine, I can tell she's wound up and can barely contain her nerves. And it's not the customers or anything to do with the café. I know she's looking forward to her date with Aaron, but she's also afraid of how things might turn out. Plus, it's been a while since they've spent any time together. I would be a total wreck.

"Everything will be fine tonight," I reassure her. "You'll see. It's going to work out."

"I hope it is," she says and finally smiles.

I'm so excited for her. I hope they get past what happened and work everything out.

Lunchtime comes and goes and despite a super busy time that forces her to run around tirelessly for hours, she can't wipe that smile off her face.

"I didn't tell Ethan yet about my date," she says, looking at the door as he comes in.

"Why?" I ask, talking to her but watching him.

"He and Aaron are friends and I don't want to make it

weird between them," she says. "You know I haven't properly dated in two years? I tried but they were all epic fails." She scrunches up her nose. "Online dating," she says and laughs, embarrassed.

"I've never tried it," I say.

"You aren't missing much; it might make good material for a book. An absurd comedy."

Celine tells me she wants to leave the café early to get ready. I don't blame her; I would do the same. If I knew, for instance, that I was about to meet Max, I think I'd take two full days to make sure every little detail was perfect.

"You can leave whenever you want. I'll take care of everything," I say, just as Ethan is coming over to get something to eat.

His phone rings, he answers, but I can't tell much of what the conversation is about or who it's with. I hear a name— Melissa—and then he's all smiles and looking obviously excited.

"Good news?" asks Celine when he hangs up.

He smiles from ear to ear but doesn't answer. A strange kind of smile. Mischievous.

"Come on. Tell us."

He puts on an innocent face. "Not yet, but we'll talk about it more tonight."

Celine looks down. "I won't be home tonight, sorry," she says.

He glances my way and I make a face, as in: 'Remember? We talked about it? THE date!'

"That's fine, it's cool. Tomorrow night then or the day after. No big deal."

"Are you sure?" she asks.

"He's sure. Besides, I'm home, if he can settle for the less interesting half of our duo."

He laughs. "I'll sacrifice myself."

Celine's face lights up. "I owe you for the next two decades," she says into my ear.

I want to tell her Ethan knows and she shouldn't hide it from him. Not only that he knows, but he made it possible. I want to, but this seems like a thing best handled between them.

* * *

Celine leaves in the afternoon and Ethan stops writing and helps me with the orders. He's the one making most of the food and the drinks while I run the front of the house.

I make a good team with Celine and, as it turns out, an equally good team with Ethan.

"I think we're doing OK," he says proudly as the dinner service is almost over.

"We got lucky nobody asked for anything complicated," I say.

He raises an eyebrow. "Where's the faith? I've watched Celine, my mom, and my grandma for years in the kitchen. I can hold my ground."

He seems very comfortable at Café Azure and perhaps it's because he's been around it for so long. His grandparents, then his parents. It's in his blood.

"I'm enjoying this," he says, looking at me. The kind of look he gives me from time to time. I'm never sure if he's just incredibly charming because that's who he is, or if these looks are reserved for me and they mean something he doesn't want to or can't say with words.

"I'm glad you are," I say.

"Do you like it? Working here?"

"More than I thought I would." There's a pit in my stomach as I say it.

"Celine is great. She has so much patience, I sometimes question if we're truly related."

"You two are more alike than you think."

"I'll take that as a compliment," he says with a smile.

It was meant to be one. "It'll be strange once it's over. I'll miss all of this a lot," I say.

I wish I could say exactly what I think, but I can't.

"So you have a plan then?"

"Not yet. But I have to come up with one; can't stay in your house forever."

"Hmm," he says, and I don't know if he's relieved I said it first and he doesn't have to kick me out—eventually. It's hard to read his reactions. "Why can't you?"

I shrug. Why can't I? Well, because this was meant to be for a week; then it turned into two. But in a few days, things will be different. Ethan will leave, Max will hopefully come into the picture, and life—as I know it now—will change.

"You can stay as long as you want," says Ethan.

"Thank you, that's nice of you to say."

He smiles and again, I don't know what that smile means.

SEVENTY-TWO

"Do you want to take a walk? It's a nice night," asks Ethan after we close Café Azure.

It is a nice night. Few people around, the street barely lit, music playing in the distance.

I'm both comfortable and nervous when I'm with him. We're in this friendly relationship but there are moments, glimpses of something more. A look, a word, a change in his tone or mine—not to mention a trip in a hot air balloon to watch the sunrise—that take things beyond friendship. And I don't know how to navigate it. We're in each other's lives and space every day and every time I want more. More of his time, our talks, more of him. And it's so confusing.

Like now, just walking with no direction, talking about small stuff—he shows me a house. "I used to play in their yard all the time. My best friend lived here."

I want to know more about his life, his past, what made him the man he is today.

"Are you still friends?" I ask.

"He moved to Ireland years ago with his wife, but we talk on the phone sometimes."

"It's nice that you kept in touch."

"It must be hard leaving everything behind and starting over," he says.

"It is," I say. "And it isn't. I think it all depends on what you're leaving behind."

"What did you leave behind?" he asks.

"Except for my mom, who I miss, nothing I regret."

He looks at me as if he wants to say something, just as I stop in front of an art gallery.

"Hey, I know the artist," I say. "We should go in. Been meaning to see her work."

I knock on the glass door. No movement; it must be closed for the night.

We're walking away when I see Anna's pretty face, as she rushes to open the door.

"Maya," she says and I'm happy she recognized me. I know she sees me every morning, but we don't talk too much and I always assume I'm pretty invisible to people.

She looks at Ethan and, to be polite, I say, "This is—"

"Ethan, it's about time you stopped by. Come in, guys," she says.

The gallery is small, just like Celine said, but it's packed. One wall is covered in seascapes, just like the ones Ethan and I saw on our way to Big Sur, the second one has over a dozen beautiful, colorful landscapes of hills and mountains, vineyards, and redwood forests. The wall on the far-right side is the portrait wall. Half of them sketched, half in color and finished.

"They're beautiful," I say to her and although she's trying

not to hover, I know she's watching our reactions as we move from painting to painting.

"Anna, you're getting better by the day," says Ethan, sounding like a big brother.

She grins. "If it wasn't for Ethan, I wouldn't have the studio in the back."

"I'm sure you would've found a solution. Besides, I didn't do much."

"He got the landlord to drop the rent by seventy percent. I could've never afforded it otherwise."

"How did you do that?" I ask Ethan.

"I told her I'll be using this location in my upcoming novel," he says. "She's a fan."

"Ethan is popular with the ladies. They gobble up his books," says Anna, laughing too.

"Especially eighty-year-old ones," he says.

"Hope your magic continues to work. The landlord is getting antsy about the two-bedroom upstairs. She asked me if I'll rent it, if not, she wants to put both levels on the market."

"I'll see what I can do," he says.

"I tried to find a tenant, but single people who'd be OK with a noisy art gallery below—I listen to music when I paint— don't need two bedrooms, and families want peace and quiet."

"Is this Hugo?" I ask, realizing one of the sketches bears a striking resemblance to him.

She smiles sheepishly. "Not done yet. He's just so handsome, isn't he?"

I have an idea. "Is the space big enough for an office and a single person to live in?"

"For sure. Why?"

"Hugo is looking for a space to rent, both to live in and to open his new business."

"Is he?" she asks and her eyes light up.

"You should talk to him."

"Tomorrow morning, first thing. Thank you so much, Maya. Both of you. Thank you."

This story is writing itself. I'll just sit by, watch and take notes.

SEVENTY-THREE

"Is this what you do in your free time?" asks Ethan after we leave the gallery.

"What?"

"Play matchmaker?"

"What are you talking about?" He's onto me, I think, and try to keep a serious face.

"First Celine, now Anna. I wonder if there are others. There must be others."

"Ha-ha. You're just imagining things."

"Sure."

As we turn on Scenic Road, I point at the beach. "A bonfire. Do you want to go?"

He seems hesitant.

"Just for a few minutes?"

It's a different spot than last summer, but it's the same beach.

Ethan shakes a few guys' hands and chats to a couple of women. He introduces me to everyone, and while I make small talk, he shows up with two tin mugs and a thermos.

"You're resourceful," I say, laughing. "Where did you get these?"

"I have my connections," he says as he pours.

"What is it?" I ask and taste.

"Hot cider. If you don't like it, I'll get you something else. Sorry, I didn't ask."

"No. This is perfect, thank you. I've never had hot cider. It's quite good."

I look over at a group of people and see they have thermoses and tin mugs and offer them to anyone who wants them because they brought too many. "Ahaaa, I found your secret source."

He laughs. "We grew up together," he says. "I know who has the goods."

One of the men gestures for Ethan to come over. "Excuse me a minute," he says to me.

Ethan sits in the sand, on the other side of the bonfire, talking to the man. I keep looking at the fire, then at him, and suddenly it hits me. Wow. Déjà vu.

He comes back a few minutes later.

"I just realized I've seen you before."

He stares.

"Last summer. You were at a bonfire."

"There are bonfires almost every weekend in the summer; I go to some of them."

"Your hair was shorter, I think, but it was you. I'm sure of it."

"Yeah, I'm pulling a Rapunzel now," he says with a smile.

"Do you remember?" I ask.

"What?"

"Me," I say, but I don't wait for an answer. "No, I guess you wouldn't. You would've told me already if you did. And it's not even important if you do. It's just, wow! I knew there was something familiar about you from the moment we met; I just couldn't put my finger on it."

* * *

Celine isn't home when we get back.

"Tired?" he asks. I am exhausted and I'm surprised he's in such great shape since we've both been awake since three o'clock.

I nod. I wish I wasn't tired, to be honest. I wish we had more time. I wish I met him first. There. I said it. I wish I met him first.

I should go to sleep. This is not helping.

I finally feel like I got a decent amount of rest, despite waking up around three and then struggling to go back to sleep for an hour.

I called Alisa last night and although she couldn't talk for too long because she was going into a meeting, I told her about the hot air balloon and sent her a couple of photos.

Her reaction was a mix of 'Yay! That's so nice. Tell me more' with 'I'm still confused. Don't confuse me even more with details. And tell me again why you're always with this guy?'

Ever since I started spending time with Ethan, my relationship with Alisa has suffered. Usually, we're on the same page. We agree on everything. Now, every time I call her, I feel like I have to defend myself and my choices, and it's exhausting. Besides, it's hard to defend something I can barely explain or justify to myself. I don't need someone making me second-guess every single thing I do or say something. I already second- and triple-guess myself as it is.

* * *

The first thing I notice when I get out of bed is that the sun is up. When I check my clock, I panic. It's nine-thirty. I didn't hear the alarm go off at six; I didn't even hear my mom's call.

I run out of the room. They're both gone.

* * *

Minutes later, my hair still wet from the shower, I rush to Café Azure when my mom calls again.

"I was worried. You usually call me early in the morning," she says.

"Sorry, Mom. I overslept," I say.

"Are you running? You sound out of breath."

"No, no, I'm just late... meeting someone."

"Someone as in him?"

"No, not him, Mom. Friends."

"David stopped calling," she says.

"Good," I say.

"I think you made a mistake."

"He cheated on me, Mom. And not just once. I deserve better."

"I'm sorry, honey. I didn't know. Why didn't you tell me? Weasel."

"And Mom, before you ask when I'm coming back. I quit my job in NY and I've been working in Carmel and I love it here. Please don't be mad at me."

"Thank God," she says. "It was about time you taught that witch a lesson."

I start laughing and she laughs too.

"All I want is for you to be happy. If you found what you were looking for there—"

Did I find what I was looking for? Isn't this the question of the century?

SEVENTY-FIVE

When I walk in, the café is packed. Celine takes an order, and Ethan makes coffee.

"I'm so sorry," I say to Celine when she comes back to the counter.

"Good morning, sunshine," she says, all smiles.

"I'm sorry," I say again.

"What for?" she asks.

"What do you mean what for? For getting here at ten. I didn't hear the alarm."

"It's OK, Maya. You don't have to be here all the time; don't feel bad. Besides, Ethan was here and he's much better in the kitchen than I remembered."

I smile and look at him and he smiles back. I don't need to say anything or hear anything from him to know what his smile means. I wonder if he knows what mine is saying.

"Thank you for helping Celine out," I say.

"I'm expecting compensation for my work," he says in a serious tone.

"From Celine, I assume."

"No. From you. It was your shift."

"Let's see," I say and check my pockets. "I have five dollars."

He chuckles. "Tempting but I'd rather be paid in time."

Time. That's one thing I can't control. And time is slipping away from me, from us.

"Time in general or...?"

"Time with you," he says, lopsided smile and all. "I have something in mind for this afternoon."

"And leave Celine alone again? I was already late this morning."

"She'll be fine," he says. "I heard she has company coming to the café this evening."

"She does?"

He winks. "So, four?"

"Four," I say.

* * *

"How did it go last night?" I ask Celine as soon as Ethan goes to his table.

"We were so awkward at first; we talked about the weather and politics for an hour."

"What happened? How did you get past that phase?"

"I said, 'It's been too long and probably what we had is gone. Let's just be friends.'"

"And... And?"

"He came over and kissed me." She blushes as she tells me this. "And then he said, 'See? It's still there. I don't just want to be friends. I want to be with you. I love you.'"

She's beaming.

"Aww, that's so beautiful," I say. "I'm so happy for you."

"I can't believe he finally gathered the courage to talk to me. I wonder what made him."

"Who knows? The important thing is that he did it."

"You bring me luck; that's what this is. If he hadn't seen the photo in the paper, we wouldn't have talked. I doubt he would've reached out, otherwise."

I take a deep breath and smile. "I heard you told Ethan."

"I did. He's happy for us."

"Of course he is. He's your brother; he loves you and wants to see you happy."

"Did you know Aaron and I used to work together at Café Azure in high school? It'll be like good old days."

I laugh. "Are you making me redundant?"

"Never! I'd be dead without your help."

About that," I say. "Is it OK if I leave around four?"

"With Ethan?"

My cheeks are on fire. Am I blushing?

"You two have been spending quite a lot of time together," she says, and I don't know if she's judgmental, confused as Alisa (and me, as a matter of fact), or just observant.

"We have, yes. He's been showing me around—"

What a lame excuse. And it comes out just as lame as it sounds in my head.

"I'm happy," she says. That's all. No questions, no probing, no: 'What are your intentions?' She's just happy. And she looks happy.

SEVENTY-SIX

"Am I dressed properly for whatever it is that we'll be doing?" I ask when Ethan and I are getting ready to leave. I have no idea where, but I can only assume it's super close since I don't see either the Mustang or the Porsche out front.

As I say the last word, I look at him and realize we're both wearing the same kind of clothes and shoes—jeans, a T-shirt, Converse. My T-shirt is turquoise, his black, so at least we have that going for us. The last time we had matching clothes, it didn't go so well. Or did it?

He gives me a funny look and I wonder if he's thinking the same thing.

We leave the house and walk for a bit before Ethan stops in front of the café. "He should be here any moment now," he says.

"Who?"

"Our Lift driver," he says and smiles innocently.

Wouldn't this be the most ironic thing ever if this is Max? Life can't be that cruel.

A black Ford pulls in front of us.

"Ethan?" asks the man when we open the back door.

Ethan nods and we get in the back seat.

OK. Clearly, they don't know each other. So, no, it's not him. Thank God!

"How come you're not driving?" I ask.

"You'll see."

"No drivers here in Carmel, eh?" asks the driver who tells us to call him 'King'.

Ethan and I look at each other and after muffled snickering, we go with it. Why not? He looks a bit like Michael Jackson, and I think he's a fan, based on the music he's playing and the memorabilia all over his dashboard—a photo of MJ, a black glove.

"Not that many, no. Maybe a couple," says Ethan.

I already knew that from Aaron, of all people. And none of them are Max, which Ethan confirmed. He could live anywhere in the Bay Area or anywhere in the world. People can be friends even if they live thousands of miles from each other. Just look at Alisa and me. Thinking about her makes me realize how much I miss her. I'll call her tonight and be on my absolute best behavior, no matter what she says to me.

"I thought so since you waited thirty minutes for me to arrive from Monterey."

Ethan smiles. "It's worth it," he says and looks my way for just a fraction of a second before fixing his sight on the road ahead.

SEVENTY-SEVEN

Ethan and I try to decide between H.P. Lovecraft and Shirley Jackson for the best horror stories—I fight for Shirley. We then move on to music, when King jumps into our conversation. 'Is Roxette a European group?' leads to a lengthy discussion about Swedish music that ends with a debate about whether David Guetta and Daft Punk are American. I lose that one; they're not.

"I've been reading more of your manuscript," says Ethan, unrelated to anything we've been talking about since we left Carmel. That was about an hour and a half ago, and I still have no idea where we're going, only that we're following familiar road signs to Napa.

"You have?" I ask.

He nods. That's all. Is he waiting for me to ask what he thinks?

"It's not going to be long now before I finish it," he says.

"Good."

That 'good' sounded so hollow, it almost echoed in the

car. Is it good? He finishes, we're done. *This*, whatever it is, is over. It has to be over; I know it. I've known it from the moment we made the pact. That was the whole point, wasn't it? I knew it even before that. From the moment I saw him standing in front of Celine's front door—his door—and understood who he was. Ethan Delphy, bestselling author who is going on a book tour on June 17 and then on a movie production set for an unknown number of months, on the other side of the world. Ethan Delphy, friend of Max. Ethan Delphy, the biggest surprise of my existence. I knew it, but it doesn't make this looming deadline any easier. All the denying and ignoring won't make it disappear and turn into something it cannot be. He will still leave, I will still stay, and Max is still Max.

"Good," he echoes.

I know we're in Napa Valley. I recognize this much. But I still don't know what he has planned, although judging by our escapades so far, it'll be something I've never done before. There are so many things, though, so it's hard to narrow it down.

"Plane, car, bike, motorcycle, walking, train?" he asks.

"Say what?"

"Which one is your favorite?"

"Plane is last. I love walking. I recently—you know this already because you wrote my story—rediscovered biking. Motorcycle, no thanks, car... sure, that's always OK. Train, it's been years since I've been on one. Maybe since I was a kid. But I remember I found it fascinating.

"I probably should've asked this before," he says and smiles.

As the car comes to a stop, I know what he means.

Not far from where we are, there's a railroad, and a train

unlike any I've seen in New York or Connecticut is waiting in an adorable, miniature station.

"Don't tell me we're going on a train ride," I say, not hiding my excitement.

"Hope that's OK," he says.

"More than OK," I say and as soon as we get out of the car, I grab his arm and basically drag him to the train.

It's old, luxurious and for some reason it makes me think of the Orient Express.

"Welcome to the Napa Valley Wine Train," says a woman dressed in a red and white outfit, like she's a character in a book or a play. One of those European folk dancers I used to see on TV when Eurovision was on.

Ethan takes pamphlets or maps—I'm not sure—from the woman and gives her two pieces of paper, which I assume are our tickets. She checks them and leads us to one of the carts.

"You are here," she says and we get on the train. "Have a lovely evening!" she wishes us.

"Wine Train," I exclaim and give Ethan an amused look as we're sitting on deliciously comfortable royal blue plush seats. "So there's drinking involved?"

"Relax," he says. "I'm not planning to get you drunk and take advantage of you."

I roll my eyes, but a tiny part of me says, 'Bummer.'

"This is amazing. And so comfortable."

"It's pretty nice," he says coolly. "So," he says and unfolds the pamphlets. "We have three stops. Each quite different, it seems. And we also have dinner and just a small, insignificant amount of alcohol. If you want to. You don't have to. I know you're not a big wine drinker."

"That's not true," I say, sounding like I'm trying to convince him I'm an alcoholic. "I appreciate a good wine, for instance. And this is the Wine Train. I assume that's what we'll have. I just don't do beer or hard stuff; never liked them."

"It's OK. I'm not much of a drinker either."

"I noticed," I say.

I did notice. I noticed many things. How he looks first thing in the morning and right before sleep, how he frowns when he's frustrated, how his eyes crinkle when he laughs, and how he stares into my eyes without saying anything. Like now.

"I'm so ready for this," I say, fidgeting.

"I can see that," he says and chuckles.

We sit opposite each other on two oversized benches, a gorgeous dark-brown lacquered table between us. I try to keep my legs to myself and not play footsie under the table.

SEVENTY-EIGHT

The train leaves the station a few minutes later, and I stare out the window, admiring stately properties and expansive vineyards that stretch out as far as the eye can see.

A man wearing a navy-blue uniform comes over with a gold-plated tray with food—ciabatta, smoked salmon, and Greek yogurt smoothies. It's a lot more food than I can eat right now, but I want to try it all. He also brings up two glasses of sparkling wine.

"Welcome aboard our wine train," he says, smiling before moving on to other passengers.

Ethan raises his glass, and I do too.

"What should we toast to?" he asks, his eyes on mine, his smile mirroring mine.

"How about a beautiful day?" It sounds boring and safe. I want to be boring and safe.

He twists his mouth. "How about we toast to the unexpected?"

"The unexpected? I like that."

Our glasses clink together, mellow music in the background, the light slightly dimmed. This is playing out like a scene from one of my stories, isn't it? The main characters look into each other's eyes and realize what they really feel. There are violins and fireworks. Nope. Not going to happen. Ethan and I, we're the wrong characters. I avert my eyes and focus on the landscape. He does the same.

* * *

Before long, the train that wasn't speeding anyway, slows down even more until it comes to a halt. A voice announces over a loudspeaker. "Domaine Chandon. One-hour stop."

"Let's go. Lots to do in an hour," says Ethan and I follow him off the train.

I've been to a couple of East Coast wineries, but this is one of the most impressive estates I've seen. Lush gardens, acres of vines, and a mansion-like property in the center of it all.

"Domaine Chandon was the first winery to be established in the United States by the French wine and spirits producer, Moët Hennessy," says one of the guides, a tall, loud woman.

The rest of our travel companions gather around her. We're all now standing in a semi-circle, listening to her talk about Chandon's history. From time to time, I glance at Ethan, and he looks just as 'entertained' as I am. It's not that I'm not into the history of the winery, I am, but—

"Come," he says and reaches out his hand as if to take mine. I follow, but I keep my hands to myself. "This way," he says, unfazed by my reaction. "I think."

Sometimes, if not most of the time lately, there's this quiet, invisible tension between us. What am I saying? It's not even subtle or hidden anymore. It's loud, deafening.

We pass by an expansive lawn where a private event of a few hundred people is in full swing, walk through a clearing and go around a patio that's blasting Eighties pop songs.

Ethan starts mock dancing and mouthing 'I'm so excited' as we walk, and I can't help but burst out into laughter. He's such a clown. "About to lose control... I think I like it," he bellows.

A woman dressed elegantly, who's dancing on the patio, stops and stares at us and it's not a friendly stare. She says something to the man she's with and he takes a step toward us.

"Oops, we're in trouble," says Ethan. He grabs my hand and pulls me behind an old oak.

My back against the tree, Ethan inches from me, my hand in his, the exuberance of this adventure takes my breath away. Sparks fly around us. Invisible sparks, but I see them. Does he?

Our eyes meet and he holds my gaze for a second, before stepping back and letting go of my hand. "We're kind of trespassing on a wedding it seems. But I wanted us to explore this place, not just stand there and listen. Let's see what's over there," he says.

Right behind the trees is a cave. Nobody's around, but we can still hear the music. There's a small body of water below it and next to it, stone steps.

"Want to see where they take us?" he asks and points at the stairs.

"Sure."

It's a terrace with iron tables, each with two chairs and a bouquet of flowers in the center.

He tiptoes to one of the tables, pulls a chair for me and we sit, not before looking around to see if we're going to be chased away from here too. We're pretend drinking and dining, and laughing like silly kids, when we hear a noise behind us.

"You can't be here. It's a private event," says a man dressed up in a red uniform.

"We were just—" says Ethan, and we both burst out laughing, and run for it.

"You're going to get me in trouble," I say to Ethan when we're back on the train and en route to our next destination.

"What are they going to do? Tell on us to the tour guide?" I giggle.

Our second stop is Raymond Vineyards. This time, I'm the instigator who takes us through an 'off-limits' wine cellar. We find ourselves surrounded by stainless steel tanks, mirrors, and tens of scrutinizing eyes. It turns out I'm better at sneaking in and out, since nobody ran after us, so Ethan put me in charge of our third and final stop.

"I'll just go where you tell me to," he says as we're enjoying the new course our waiter brings us on the train, in between stops. A delicious meal, by the way. Asparagus bisque with white truffle oil and aged parmesan with mixed greens, mission figs, spiced walnuts, and blue cheese. Yum! We also have a glass—or a quarter of glass each—of rose wine. Equally delicious.

SEVENTY-NINE

Inglenook is the last stop. It's a majestic chateau with a breathtaking vineyard, once owned by a Finnish sea captain and later restored by Francis Ford Coppola, according to the guide. There's something magical about this place, with its terrace that reminds me of Italian piazzas in old movies and mysterious infinity caves like you'd see on exotic islands.

It's dark out, and the estate is lit by hundreds of fairy lights. A small party is happening on a brick platform at the edge of the property. Ethan and I sit on the lawn, both a bit tired, listening to the slow music and watching couples dancing.

"I've lived in California all my life, and it's my first time seeing this place," he says.

"You didn't know about it?"

The music stops for a moment before the next song begins. The night is silent around us, except for a lone cricket in the tall grass.

"No, I did. I just didn't want to come here alone."

Lonely Ethan. I find it hard to picture. He has it all; why wouldn't he also have someone?

"What about your ex-wife?" I ask.

"What about her?"

"I don't know. Just wondering why you didn't bring her here."

"Isabella and I were wrong for each other from the start. Nothing in common."

"Do you think you need to have something in common with the person you're with?"

"At least your values, yes. Principles. I'm not talking about a shared passion for stamp collecting. Just the high-level stuff."

I nod. Maybe they had opposing views regarding kids or careers. I'm not sure.

"I seem unable to pick a partner who views monogamy as a rule, not the exception."

"I'm sorry," I say. "I didn't realize—"

He shrugs as if saying... it is what it is.

Who would've imagined? Ethan, cheated on? It makes me sad knowing someone caused him the pain I experienced because I know how it changes you. It diminishes you and makes you question your worth. Ethan should never question himself. He has it all, and so much to offer.

"If nothing else, we have that in common," I say sourly.

He turns to me. "That's the last thing I want to have in common with you."

Ethan seems angry suddenly, and I don't know if he's mad at me or in general. I can't read his reactions right now. "Enough of this," he says. "If I'm not back in five minutes, send back-up," he jokes and gets up.

"Where are you going?"

He puts a finger to his lips and goes in the direction of the party.

* * *

It's been five minutes, and he's not back. I'm on my feet, looking out in the distance, but I can't see him anywhere. Then I suddenly hear voices coming from somewhere to the right of where I'm standing. From the darkness, a group of people approaches—two women, wearing long dresses and holding their shoes in one hand, a glass of wine in the other, two men in black suits, and Ethan.

"I got hijacked," he says when they reach me.

I don't know if they just met or they've known each other before tonight, but they all seem super comfortable with each other.

"Cleo, Rebecca, Greg, Ian, this is Maya," says Ethan.

They all smile and shake my hand.

"Nice to meet you," I say, slightly uncomfortable.

The men huddle around Ethan, close enough that I see him looking my way from time to time, far enough that I don't hear their conversation.

"Want to sit?" asks Rebecca. "My feet are killing me."

"Sure," I say.

"We're taking a break from the chaos," she says, pointing at the terrace. "My sister's engagement."

"Congratulations," I say.

"Thank you. It was such a nice surprise to see Ethan here," says Cleo. "Small world."

"Are you guys friends?" I ask.

"Rebecca and I work at a magazine in Monterey. *Breeze*. It's OK if you haven't heard of it," she adds, guessing by my stare what I was about to say. "We met Ethan a few years ago when he started writing articles for *Breeze*."

"Nice," I say.

"Are you two—" asks Rebecca.

I smile awkwardly. Thank God it's somewhat dark here. I think I'm blushing.

"No. No. We're just... friends," I say.

"Too bad," says Cleo.

You tell me?

"Are you a reporter or an editor?" I ask Cleo.

"I'm a sportswriter."

"That's cool. What kind of sports?"

As she starts talking about some of the events she's excited to cover this summer, I find out most of them are car-related, and I immediately think of Celine.

"Monterey Car Week is in August. This will be my second time covering it," she says.

I ask for more details, and she gladly offers them and then some.

"It starts on Friday with the *Mazda Raceway Laguna Seca* and a classic car show in Downtown Monterey. Just imagine: over thirty classic race cars lining Alvarado Street. It's incredible. On Saturday, it's the *Monterey Pre-Reunion* where I get to photograph 300 race cars that will be competing before the Rolex Monterey Motorsports Reunion. On Tuesday, it all moves to Carmel for the *Concours on the Avenue* on Ocean Avenue. It all gets closed to traffic and filled with almost 200 cars on display in groups of juried classes. There's luxury cars, muscle cars, hot rods, and sports cars."

Celine would be so happy to be in my shoes right now and have this conversation.

"I have a friend who is a race car mechanic. Race cars and sports cars, I guess."

"Is he based out of the Bay Area?"

"She. Her name is Celine. And yes, she is in the Bay Area," I say.

"She? Even better. I know the organizers are always looking for good mechanics in the area, especially for Laguna Seca, but for other parts of the week as well. Is she any good?"

"She's amazing. She's Ethan's sister by the way," I say and give her the phone number.

"Ethan's sister? Wow. I'll call her for sure. This will score me points with the organizers. Last year Tomassini had problems with some cars, and all the good mechanics were booked."

I have no idea who Tomassini is and, honestly, don't care. All I care about is that Celine will finally be doing what she's dreamed of for years if this works out. And if I get to play a small role in that, I'm happy. This is the least I can do to pay her back for everything she's done for me since I arrived in California.

EIGHTY

It's time for us to go back to the train and, from there, back to Carmel. I'm sorry this evening has ended. I wish it could've lasted longer. Of all the days we've spent together, I think this was my favorite, because we got to do a bit of everything, and I enjoyed it so much.

"I hope you had a good time," Ethan says to me in the car.

"I did. Thank you."

We drive in silence for a while. Even the driver is quiet.

"How are we on the hating part?"

"The what?" I ask.

"You hating me and all that? Have I scored any points today?"

He smiles, but it's only a half-smile.

"Not that many," I say. And I obviously mean it as a joke. Isn't it clear I don't hate him? I think I'm as far from hating him as anyone can possibly be.

"Too bad," he says. "I'm running out of time."

I have a knot in my throat. I didn't want to think about

this. Time. Our time together. The looming deadline. I'm not ready for it to be over. Not ready at all.

The driver drops us in front of the cottage.

"I'm not looking forward to Monday," Ethan says out-of-the-blue once we're out of the car.

June 17. The day after tomorrow. This will probably be the day when he will tell me who Max is. I should be jumping up and down, but I'm not.

"Why? Is it chaotic?"

"It's not that. It's just that Monday is the beginning of the book tour and—"

"I know. Two months, right?"

He nods.

"It must be exhausting to be on the road so long, but exciting too, right?" I say, trying to keep a positive attitude and not think about my feelings or internal turmoil. This is about him, not me.

"Yes. No. It's exciting, for sure. And I get to meet my readers. But I just don't want to leave right now."

Only platitudes. That's all my brain can produce now. Anything that doesn't sound like 'why'. I can't ask why. I can't go there. Because I don't know if I'm ready to hear his answer. I might just be imagining it. It might all just be in my head. This undefined, unnamed, intangible thing between us. But if it's not, I can't ask 'why'. Because there's no turning back after I hear his answer.

I choose not to say anything. Like I didn't even hear it.

He turns to me and looks into my eyes. "You're not going to ask me why, are you?"

I try to hold his gaze, but I can't. I look away when I say it. "No."

He nods as we walk into the cottage, not saying another word until we're inside and we both go to our bedrooms with frugal 'good nights'.

I close the door behind me and let myself fall on the floor, head in my hands and try to breathe but I can't.

Yesterday ended with a call to Alisa; she rejected it and texted she was having breakfast with an out-of-town author.

It's OK, I replied. *Nothing urgent. Just wanted to hear your voice. I miss you.*

I miss you too. And sorry if I've been prickly lately. I'm sure you know what you're doing. I just don't want you to get hurt.

You're not prickly, you're honest. And... I don't know what I'm doing, but I do know I'm terrified of getting hurt. And I think that's the problem.

A problem you can solve. You're a smart cookie. You'll figure it out. I believe in you! she said in the last text before I went to sleep.

* * *

Today is the last day before Ethan's book launch. It's going to be a bittersweet day, I know it as soon as Celine and I arrive at Café Azure.

"I was thinking of closing the café tomorrow, for Ethan's book event. The problem is I have to rush back because last time everyone came to Café Azure when the signing was done."

"I can stay here while you go with Ethan," I say.

She squints, "You're not coming?"

I don't answer because I don't know. I haven't thought about that yet. I feel like I should start tearing myself away from him, so tomorrow, when he leaves for the airport, it's not going to be like ripping a Band-Aid off a fresh wound. It will be more like an existing, already bandaged cut.

Who am I kidding? How much of this forced separation can I accomplish in one day?

Especially with him sitting, like always, at his table. As if tomorrow is just another day. Maybe it is. For him. Although, thinking back to last night... I'm starting to have doubts.

"He'd want you to be there," she says.

And I would want to be there. "I just don't know if it's a good idea," I say.

"Because of the paper thing?" she asks.

Anna interrupts us when she comes from behind me and hugs me tight.

"Thank you! I now have an upstairs neighbor and, as it happens, a date for tonight."

I smile. "I'm so glad it worked out."

"Not more than I am," she says and after getting her order 'to go' from Celine, I see her meeting our charming Hugo outside. The 'Blue Valentines' Club' is getting thinner. I love it!

* * *

Ethan stops writing after a while and I see him taking out my manuscript. He must be almost done with it. He's browsing through some pages, back and forth, as if he's looking for something and the nervousness is back with a vengeance. He's so focused, I don't dare to interrupt him.

The more he keeps reading and the more time passes, I feel again like last night. Out of air. I feel the walls closing in on me and pressing my rib cage. Am I becoming claustrophobic?

"Do you mind if I take a break?" I ask Celine. "I want to take a walk. Get some air."

"Of course!" she says. "Everything OK? You look a bit pale."

"I'm fine, don't worry."

As I'm about to go out the door, I feel someone is right behind me and turn. It's Ethan.

"Where are you going?" he asks.

"Nowhere in particular; taking a break," I say.

"Do you want company?"

Yours? More than anything, which is killing me inside. That's the problem, Ethan. I do want your company. Now, and later, and tomorrow and the day after tomorrow.

"Is it OK if I just do this one by myself?"

"No, of course." He touches my arm. "Before you go—" He pauses. "I finished your book."

My heart is thumping.

He looks at me, through me, and straight into my soul.

"I now owe you some answers. As was the deal."

I swallow nervously and realize I haven't said a word.

"Can I text you later? I have to see... someone. Arrange a meeting." His smile forced.

He's seeing someone to arrange a meeting? Max. He's

going to see Max, tell him about me, and get us in front of each other. Ethan finished reading and he believes me. This is what I've wanted. Then why is my heart hurting right now? Why am I feeling sadness instead of joy?

"Yes, sure," I say and walk out of the café and into the sun. I'm shivering, although it's eighty degrees out. This coldness is coming from inside. It's panic. And not panic that I will finally meet Max. It's the panic that when meeting Max, I will lose Ethan.

EIGHTY-TWO

I've been back at Café Azure for about an hour when my phone beeps. A text from Ethan.

Can we meet at Mission Ranch? 9 PM? There's someone I want you to meet!

I'm about to meet Max. This is really happening. Can the choice of restaurant be more obvious? It's where I had dinner last year in Carmel. Yet, I hesitate before I reply, *Of course.*

I walk to the cottage as fast as I can, get ready for my date with him—I can call it a date, can't I? I put on the long, black dress Alisa gifted me for Christmas and black stilettos. I do my hair and put on makeup. The works. I do it all like a robot, not stopping to think for a second.

I'm ready. Am I ready? I take a deep breath, then another and another. And minutes pass. I can't back off now, although every fiber of my body is telling me I should. But why? This is the reason I came to Carmel. This is what I've been dreaming of for a year. I have to do this. I owe it to myself to meet him and I owe it to him.

When I arrive, the hostess says my party isn't here yet and invites me to follow her.

I missed this place and after reading Ethan's book and seeing it from Max's perspective, it has even more meaning. He was here, somewhere, and now, he will be here with me, at the same table. I try to picture his face like I have done so many times, but Ethan's face is all I see. I close my eyes, forcing the image out. I am here to meet Max. Max, not Ethan.

I focus instead on how I look and what he's going to see. I arrange my dress a few times, push back a strand of hair, look in my small mirror, making sure I don't have any lipstick on my teeth or anything. I look good. I'm ready; I have to be.

I hear Ethan's voice and turn. I was wrong; I'm not ready. Not for this. Who is she?

Next to Ethan is a beautiful woman whose outfit makes my dress look like I bought it from Zara for $24.99. Her hair is perfect, her skin is flawless, her makeup impeccable, just like that flowy summer dress that screams 'I'm not even trying'. Of course she's not. She doesn't have to.

I get up, not knowing how to react.

He smiles and wants to say something, but the woman, without waiting for any introductions or anything, jumps at me and hugs me.

"Maya, so nice to meet you. Ethan told me so much about you," she says, a huge smile on her face. Yes, her teeth are perfect too.

"I couldn't say the same," I say. Nasty. I know. I didn't mean to say it out loud... I think.

"This is Melissa," says Ethan, his whole face smiling now. My God, he looks happy. Melissa? I heard that name before. He was on the phone with her the other day, wasn't he?

"Melissa," I repeat.

Is she his girlfriend? I assume so. Where did this come from? Where did she come from? I came to the restaurant to meet Max, and instead, I'm meeting Ethan's girlfriend? I'm so confused. And the most confusing part is not that Max isn't here, but the fact that Melissa being here is causing me so much heartache. Why would I care? It's his business who he sees and who he spends time with. I guess it's the surprise of it all. I didn't know he was with someone. Truth is, I never asked. Not once. Just because he's divorced, it doesn't mean he's alone. Why did I assume that? Because he spent time with me? It didn't cross my mind and it hurts seeing them together, smiling at each other and exchanging loaded looks. It really does hurt.

"You're just like I imagined you would be," she says and laughs.

A crystalline laugh, like the kind you hear in Japanese cartoons.

"Let's sit," says Ethan. He holds her chair, and my stomach churns. I'm jealous. There's no way around it: horribly jealous. Instead of thinking of Max, I'm thinking of these two kissing and whatnot and I feel like getting up and leaving the restaurant. What's this charade?

Ethan orders wine. "We'll need a few to decide on the food," he says to the waiter.

After he pours the wine, the waiter hands Melissa the bowl.

"What is this?" she asks.

It's the 'fortune cookies'. I still have mine from last year, carefully taped in a notebook.

Ethan looks at me for a moment, but I look away.

The waiter explains the fortunes to Melissa, and she gets one. Then me, and then Ethan.

"You can't have everything. Where would you put it all?" she read out loud and starts laughing. "That's true," she says and Ethan laughs too.

I don't.

I unfold mine. *Life is a strange restaurant where odd waiters bring you things you never asked for but unknowingly need.* That's funny. Very funny.

"What did you get?" she asks him.

"The love of your life is right in front of your eyes," he reads and smiles at her.

I gulp down some wine and as I do, I see her from the corner of my eye, leaning toward Ethan and whispering something in his ear, and I feel like I'm going to get sick. Physically sick.

"Can you excuse me?" I say and without waiting for an answer, I head to the bathroom.

I lock myself in a stall and start breathing in and out through my mouth, trying to calm down. I hate him. And I hate myself. And I hate that perfect Barbie doll he's making googly eyes at. I just hate my life right now! Can nothing work out the way I hope it will? Nothing? Why would he bring her here to meet me? It's ridiculous.

EIGHTY-THREE

I grab the phone from my bag and not even thinking how late it is in London, I call Alisa.

It doesn't go straight to voicemail. There's hope. Please, pick up. Please!

I hear a mumble and then Alisa's sleepy voice.

"Maya, are you alright?"

"Alisa, I'm so sorry to wake you up. I just, I need to talk to you."

I hear a noise, and I picture her sitting up, turning on the light, and staring at her clock.

"It's OK; I was planning on waking up for the gym," she says, and I know it's a lie.

"I love you, you know?" I say.

"I love you too," she says. "What's going on? I assume you didn't call to declare your love," she says and giggles.

"I should've," I say. "You're the best friend anyone could ask for."

"Just returning a little bit of how much you give me. So, what's up?"

"He has a girlfriend," I say, the desperation coming through every word.

"A girlfriend? That's messed up! How do you know? Did Ethan tell you?"

"No! I'm not talking about Max."

"Huh?"

"Ethan. Ethan has a girlfriend. And she's a hundred times prettier than me, clearly younger. She's like this perfect thing and so nice, you can't even be mean to her."

"So what's the problem? Why do we care about Ethan's girlfriend?"

I bite my lip and don't respond.

"Do we care about Ethan's girlfriend?" she asks tentatively.

"We shouldn't, should we?" I ask, playing her game. I'm so all over the place. And I sound childish, I know that. But Alisa is the only person I can be messed up with. Hmm, weirdly enough, I also felt lately I could be my insecure, chaotic self with Ethan.

"No, we shouldn't."

"Right. You're right. We're just friends. Not even."

"Indeed. You're just friends until he tells you who Max is."

"But—"

"No buts. And where are you anyway? It sounds echoey."

"In the bathroom. At a restaurant."

"Let me guess. He's in the restaurant with her."

"He is."

"And you pulled the toilet pass. Ouch. I don't like what it means."

"It doesn't mean anything. Just a momentary blip."

"Is it the same blip that took you to Big Sur, Napa and that show in San Francisco?"

"I—"

"If it's the same blip that made you kiss him, maybe you should stop for a moment and think about what you truly want. I know it's easy to get caught up in a plan and walk blindly forward until you reach your target. But sometimes the target moves."

"Stop saying blip. And what are you even talking about?"

"Plans change. Targets change. Feelings change. People change. I'm not Ethan's fan. I think he's a sucky friend and I think he knew what he was doing, spending all this time with you, but I'm pretty sure you're not the only one who has these feelings. Unless he's the world's biggest player or he's trying to get back at you for something, all these things he's doing, these super nice things can only mean one thing. Even from thousands of miles away."

"No! Plans don't change. I'm tired of plans changing and never working out as I want them to. It's just a... blip. There, you made me repeat it. But that's all this is. We've been spending some time together lately, that's all."

"Some? No. A lot of time. Tons of time. *All* the time. You sounded happy on every call, and I don't remember Max being mentioned too much in our conversations. It's not always as black and white as you want it to be. Especially when it comes to matters of the heart. If you'd just be honest with yourself, you'll see that all signs point to... you having feelings for him."

"The only person I have feelings for is Max."

"Max is a unicorn. A one-day adventure. What you and Ethan share is much more—"

I interrupt her. "Either way, did you hear me? Ethan has a girlfriend."

"Yet he spent all of his time with you. I wonder about this out-of-the-blue girlfriend of his."

"It doesn't matter anyway. I'm in love with someone else."

I walk out of the bathroom and into the restaurant as stealthily as possible. I'm one with the wall, away from their eyes. I peek around the corner and see them talking and laughing.

"Maya, you sound like a robot. Listen to yourself. In love? You are in love, alright. But it's not with Max. I hope you won't regret this stubbornness of yours and you won't wake up too late to see what's in front of you," she says and that stings. Because it is too late. And the proof is wearing a summer dress and smiling with her perfect teeth at this man who is not a blip, and who is not Max, and who was not in my plan. But who I love! Oh, God! I do. I love him. Despite everything, despite myself.

Instead of walking toward the table, I do a 180 and go for the door.

Did he do this to humiliate me? He never planned to tell me who Max is, did he? All he wanted to do was play with me. Is this his way of taking revenge on what he thinks I did to his friend? He read my book, he knows how much that day meant to me. How could he do this?

I can't love him. I should hate him, just like I told him so many times; instead, I hate myself for feeling so strongly for him. I'm not mad because Max is not here, am I? I'm not mad that Ethan's not telling me who Max is. I am mad because sometime between my arrival here and today, I fell in love with Ethan. Although I knew it was a bad idea. I knew it, and it still happened. And now I'm hurt beyond measure. He used me to get publicity, which is probably why we continued to go out to all those places. Always public places. People saw us together all the time. How foolish I have been! How stupid and gullible. How could I fall in love with a man like him? With his charming smile and his good manners, his perfect sense of humor and playfulness. He knew exactly what buttons to push to keep me hanging and only ever gave me enough to hope, but never to be sure.

Alisa is absolutely right. I have denied it all this time. I kept telling myself it was all for Max, when in fact Max was the last thing on my mind. I don't deserve a man like Max. I have hurt him enough. Even if I met him now, I'd have nothing left to offer him. I can't give him my heart. Unfortunately, I gave it away already to someone else. Someone who broke it into a million pieces and then trampled it.

What did I do?

I go back to the cottage, and pack. I'm done. Maybe a cheat and a liar like David is the best a person like me deserves.

EIGHTY-FOUR

I booked myself a ticket to New York for tomorrow morning, but I have no intention of spending one more night in the cottage, so I change and plan on heading for the airport. I'd rather be stuck on a chair for hours than be anywhere near him.

On my way to the airport, I stop by the café to tell Celine I'm leaving. I have to find a reason, something that won't sound completely made up. But before I get a chance to open my mouth, she starts telling me all about the fantastic news she had.

"I'm going to be in Laguna Seca," she says. "I got a call, and they need mechanics and I'm going to be part of it. And while I'm busy, I know just the perfect person to take over the café, someone who would undoubtedly do a much better job than I did." She winks. "I've never been this happy. All my dreams are coming true. First Aaron, now this."

"You deserve it, Celine," I say. "You deserve all the happiness, but I'm afraid you will have to find someone else for Café Azure," and as I say this, I have tears in my eyes.

"Why? What's wrong?" she asks, taking my hands in hers.

I tell her I have a family emergency and I must return to the East Coast immediately,

She's speechless.

"When are you coming back?" she asks, still in shock.

"I don't know," I say.

"Maya, you would tell me if there was something else, right?"

I wish I could. I wish I had done things differently. I will miss her so much. I will miss...

No! I can't think about any of that. This is the most logical decision I've made in the last few weeks. I should've never come here.

"I'm going to miss you so much," she says through her tears, echoing my thought.

I hug her and try not to cry. As I make my way out, I feel her eyes on me and can only imagine what she must be thinking.

* * *

At the bus station, I check the schedule and the next one is not for another hour from now, so I walk to the beach, killing time.

With my luggage at my feet, I sit on the bench. THE bench. I want to say goodbye. To this place. To my dreams and hopes about it. To what could've been.

I wipe a tear with the back of my mind and continue looking out at the ocean.

Who would've imagined? Who could've possibly imagined a

year ago this is where I'd be today? What about two weeks ago? Not me. The last image of him, giggling with that woman, still fresh in my memory, I clench my jaw and promise that, no matter what, I'll never let myself be hurt like this again. Never ever again.

Someone is standing in front of me and I look up to see who it is.

I feel the blood draining from my face, my body, into my legs and onto the ground.

My head snaps to the side, and I wipe my tears so he doesn't see I've been crying.

"You shouldn't be here," I say, poison dripping from my every word.

He stands next to the bench, his face expressionless.

"Why?"

I get up, my fists clenched next to my body. I can feel I'm trembling; I am that furious.

"Because I hate you, that's why," I say.

He starts laughing and I feel like I'm going to lose it. "Nothing new there, eh?"

"This time it's for good. It's the real deal. To the moon and back again."

He seems so calm, it's driving me crazy.

"That's a lot! Dare I ask what brought on this new wave of hate?"

"Really? Are you really asking me that? What was the point of tonight? Instead of bringing Max, you brought your girlfriend to rub it in my face that I can't be with him, but you can be with her, or what? I don't get it."

He laughs and I want to throw my phone at him. "Is that what this is all about?"

"No! Why don't you just leave, Ethan?"

"I don't want to leave and I don't want you to leave either."

He takes a step toward me and I take a step back.

"What more do you want from me?"

"I think there's something you want from me."

"That's funny. We both know you're not going to tell me who he is. I don't think you ever intended to."

"No," he says and I'm taken back by his honesty. "It's true. At first, I didn't. I wanted to send you on a wild goose chase after random Lift drivers until you got frustrated and went back to New York. I was convinced that day meant nothing to you and you only came back to use my book as a launch ramp for your own writing career."

I scoff, disgusted. "At least you admit it."

"At first," he repeats. "But then... I realized I was wrong. All this time we spent together, and reading your book and—"

I stare at him, the fury still raging in me.

"I don't believe you. I think everything you've done since you met me was for your personal gain. What better way to sell books than to parade yourself around town with the main character? That's what I was to you. The main character in a story. A poorly written story," I say bitterly. "You used me and you misled me and—"

"How did I mislead you?"

I want to tell him that he made me feel like there was something between us. But how would that sound? I could never say it anyway because I have too much pride. Knowing his perfect Barbie is waiting for him, I would never humiliate myself like this. What's the point? Just to get it off my chest? No, thanks. I'll keep it on, until it suffocates me in my sleep. I'd rather that.

"Maya," he says and again takes a step toward me. Again I back off.

"OK," he says. "I get it. I'll stay here. Far from you. Is this far enough?" he says and takes five, six steps back. Seven, ten. Fifteen. "Why are you leaving?" he yells and I barely hear.

"Why do you even care?" I yell back.

"Well, for one, because I..." he yells again but I can't hear what he says at the end.

"What? I can't hear you."

I want to leave. I don't want to talk to him anymore. "I'm going now," I yell.

I grab the handle of one of my suitcases, and all of a sudden, I feel like I'm flying. He's holding me up in his strong arms and his lips are on mine. He's kissing me like I've never been kissed before. Passionately and possessively, like he can't get enough of me, like he's been hungry for me. I feel the world is spinning and I can't breathe. I can't think. I try not to return his kiss, but it's beyond me. I kiss him back and I let this moment take over all my senses.

He puts me down. "I said... because I love you," he says and looks straight into my eyes.

I'm trying to catch my breath and regain my composure, but my cheeks are on fire and my legs are weak. "Too bad," I say, "because I don't love you," and I step back.

How dare he tell me he loves me after everything that happened? No, no! I get that I can't control my urges when he's near me, but I can control what I say and how I behave from now on.

"I don't believe you," he says, his face now serious.

"Well, I don't," I say, and look away.

He comes in closer, so close I can now feel his warm

breath on my face. His cologne is making me dizzy. "Look at me," he says, his voice firm now, but I don't.

He gently grabs my chin and turns my face to him. "Maya —" he insists.

We look into each other's eyes, and the chemistry is overpowering. But I won't give in. I clench my jaw and do my best not to let him see how my body responds to him, how I long for his touch—but it's stronger than me. I don't know from where or how it happens, but I find myself pressing my lips to his with thirst and desperation I didn't think I was capable of.

"Maya," he whispers. "I never meant to hurt you," he says as a tear rolls down my cheek.

"Please, I'm begging you, don't cry. I promise you have no reason to cry."

"Don't make promises, Ethan."

"I want to explain everything. First, what happened tonight at the restaurant. But for that, you will have to come with me to Café Azure."

"Some things are better left alone. And anyway, I have a plane to catch," I say, feeling my arguments are weak and my defenses are going down. Again.

"What time?"

"Ten tomorrow morning." It sounds ridiculous, I know. That's twelve hours away.

"Plenty of time," he says and grabs my luggage.

EIGHTY-FIVE

When we walk into Café Azure, nobody's more surprised to see me than Celine.

"You got her back? You got her to change her mind?" she asks, in tears again.

"Not yet," he says and winks.

Celine goes into the kitchen and I don't even notice Melissa until Ethan shows me to a table by the window.

She gets up and reaches out across the table to hug me. My body is limp in her embrace.

"Ethan told me you weren't feeling well. Are you a bit better now?"

I look over and Ethan, who nods, so I go with it.

"I am," I say unconvincingly.

"I won't keep you long. We can talk more tomorrow, after Ethan's book launch."

"Talk about what?"

She looks at Ethan and then at me. "Your manuscript," she says. "I read it, and it's absolutely brilliant. It's beautiful and heartwarming and heartbreaking. And considering I have already read Ethan's ten times and edited it before sending it to publishers, it still kept my attention all the way through. It is the same story, in a way, but in so many other ways, it is so different. They're like the perfect halves of a perfect story," she says and sounds excited.

I am nothing if not confused. "Sorry, I don't understand."

"Ethan?" she says, an eyebrow raised. "You didn't tell her?"

"No, I wanted it to be a surprise."

"That explains your reaction," she says and laughs. "OK. I'm sure he'll tell you more about it, but Ethan sent me your manuscript as soon as he finished reading it, about ten days ago. He said he stayed up all night after you gave it to him, and he couldn't put it down. And I know why. I did the absolute same thing. He asked me if I would represent you and if I had editors in mind I could send this to and a plan for how to market it."

"You read it that first night?" I ask him. Of all the things she's telling me, that's the one thing that stuck to me.

He nods. "I told you it was fabulous."

"You also told me you're a slow reader," I say.

"Not this time," he says with a smile.

"Not only do I have a list of editors, but I already pitched it, and both editors and scouts are dying to read it. I couldn't send it without your approval, though, so I had to wait until we met. I also have the best plan for it. Think Eamon and Frankee. Justin and Selena. Taylor and Harry. Same story, two sides. This is going to be huge! And they're both going to feed off each other, and Ethan's book is already doing so incredibly well," she says, turning to him. "Not that I had any doubts, of course."

"So, that's why you're here?" I ask.

"To meet you, yes. And for Ethan's launch, and because my husband wanted to visit California, so we packed up the kids, got on a plane and here we are," she says, laughing again.

I like her. I liked her even when I hated her.

Husband. Kids. My manuscript. Ethan. Everything is spinning and spinning.

"And you want to represent me?" I ask.

"I would love to. If you want me to, of course."

I look over at Ethan, and he's all a smile. A grin.

"I do," I say. "Thank you."

"No. Thank you for this special love story. It's just, ah, it melted my heart. Alright," she says, "I have to go now, or else my husband will declare me missing. I will send you the contract via email tonight, so we can go over it tomorrow if you have any questions. I hope you both have a lovely night," she says and leaves.

Is flabbergasted the right word for my state right now? Maybe. I don't have any other.

I look at Ethan. He looks at me. I can hear my breathing; it's that quiet between us.

"Thank you," I say. "For that."

"Nothing to thank me for. You deserve it and like you said, I kind of stole your story."

I can't even smile, I'm so shocked about this new development.

"We had a deal and I'll keep my end of the bargain. I promised that once I finish reading the book—I didn't say how many times though—if I believe you, I'll tell you who Max is."

I hold my breath.

"I finished reading your book for the fourth time this morning and I do believe you. It's time for you to meet Max."

I don't want that anymore, I want to say, but the words

don't come out. Instead, I sit across from him, trying not to cry.

"I have something for you. Something that will explain everything I couldn't," he says and gives me two typed pieces of paper.

"What are these?"

"The missing pages from my novel. The ones I told you about the day we made the pact."

I take them and my fingers tremble as I hold them.

"Once you read them, you will have the answers to all your questions—"

"Ethan, what does that mean?"

He leans down and kisses me on the top of my head, then leaves the café without a word.

June After Midnight

Chapter 21 (Draft 1 Version)

I'm sitting by the fire, holding a beer and looking out at the ocean. I know she will show up in a few minutes, but I do my best to stop staring in the direction of the path. I have to seem casual. Luckily, there are over twenty-five, maybe thirty people here and more come. People drink beer and wine, roast marshmallows, a woman brought two thermoses with hot cocoa. I believe some of them are tourists or new to the area, but still I know at least half of them, even if just by sight.

I chat with a few of them, nod to others, then continue sitting. And waiting.

It's risky what I'm doing, and I know it. But I'm still here. I don't know if I should continue this; it's gone so well so far. She's had a blast, a wonderful birthday she will surely remember. But she's still leaving in a few hours. I'm not sure why I'm here. Just couldn't stay away, I guess. Wanted to see her up close. I've been watching her all day, but from a distance. It would be nice to sit together—not together but almost—by this fire, to see her smile, maybe even laugh. I'm curious what her voice sounds like. I only heard it for a few seconds when we were doing the bike tour, but I was in such a state of panic that she'd discover me, I didn't truly pay attention. I'm curious what color her eyes are. I really don't know what I'm doing here. Will I tell her who I am? Will I just go over there and introduce myself?

She sits across from me, on the other side of the fire and right next to Remy.

As he's singing, she lifts her eyes and looks at the fire.

I try to look away, look somewhere else, act busy or distracted, but I don't. I can't.

So I look too. And our eyes meet.

At first, I think she might be looking at the fire or right through me, but judging by that feeling in my stomach, she's looking straight at me.

I hold her gaze. My God, she's beautiful.

The woman with the thermos offers a cup of cocoa and Maya gladly takes it.

The staring contest is over. The moment is gone.

I'm almost on the street, when I see something in the sand, not far from where I am, in the spot where Maya and I sat earlier today, ate our snacks and drank our juices. Together but separate. It makes me sad thinking I missed the opportunity to get to know her better, to spend this day with her, not just watching her and watching out for her, but looking into her eyes and hearing her voice. I wish I had been braver, bolder. But it's too late now for regrets.

At first, I think I'm imagining it. I walk closer, and yes, it is her. She fell asleep on the beach, her backpack next to her.

I approach as slowly as I can, afraid I might wake her up and then stand there looking at her, wondering what could've been had we met under different circumstances.

I take my hoodie off and cover her with it, then grab my pen— always with me—and the travel notebook from my pocket and write down quickly my hopeful thoughts for the beginning of our life together... before I bend down to put them in the hoodie's pocket and kiss her hair. She smells so nice, like cherry blossoms in the spring. "I will see you soon. I hope..."

Maya moves a bit, and in a panic, I rush away from her and to my meeting point with David—I don't want to call him her boyfriend, because I'm still holding on to the hope.

EIGHTY-SIX

I text Alisa the moment I finish reading.

Not precisely that very moment. First, I thought I misread. So I read that part again. About the fire and him being across from me. Us looking into each other's eyes. I told him I remembered him from the fire, but he pretended like he didn't know what I was talking about. I just imagined it was a coincidence. After all, he lives here, and he said he goes to these bonfires every couple of weeks in the summer. When I read his early copy, there was no mention of him being by the fire, so of course I put that out of mind. I kept reading and rereading. It was him across the fire. That moment we had was real. I felt it then just like I've felt it every single second ever since we both returned here, to Carmel.

Then I got to the part about me sleeping in the sand and him kissing me on my hair, just like he just did now. Him putting his hoodie on me, to keep me warm. And then to the last part. The message he wrote me; the message I never got. I jumped out of my chair, grabbed my luggage. I knew it was still there. It had to be. I never washed it; I never even touched it in the last year. But I kept it...

Alisa, I FINALLY KNOW WHO MAX IS!

EIGHTY-SEVEN

I get the hoodie out of my backpack and put it on, before stuffing my hands in the pockets. I can't believe it. It's still there.

I may have just imagined this whole thing. You. Today.

I may have just imagined us looking into each other's eyes tonight, across the fire.

I may be the only one feeling all these incredible feelings today.

I may be that crazy guy who falls in love in just a few hours, maybe minutes.

I may very well be... and if I am, then you will leave with him and I will never see you again. But if I'm not, know that I will be waiting for you here. Tomorrow. The day after tomorrow. Whenever. To see the sunrise together. Like I promised. All you need to do is text me and I will come running. (my name and phone number are on the back)

PS: And yes, I do want to know what your question #50 is. And I can't wait for you to tell me...

The sunrise is hours away, but I don't care. I've waited a year for this. I've waited a lifetime for this!

"Maya, are you leaving?" Celine asks when she sees me heading for the door.

I stop short and turn around. "I have to tell you something, but I want you to know that I never meant to hurt you or lie to you and I care about you deeply. You are a wonderful friend."

She squeezes my hands and smiles. "Maya, I know. I've known who you are and why you're here since the moment I saw you back in the café. I should be the one to apologize. I wanted to tell you, but he asked me not to interfere."

We hug, both with tears in our eyes.

EIGHTY-EIGHT

I get out of the café and run toward the bench. With trembling hands, I text him the moment I see the bench. Our bench. *Number 50, you ask? OK. Do you believe in love at first text?*

Minutes pass and nothing happens. More minutes. He's not coming. No, he has to come!

I don't want to cry, but I feel so overwhelmed by this moment. By the realization of what happened last year, these past few weeks. By my love for him and his love for me.

I hear someone running toward me. My heart is beating like crazy and I'm afraid to open my eyes. This feels too much like a dream. What if I wake up?

Then I feel he's gently kissing the top of my head like he did it a year ago, but this time I'm not leaving. And I'm not breaking his heart. "I do," he whispers. "I do believe."

No, this time I open my eyes, and we stare at each other for a moment before we both say, "I love you," and I pull him to me and kiss him.

"Can we stay here until the sunrise?" I ask.

"I wouldn't want it any other way," he says, before he kisses me again. "Are you mad at me for not telling you earlier who I was?"

"No. I'm not mad. I hate you," I say and chuckle.

"It figures. Just put it in the black book."

"What do you think I've been writing in that notebook you gave me?"

He laughs.

"I understand why you didn't tell me the truth when I came back, although I think, at first, you wanted to, right? In San Francisco? I can see how this all must've looked to you. You were just guarding your heart," I say, holding his hand tight in mine.

"What a great job I've done," he says, pulling me closer.

"I don't get one thing, though. The Lift. Nobody ever told me you're a Lift driver and I doubt you drove people around in the Porsche or Mustang."

"Good catch. I had a Prius I sold to Aaron when I left for Florida. I Lifted from time to time—maybe a dozen times in total—hoping the people I met would inspire my stories."

"And did they?"

"Funny you should ask. I think you should read my latest book. It's the story of my last Lift ride. It publishes tomorrow."

"No free copy?" I ask and wink.

"An author's got to make a living. How else can I afford this?" he asks and from his backpack, which I didn't even notice until now, he takes out a square package wrapped in paper.

"What is this?"

"A small gift. Happy early birthday, Maya."

"You remembered." I try not to start crying again.

"Maybe," he teases.

I unwrap it and throw my arms around his neck and hold him close to me. It's the small painting I wished for. The one from Big Sur, with our sunset. "Thank you," I say. "It's perfect."

"We'll have to find a place to hang it," he says.

"How about Café Azure? Oh, did Celine tell you the big news?" I ask.

"She did. And I have a different suggestion for the management of Café Azure for the next few months at least. I'm hoping you'll be unavailable, and Aaron knows plenty about the place to be just fine."

"I'll be unavailable?"

He smiles. "I'm hoping. As for the painting, I had a bit of a different thing in mind."

"You did?"

"Yes. Something like Dolce Far Niente, perhaps? I heard it's up for sale."

"What?" I stare at him, and I get lost in his eyes and this overwhelming moment.

"When we get back, I know someone who would love to sit on the balcony and watch you watch the ocean and be happy."

I smile. "Get back from where?"

"Well, let's see. I know about Hawaii, but how high is New Zealand on your wish list?"

"Number two. IF it includes a one-day layover in London. There's someone who's dying to meet you."

"Alright. I'm intrigued. What's number one?"

"A two-month tour of America for some bookstore visits," I say, laughing.

"Was hoping you'd say that. How many points on the hate scale will both win me?"

"A few. I think you'll need much more time to win enough points, though."

"We're talking decades here, right? Just asking because I have something in mind—"

"Of course you do," I say and kiss him again.

And for the first time in my life, all I feel is absolute happiness and love.

THE END

ACKNOWLEDGMENTS

I've truly loved writing Maya's story. I started it at a time when the world seemed to be at a standstill, and everything felt dark (during the first weeks of lockdown in the Bay Area in early 2020). I knew I wanted to tell the kind of story that recharges your batteries, helps you feel hopeful and dream again. An uplifting, heartwarming love story set in a dreamy location, with characters I would love to spend time with...in real life and become friends with. I'm not ashamed to admit I've lived vicariously through Maya and her adventures in California.

First and foremost, I want to thank you, the reader. Thank you for picking it up online, in a bookstore or library (I know you have many choices for your next read, and I bet your TBR pile is ever-growing, just like mine). Thank you for reading. Thank you for telling your friends and family about my book(s), posting reviews, sharing photos and all your support. Thank you for coming along for the ride, whether this is the first of my books you've read or you've also read *Someday in Paris*, my debut.

I hope you enjoyed *The Meeting Point*, and it made you smile, believe in love (be it, at first sight, text...in any shape or form), and it helped you discover (or re-discover) the magical small town of Carmel by the Sea. Hopefully, you will also get to see it in person. Don't forget to take your copy of the book/or your reading device with you so you can retrace Maya's steps. If you do, I'll be on the lookout on social media for the #TheMeetingPoint and your lovely photos. I will definitely do the same. Returning to Carmel—my absolute favorite place on the West Coast—, after missing it dearly for a year, is my birthday gift to myself in 2021.

As always, a big thank you to Hannah Sheppard, my talented, patient, lovely literary agent who's been my biggest supporter from day one! I'm lucky to have found you. And thank you to everyone at DHH Literary Agency.

My editor, Hannah Todd, and the Aria Fiction/Head of Zeus team, who brought *The Meeting Point* to all of you and who worked me with at every step of this incredible journey...from the first draft to the beautiful, happy cover, to publishing day (and everything in between and beyond). Thank you for everything!

And last but certainly not least, thank you and limitless love to my family for your unconditional love, support, extra cups of coffee on late writing nights, giving me space and time to be creative and keep doing what I do, knowing that it makes me happy. Thank you for all the small things (and big) you do every day. I am blessed.

ABOUT THE AUTHOR

Olivia Lara was born and raised in Bucharest in a family of booklovers and storytellers. Since university she has worked as a journalist and marketer in Romania, France and the United States. She is currently a marketing executive in San Francisco and lives in the Bay Area with her husband, young daughter and four cats. Olivia's debut, *Someday in Paris* was published in 2020. *The Meeting Point* is her second novel.

Visit her online at Olivia-Lara.com. Follow her on Instagram at @olivialara.writes, Twitter at @olilara_writes, or Facebook at @olivialaraauthor.